MISSING PRESUMED DEAD

Arlene Hunt is originally from Wicklow, and having spent five years in Barcelona, now lives in Dublin with her husband, daughter and mêlée of useless, overweight animals. *Missing Presumed Dead* is her fourth novel.

Also by Arlene Hunt
Vicious Circle
False Intentions
Black Sheep

ARLENE HUNT

Missing Presumed Dead

HODDER
HEADLINE
IRELAND

For Terry

1

1980

It was a scene for the photo album, a picture-perfect magical day. The seaside was packed. High above the curved golden dunes of Brittas Bay, the clear blue sky stretched unbroken from the horizon to behind the purple-hued mountains, and sails dotted the cobalt sea. A warm breeze carried the sounds of children playing and the gentle lap of waves on the sand.

Charlotte Jones, propped on her elbows, watched the boats, wondering idly where they had come from and what sort of person could afford such a thing in this day and age, with unemployment rife and everyone struggling to make ends meet.

She put on some more oil even though she was certain her chest was beginning to burn. Well, what harm? She'd be brown the next day – and when would she get a chance to sunbathe again this year?

It had been her idea to come to the beach, and now she relaxed and allowed herself an unusual moment free of worry. The sun was abnormally hot. Thirty degrees, the weather forecast had predicted that morning as she had stood making sandwiches in the tiny kitchen of her council house in Ringsend. Thirty degrees – imagine! Near enough to foreign temperatures.

'*Mam!*'

Sam raced across the hot sand towards her. He looked like a miniature, skinnier version of his dad. And she knew from his pinched expression that he was vexed about something.

'What's wrong, love?'

'Tell that boy to go away. He's *wrecking* my fort!'

Charlotte looked over Sam's freckled shoulder to where a tawny-headed child was acting innocent. 'He's just a little kid. C'mon, Sam, I'm sure he won't do it any harm.'

'Huh.' Sam's expression said he didn't believe a word of it.

Charlotte pointed at the sandcastle. 'That's some place you're building there, love. It's only massive.'

Sam nodded. Charlotte waited for him to say something else, but as usual he held his tongue. At eight, Sam was as reticent as ever. Sometimes she couldn't make him out and, the older he got, the further away he seemed to draw from her and the world in general. He was a delicate boy, thin, gawky and prone to silences. He had no real friends, either in school or from their neighbourhood, and lately, she'd noticed, he'd been happy to come home, grab a bite to eat and shut himself in the bedroom to build great structures with the Lego sets he asked for every birthday and Christmas.

She shielded her eyes and looked up at him. 'Is Katie bothering you too?'

Sam stopped scowling and glanced down the beach to where his sister, clad only in blue pants and a pair of orange water-wings decorated with dancing Donald Ducks, was scrabbling about in the sand, her red plastic bucket gripped in one chubby hand. Katie was a fat, blonde, curly-haired doll with the bluest eyes – like her daddy – dimples and an infectious chuckle.

'No, she's helping to find shells for the ramparts.'

'Well, make sure she doesn't wander too far to get them.'

'I will.'

'You want anything to eat?'

'Nu-uh.'

'Okay then.'

He smiled, and then he was gone, running across the sand on his spindly legs, eager to get back to the damp sand before it dried out and wouldn't stick together. Charlotte watched her children for a few more minutes, then she lay down on her towel.

'You hungry, Tommy?'

Her husband opened an eye and grinned. 'I wouldn't say no to another of them Fig Rolls.'

'You ate them all!'

'Well, you have me working up an appetite.' His eye, the colour of a cornflower, twinkled mischievously.

She smiled at him, blushing. 'Go on with you out of that.'

He patted her breast affectionately, letting his finger brush against her nipple just long enough for it to harden.

'Hot, isn't it?'

'Sure is.' Tommy's voice was soft and sleepy. Charlotte decided to let him be. She looked at him, taking in the tanned neck and arms, the milk-white back. Those arms were roped with muscle that had developed from hours of graft, loading and unloading supplies on the docks, a back-breaking job that aged men, made them stooped and weary before their time. No, she would leave him sleep in peace and she would be grateful that her Tommy was a hard worker and a good provider. And how many women could honestly say their husband was happy to spend a rare free day with his wife and children.

Maybe she'd relax for a second. The kids were playing and it was such a beautiful day.

She closed her eyes ...

Something's wrong.

Charlotte sat up with a bolt of fear. Dazed, she realised she had fallen asleep, but surely it had only been for a second. She looked around. Did the beach seem emptier? She realised the sun wasn't where it had been and the air was cooler.

She looked around, wiping her eyes. Tommy was still asleep, but he had rolled over onto his side and was facing away from her.

She looked to where the kids had earlier been building the sandcastle, but they were gone.

She scrambled to her feet and looked around wildly. '*Tommy!*'
She slapped his shoulder.

'What?'

'The kids.'

Before he had opened his eyes, she was off and running towards
the sea, her feet scrabbling in the soft sand and over the crab grass,
oblivious to the discomfort. She heard Sam before she saw him. He
was standing chest high in the water, screaming blue murder, and a
crowd of anxious people had gathered behind him on the beach. A
young woman in a blue and white polka-dot bathing suit had waded
in after him and was trying to coax him back to shore, but Sam kept
screaming and struggling against her.

Even as he and Charlotte ran towards them, Tommy knew
something was terribly wrong. People were pointing at something on
the ground and a woman had a hand over her mouth.

'Sam!' he shouted. He sprinted as fast as he could to the shoreline.
He had never heard Sam make that sound before, not even when he
had fallen down the stairs and sprained his wrist. 'Sam, I'm coming!'

The group parted. He ploughed through them and plunged into
the water.

'Here they are! Here they are!' the woman in the bathing suit said.
'It's all right, honey, your daddy's here now.' She was holding Sam.
No, Tommy noticed, with a splinter of shock. She was hanging on
to him to stop him going out further into the sea.

Tommy swept his son into his arms. Jesus Christ, he thought, he's
frozen stiff. He carried Sam back to the shore and lowered him onto
the sand. The boy's lips and skin were blue and his eyes were glazed
in shock.

'Sam, it's all right now.' Tommy tried to keep the panic out of his
voice. 'Listen to me carefully, son. Where's Katie? Did you see her go
in the water? Sam, did you see her go—'

But Sam would only scream. Tommy felt his scalp tighten as fear
rushed through him. 'Sam—'

'*Katie!*' Charlotte rushed into the water up to her thighs.

Tommy looked around frantically. '*Katie!*'

'There was a little one here earlier. Are you asking about a little girl?' an old man in a battered hat asked, squinting in the late-afternoon sun.

'Yes. She only a baby, she's—'

'I saw her playing here earlier. She was picking up shells in the shallows there.' He pointed along the beach. Charlotte came screaming out of the water and ran in the direction he had pointed.

Tommy prised Sam off and raced after his wife. Before he reached her, Charlotte slid to a halt. 'What is it?'

She sank to her knees on the wet sand. Beside her lay an overturned bucket. The shells Katie had collected lay at the edge of the water. A deflated water-wing, decorated with dancing Donald Ducks, bobbed in the surf.

Charlotte began to wail.

People were starting to run towards them. *No, no, she's wandered off somewhere, she's playing, maybe she fell asleep up in the dunes, kids get tired, they fall asleep all the time...*

He turned and began to run. '*Katie!*'

But even as he stumbled across the sand frantically calling her name, he knew he wouldn't find her.

Katie, their little golden angel, was gone.

2

2006

Seamus Ryan was having a tough morning. His guts were killing him. He had spent much of the previous night playing cards and drinking with a group of friends and now he wished he hadn't bothered turning up for his shift. Though it was early, the traffic at Busárus was at a standstill and the winter sun beating through his windshield was blinding.

Shit cards, shit food and now, he was paying the price for it. He belched softly.

'Whereabouts in Howth is it, love?' He glanced in the rear-view mirror.

The blonde girl stared silently out of the window. He had tried to engage her in conversation twice since he had picked her up outside her hotel in the city centre, but she wasn't a talker. A looker, definitely, with her curly blonde hair and her huge blue eyes, but not friendly. And what was with her get-up? Sean thought. Sloppy-looking gear. A grubby smock like the kind his old mother had worn when she cleaned the house. What was wrong with women these days? Why didn't they want to look like women any more?

'Whereabouts in Howth?' he repeated, a little louder.

'Asgard Road.'

'Asgard Road?'

'Yes.'

'Nice area, that.'

The girl didn't reply.

'Traffic's only brutal. But we should be there soon anyway.'

Silence.

'You must be half frozen, have you no coat with you?'

The girl sighed and closed her eyes. 'I'm fine. Could you just drive, please?'

He grunted and tossed a piece of nicotine gum into his mouth. If she didn't want to chat, that was fine by him. Stuck-up sort of a yoke. Oh, he knew the type, all right – ten years driving in the city and he knew them all. He took a slug from a bottle of warm Ballygowan and rammed it back into the side pocket of the driver's door.

Forty minutes later he turned onto a tree-lined avenue. He looked in the rear-view mirror expecting her to tell him when or where to stop. He noticed she was staring at a piece of paper. 'Where to now, love?'

'Over there on the right, please.'

'Where?'

'Outside the white gates.'

Seamus pulled in at a large, three-storey, red-brick Victorian house. It had two bay windows, and the south side of the house was covered with ivy. He pulled up the handbrake and checked his meter. 'That'll be thirty-two euros.'

She passed him a fifty and climbed out.

'Here – don't you want your change?'

She closed the door and walked in through the open gates without a word or a wave, clutching her shoulder bag.

Seamus folded the money and put it into his clip. He watched her open the gate and walk through. She peered at the house and then made her way to the front door. She rang the bell.

Seamus glanced at his watch. He still had hours to go on his shift. He groaned and lowered the handbrake. He checked to make sure there was no oncoming traffic before he pulled out, and that was when he saw the notebook on the back seat. He reached for it and opened it. It was empty but for two addresses.

Stuck-up or no, he'd better give it to her, he thought. He picked it up and got out of the car.

He said afterwards that he wasn't sure how he knew something was wrong, but he did. He told the gardaí it was the expression on the face of the old man who opened the door. The look he'd given the girl – Seamus had never seen anything like it. He told the gardaí that his passenger and the old man had exchanged a few words, and then the old man had looked terrified.

That had been when Seamus Ryan had told the officers that some instinctual part of him had known something was very wrong.

He said he had just stepped out of the car with the notebook when he heard the shot. He had immediately run towards the house. (He had done no such thing, he had ducked behind the driver's door so fast he had cracked his right knee on the handle hard enough to leave one hell of a bruise, a bruise he touted proudly for days as he relived his 'experience' with other drivers.)

He said he had looked in the bay window and had seen nothing, he had banged on the door and rung the bell but no one answered. He said he had begun to feel really creeped-out when no one came. Then he'd heard the second shot. This time, he told Sergeant McBride, he'd decided not to take any chances. He had walked back to the car to phone the gardaí.

Not quite true.

He had raced back to the car, dived into the driver's seat and started the engine. He had slammed his foot on the accelerator but, in his panic to get away, he'd stalled. 'Oh, sweet sacred heart of the divine Jesus!' He was turning the key frantically in the ignition again when the front door of the house opened and the girl fell out onto the pale gravel.

He sat still, ramrod straight, unable to move or tear his eyes from her. She struggled to her feet and spun clumsily in his direction.

Shit, Seamus thought. Was she coming for him?

He turned the key again.

He needn't have worried. She took two more steps, then stood still, wraith-like, her hair a golden halo round her pale face. She didn't seem to register that he was there and blood was spattered across her face. She lifted a gun and staggered. She turned her head and he could see blood running down the side of her face onto her neck. She opened her mouth and pointed the gun towards the taxi.

Seamus Ryan stopped breathing. He placed his outstretched hand against the windscreen. 'Wait now, don't—'

The blonde lowered the gun, dropped to her knees and fell forwards onto her chest.

3

'Mam! Come on, shake a leg or we'll be late.' Sam Jones tapped his foot impatiently. He glanced at himself in the hall mirror, adjusted his tie, licked the tip of a finger and smoothed his eyebrows. 'Mam!'

Why did it take her so long to get ready? It drove him crazy – every Friday the same. He had a string of appointments set up for the afternoon and couldn't afford to get behind.

Today was especially important. He and his partner, Saul Winters, had a preliminary meeting with a German property developer at three. The man wanted to build a massive apartment complex in the grounds of an old convent in Sligo and Sam needed to go over the plans once, even though he knew every inch by heart. It was the most ambitious project Jones & Winters had ever attempted.

'*Mam!*'

'Hold your horses, Sam. I'm just checking that everything's unplugged,' his mother called from the kitchen.

Sam huffed. He knew she'd already checked but that she'd do it again, no matter what. Since his father had left, his mother had developed a series of rituals that had to be carried out before she set foot outside the front door. 'I'll go and start the car,' he called.

'Okay.'

He let himself out and walked down the path to his Land Rover Discovery. At the gate he looked back at the tiny house.

Sometimes he felt proud to have come from such humble origins. He had worked his way through college and had spent three years learning his trade from the ground up on some of the toughest construction sites in Ireland. He appreciated his life now, his income, his talent and now his success.

He could picture the bedroom in which he had once spent every spare moment and Katie's next door. It had been five years before his mother could bring herself to remove her daughter's belongings and turn Katie's little pink room into a sewing room.

He swallowed. Even now, after all these years, it hurt to think of his sister.

'Good man yourself.'

Sam jumped.

Albert O'Shea, the postman, leaned his bike on the railings, then dug into his sack and pulled out a bundle of envelopes. He flicked through them and handed a couple to Sam. 'There you are. Two for your mother.'

'Right,' Sam said. He felt he should probably say something more, but he didn't know what to add. He wasn't a man for small talk.

Albert waited, but when no conversation was forthcoming, his eyes wandered. 'Right so. Tell your mam I said hello, will you?'

'Of course.'

Albert collected his bike and pushed it two doors down. If he was offended by Sam's lack of chit-chat, it didn't show.

A dark Ford Focus cruised up the street. Sam watched it pull in behind his Discovery. Two men climbed out. One was balding and wore a tatty blue anorak. The other was tall and thin, in a rumpled grey suit. His face was full of razor nicks – he must have shaved with hedge shears, Sam thought. They walked towards him.

'Excuse me. Is this the home of Charlotte Jones?' the one with the cuts asked.

Sam eyed them suspiciously. 'She's my mother. May *I* help you?'

'We need to speak with her. I'm Detective Sergeant Dennis McBride and this is Sergeant Sean Cullen.' The two men produced their warrant cards.

'Is something wrong?' Sam asked. 'Is my father all right?'

'May we come inside?'

Sam hesitated, then led them into the house. Something had to have happened to his father – why else would the guards be there?

Charlotte was in the hall winding a grey scarf round her throat. She took the post from Sam and smiled at the men who had followed her son in. 'Hello,' she greeted them.

'Mam, these men are police officers. They want a word with you.'

Charlotte stopped smiling. 'What's wrong? Is it Tommy?'

'Mrs Jones, I'm Detective Sergeant Dennis McBride and this is Sergeant Sean Cullen. We're with Pearse Street Garda Station.'

'What is it? Has something happened to my husband?'

'No, Mrs Jones, but we'd like to ask you a few questions, if you wouldn't mind.'

Charlotte blinked. 'Of course.'

'Look what's this about? Why don't you tell us why you're here?' Sam said. 'It's Dad, isn't it? What's happened?'

'Sam.' Charlotte laid a hand on his sleeve. 'Be quiet.'

Sam clenched his fists. His father was often drunk and maudlin, sometimes belligerent. It drove Sam crazy and upset his mother but, right at that moment, the thought that something might have happened to his dad terrified him.

Charlotte put her handbag and the post on the hall table. McBride opened a notebook and thumbed through a few pages. 'Do you know anyone called Walter Hogan?'

Charlotte's brow furrowed. 'I don't think so.'

'He's a retired doctor.'

'I'm sorry, I don't know the name.'

'How about a woman by the name of Katie Todd?'

Charlotte glanced at Sam before she answered, 'No, I don't believe so.'

'Look, what is this about?' Sam said again.

McBride cleared his throat. 'There was a shooting yesterday, over in Howth. An Englishwoman called Katie Todd shot Walter Hogan before turning the gun on herself.'

'I heard something about it on the radio,' Charlotte said. 'She killed herself?'

'She tried to. She's in a coma.'

'That's terrible, but I can't see what it would have to do with me.'

McBride sighed. 'The woman had two addresses with her, one for Hogan and one for you.'

'For me?'

'Yes.'

'But why would she have my address?'

'I don't know. We were hoping you might throw some light on it. You're sure you never heard of Walter Hogan?'

'I promise you I haven't.'

McBride nodded. 'Or Katie Todd?'

'She's already told you she hasn't,' Sam said impatiently, glancing at his watch. 'Look, we really have to get going, Mam.'

'We're very sorry to have *kept* you,' McBride said, with the faintest trace of sarcasm in his voice.

Sam's spine tightened. 'Let me show you out.'

The two guards exchange a look, said goodbye to Charlotte and walked towards the door. She watched them go, her expression thoughtful.

When Sam returned, she was looking at her post. The bill lay ignored by her bag, but the second envelope was in her hand. 'Mam, you can look at it later. Come on – I'm going to be late enough as it is.'

'Wasn't that odd?'

'Yes. Come on!'

Charlotte turned the envelope over. Her name and address were written in sharp, spiky letters in green ink. It had a Dublin postmark but there was no return address. She opened it – in what seemed like slow motion to Sam – and peered inside. 'There's something in here.'

She turned the envelope upside down, and something slid out into her hand. She gasped.

Sam, startled, grasped her arm. 'Mam, what is it? Are you all right?'

Charlotte opened her fingers slowly and Sam saw a locket on a long silver chain. His mother made a strange keening sound. She took two steps backwards and sank onto the stairs as though all the strength had drained from her body. Sam leaped towards her, frightened now. What the hell was going on? Had she had a heart attack?

'Quickly, Sam!' Charlotte choked out the words. 'Call them back.'

'The gardaí?'

'*Quickly!*'

Sam turned and ran after them. They were in the car, about to pull away, when he waved at them to stop.

Cullen wound down his window. 'What?'

'My mother! Something's happened – she got something in the post. You've got to come back.'

They followed him back into the house. He was alarmed to see that his mother was crying. 'Mam? What's going on?'

'Mrs Jones?' McBride pushed himself forward.

Charlotte handed Sam the locket. 'Open it.'

He did, and stared at the aged photos inside. He didn't recognise the one on the right but, with a shock, he knew the person on the left. 'It's Katie,' he said. 'How is this possible?'

'Mrs Jones, what is it?'

'The woman, the Englishwoman, you called her Katie.'

'Yes.'

'What did she look like?'

'Blonde, about five foot four, slim, blue eyes. Estimated age late twenties, early thirties—'

Charlotte groaned so loudly that Sam flinched. She snatched the locket from Sam's hand and pressed it into McBride's huge paw. 'This is my daughter's locket. My daughter. She … it's the locket she was wearing the day she disappeared twenty-six years ago. Her name was Katie – Katie Jones.'

McBride opened the locket and stared at the photo inside.

'You've got to take me to her,' Charlotte cried, clinging to his arm.

'Mrs Jones, I don't think—'

'*Please!* She had my address, you said so yourself – please! I just want to see her.'

'Stop this!' Sam grabbed his mother. 'Katie drowned.'

'Sam—'

'No,' Sam snapped at his mother. 'You've got to stop this.'

'But the locket.' She wrenched herself free of him. 'It's hers! Who else would have it?'

'I – I don't know,' Sam said. He turned to McBride, who was looking a little uncomfortable. 'What the hell's going on here? Are you trying to say my sister's alive?'

'Please, calm down.'

'Calm down? Are you for real? You come here upsetting my mother, getting her hopes up over my sister. Do you have any idea—'

'We didn't know about your sister,' Cullen said softly.

Sam's hand tightened over the locket. 'This is outrageous.'

'Sir, perhaps you and your mother *should* come with us. We'll explain everything at the station,' McBride said in a voice that made Sam nervous.

'I have appointments all day – I can't—'

'Sam.' His mother's voice behind him. 'It's Katie.'

'You don't know that.'

'It's her,' Charlotte insisted. She took her son's shoulders and shook him. Tears spilled from her eyes. 'Never *mind* appointments. She's *alive*. I *prayed*, Sam. I prayed my whole life – I prayed for this … *Katie's alive!*'

Sam held his mother close and patted her stiffly on the back. 'All right, Mam, all right. We'll go. Don't cry, it'll be all right.'

4

The kitten was tiny, only eight weeks old, a small tabby with a white bib, two white socks and a dark button nose.

'What do you want to call him?' he asked, kicking his feet onto the coffee table and spreading his arms along the back of the leather sofa.

'I don't know.' She lifted the kitten up and held him close to her bruised cheek. He was soft and fuzzy. She thought his fur smelled of cinnamon. She wondered where he'd got him. 'What do you think?'

'He's your cat, darlin'. Call him what you like.'

'Hello there, little one.' She smiled. He was sorry. The kitten proved it – she knew he wasn't much for animals. 'What about Ziggy?'

'Sure.' He was watching her with ice-blue eyes. All of the girls at the club were crazy about him and sick jealous that he was with her. She'd heard more than one ask what he saw in her. He was handsome, tall and athletic. He had high cheekbones, because he was, he said, part Russian on his grandmother's side. Sarah believed he was telling the truth about that.

'Just make sure you look after him proper. I don't want no mess, he's your responsibility.'

'I will.'

She nuzzled the kitten and carried him into the kitchen to give him some milk. She set him on the floor and watched him totter about on his little paws, sniffing out his new surroundings. She though he was the cutest thing she'd ever seen.

In the sitting room, the TV came on. Football.

She stiffened. She hoped his team would win – he had almost two grand riding on it, she'd heard him place his bet on the phone that morning.

She put the saucer of milk by the fridge and knelt down. 'Here you go, baby.' She picked the kitten up and tilted his nose into it. He spluttered, then bobbed his head in. After a few tries, he finally got the hang of it and began to lap furiously, his tail sticking straight up in the air. Sarah stroked his back with her index finger. She could feel him purring and was smitten already. 'Hey there Ziggy, you like that?'

She sat on the floor and watched him. He was so tiny, so defenceless. She tried not to think about that, but already a fearful doubt was nagging at her.

The kitten stopped drinking. She lifted him into her arms. He looked up at her. He had soft grey-blue eyes. 'Hello, little fella, had enough?'

He began to knead her jumper, his tiny paws working in a gentle rhythm. She sat down and brought up her legs to create a little fort round him. Inside it, he would be safe. She could protect him there. 'Ziggy.'

Sarah Kenny opened her eyes. She took a deep breath and sat up. Then she touched her cheek and was surprised to discover it was wet. She had been crying in her sleep.

Outside, the bin men clattered. She climbed out of bed and opened the curtains. It was still dark and the lawn was covered with frost. She traced a name in the condensation on the windowpane.

Ziggy.

If she wanted to, she could close her eyes and still smell him.

She wiped out the name and made her way to the bathroom. She could do nothing about her dreams, but she was damned if she was going to let memories infect the hours she was awake.

* * *

23

'So, you don't believe your wife is walking the dog?' Sarah asked, somewhat testily, later that morning. She had played beat-around-the-bush with Geoff Granger on the phone for ten minutes and her patience was about to run screaming for the door.

'Oh, no, she's definitely walking him.'

'Then I don't see—'

'Well, I think she is. See, first I thought it was great she was taking more of an interest, you know? Trigger's more my dog, really, and I suppose Carmel never really wanted him so I don't, you know, blame her for not, you know, taking him out much. I was happy enough to see her getting on with him, but then, you know, I noticed some days he was ... Oh, I don't know, kind of *clean* for a dog that's supposed to be doing lots of walking. When I take him out, he always manages to get kind of filthy, you know? And then I noticed he was especially active last Wednesday? And he was clean, really clean. But Wednesday week it was wet, right? Why would he be so clean on a wet day?'

'I see.' Sarah wrote 'clean, not tired dog' on her notepad, and 'Wednesday'.

'So I asked my neighbour, you know, did he see Carmel walk him much. And he said he saw her go out with him all right, but she always took him off with her in the car.'

'Right.' Sarah wrote 'car'.

'And then when I asked her why she took the car she said she preferred to walk him in the Phoenix Park. She said she felt safer there. More people about, she said.'

'Right. Well, lots of people do walk their—'

'But that's odd in itself because, like I already told you, Trigger's a retriever and they can be, you know, he's a bit of a shedder and Carmel hates dog hair getting everywhere. That's why he's not allowed into the house here. Well, he can go into the kitchen, but that's tiled, you see? I can't see her being happy about hair in her car.'

'Right.' Sarah wrote 'shedder'.

'And then I got to thinking, how come she didn't walk him closer to home, you know? There are plenty of places she could take him around here. It didn't make sense. You know?'

'And did you ask your wife?'

'I did, but she got angry. She said if that was how I was going to be she wouldn't walk Trigger at all. Then she said she was trying to lose a bit of weight and walking the dog helped and that she'd walk him anywhere she damned pleased.'

'Well, I suppose she—'

'So I said I thought that was great – you know, about the weight – but when I offered to go with her the other evening, she got ... all angry with me again, you know. And then she said she had a headache and she didn't want to walk Trigger. Next thing I know she's stopped talking to me. I had to say sorry, but she was mad for days.'

'Right.' Sarah wrote 'headache' and 'mad'.

'Now I'm sure,' Geoff continued, 'there's nothing funny going on and maybe I'm ... I'm overreacting, but I want to know that everything's okay, put my mind at ease, you know?'

'I understand.'

'So, can your firm take my case?'

'You want us to watch your wife walk the dog?'

'Well ... yes.'

'We'll charge you a hundred and fifty euros an hour for surveillance.'

'Okay.'

'For how long?'

'Just for a few days or so, I'd say. She'll take him out later today, tomorrow and on Friday at lunchtime.'

'Okay, then.' Sarah tucked a strand of long dark hair behind her ear and transferred the phone to the other side of her head. She checked her watch and opened a new file on the computer. 'We'll need an up-to-date photo and—'

'You'll be discreet, though, won't you?' Geoff interrupted. 'I don't want Carmel to know anything about this.'

'I understand.'

'I'm sure it's completely innocent, you know, the walking. Like I say, she has been trying to lose weight, so it's perfectly natural that she'd want to exercise a bit more.'

'Of course.'

'We've been together a long time.'

Sarah waited. She understood the hesitation in his voice and didn't push. Sometimes they changed their minds at this point. Sometimes ignorance is bliss. You can't put the genie back in the bottle when you've released him.

'So, if she was, you know, just walking him ... it wouldn't be right, now, would it, following her like that?'

'Mr Granger, we're very discreet, you know?' She slapped herself on the forehead for the 'You know', but really, it was very catching.

'Because I'm not ... you know, saying she's up to anything. I just, well, I—'

'I understand.'

'And these things, well, you know, if she found out I was ... checking up on her ...'

'I promise she won't know a thing about it.'

'Right.' He still didn't sound convinced.

'Peace of mind,' Sarah said quickly. 'That's what most of our clients want.'

'That's what I want. You understand, don't you?'

'I do.' Sarah felt slightly guilty at how pathetically grateful he sounded. 'So, about that photo ...'

'You've got to be kidding me. Dog watching?' John Quigley, Sarah's partner and co-owner of QuicK, their investigation agency, said when she had got off the phone and explained the story.

'Correction. Wife watching. The dog is secondary.'

'This is really lame.'

'From what he told me he might have a right to be suspicious. Either way, we're taking it.'

John threw his legs up onto the desk. QuicK Investigations was going through one of its periodic lulls and sitting around, staring at the four walls and waiting for the phone to ring was not his idea of fun. His hand reached automatically for the breast pocket of his faded denim shirt, and then he remembered.

He had promised Sarah – no more smoking in the office. She was right, of course. If he was caught, he'd be fined, although the very idea that the government was dictating whether or not he could smoke in his own office bothered the hell out of him. Still, the no-smoking ban was probably doing wonders for his health.

'Dog watching.' He shook his head.

'At least it's work.'

'Barely.' He reached for his pocket again and clenched his jaw.

'Look, I know it's not much,' Sarah said, 'but between that and the insurance job Rodney sent up, we're pretty much breaking even this month.' She tapped on her keyboard for a second. 'Next thing you know, one of us might actually earn a wage.'

'Yeah.'

'If I'm really lucky I might even be able to pay the mortgage this month.'

'Still no sign of a buyer for the flat?'

'Not so far, although Gloria reckons it shouldn't take long.' Gloria was the estate agent with whom Helen had set her up.

John groaned. 'Oh, all right. But tell me this, boss – which lucky sucker gets to traipse after our dog walker?'

Sarah pointed at him with her pen. 'I thought you'd jump at the chance to get out of the office.'

'You took the call.'

'I'm not the best at tailing.' Sarah indicated her ankle. Though she was improving, she still limped a little from where she had been shot by Patrick York, a drug-dealing scumbag the year before when she was working a missing person case. 'Injured, remember?'

'When it suits you,' John said. 'Didn't stop you last week when you saw that warden looking at the Fiesta. You were up the road like a scalded cat.'

'Okay, I'll play you for it.'

'You're on.'

Sarah grinned. 'Ready?'

'Wait.' John took down his legs and cracked his knuckles. 'Okay, go.'

They jiggled their hands furiously.

'Rock!' John yelled, brandishing a fist.

'Paper covers rock!' Sarah shrieked, her hand held flat.

'Ah ... best out of three?'

'Nope.'

'I hate that stupid game.' John sat up and stalked outside for a smoke.

'I really appreciate the not smoking, you know!' she called after him.

'Yeah, yeah ...'

5

'Got her.'

'Sure?'

'It's her all right,' John Quigley muttered into his mobile later that day. 'I don't see her doing a lot of walking either. You should see the get-up she's in.'

'What's she wearing?'

'White pants, slip-on white shoes and some kind of pink mac. Oh yeah, and enough make-up for a drag queen to get jealous.'

'All that to walk a dog?'

'Yep. And it's starting to rain. Who walks their mutt in the rain?'

'Don't get too close to her,' Sarah said. 'I can't believe you took Sumo – you're supposed to be discreet and he's *very* recognisable.'

'You don't say,' John said. Sumo, half wolfhound, half German shepherd, took up most of the back seat of Sarah's Fiesta. John thought it made perfect sense to kill two birds with one stone – Sumo needed exercise and he was spending the afternoon in a park.

'Well he is, isn't he?'

'Sarah, it's a fucking park, people walk dogs in the park. She could see me there every day for a year and find it less weird if I had him with me than not.'

'He'll slobber all over my car.'

'I'll ask him to refrain.'

29

'Just make sure you don't lose her. Maintain a visual.'

'A visual?'

'Yes, John, where you can *see* her.'

'Oh, ten–four, buddy. Target in range, repeat, target in range, over.'

'John Quigley, I swear to God …'

'I've got to go, Commander. She's getting into her car. Repeat, target and four-legged target are moving out. Roger.'

She hung up on him. John slipped the mobile back into his tracksuit pocket. He adjusted his hat and waited for Carmel Granger to drive past. He gave her another few seconds to get down to the green before he followed. Sumo whined behind him, eager to be off.

'Hold your horses, big fella,' John said as he started the engine. He slipped out onto the road and accelerated a little. 'We're stalking a housewife walking her dog. We need our wits about us.'

Sarah flung her phone onto the desk and rolled her eyes. There was no point in talking to John when he was like this, and he always was on stakeouts. He really hadn't the patience for them.

She glanced at the open cardboard folder on her desk and began to type the details from it into her computer. She was transferring every file they had onto the hard drive so that, in future, if they needed to access one they could do it by computer instead of rummaging through a mountain of paper. It was dull work, but it kept her mind occupied.

Except it didn't, and after a few minutes, despite her best intention, her hand strayed to the phone. The home help answered on the third ring.

'Hi, Belinda.'

'Hello, Sarah.'

Did she sound irritated? It was so hard to tell what Belinda felt, Sarah thought. 'How's Mum doing?'

'Pretty much the same as she was when you last called.'

Sarah winced. She hadn't known Belinda long, but already she could recognise exasperation in her voice when she heard it.

'Still unsettled, then?'

'A little.'

'Did she eat?'

'A little. She says she's not hungry.'

'She hardly touched her dinner last night.'

'Don't worry, I've made chicken soup. She'll have that during her film.'

'Great,' Sarah said. It felt wrong to talk about her mother as if she was a petulant child. 'Well, I'll see you later.'

'You will be home by seven today, won't you?'

'Sure will.' Sarah winced again. She had been late twice in the almost two months that Belinda had worked for her and the care-worker never let her forget it. 'Bye.'

Sarah hung up and chewed her lip. Helen and Jackie, her elder sisters, were contributing the bulk of Belinda's salary because Sarah had insisted their mother should not go to a nursing home. But was it working? Sarah knew that their mother hated having a stranger in her home, but her Alzheimer's was progressing at an alarming rate. Just a few months ago she had seemed a little eccentric, but now, it was clear that the disease had taken a much firmer hold.

She still had clear and perfectly lucid days, but the bouts of confusion and irritation were increasing. Sarah knew Helen in particular was biding her time until she got her way and carted their mother off to a nursing home – or 'care facility', as she called it.

Sarah lowered her head into her hands. She felt trapped. She needed her sisters' help to keep things running, at least until she sold her flat and released some capital, but she chafed under their interference. Between Jackie's moist-eyed kindness and Helen's blunt efficiency, it sometimes seemed that she would never escape her family.

She wondered if she was being too hard on her sisters, too quick to snap. It wasn't like any of this was their fault. The apartment had only been on the market a month and, with the way property went in Dublin, it was bound to sell. Gloria, the agent, Helen's friend, had agreed to handle the sale for a vastly reduced fee. And she had phoned to say there was a viewing that evening. Sarah would be sad to see it go, her little haven, but family came first.

* * *

John followed Carmel Granger's Punto all the way to the round-about where Carmel should be taking a right – if she was going to the Phoenix Park. He watched as she went left and drove towards Mulhuddart Village.

'Okay, Sumo, you might as well get comfy. Looks like we're going on a road trip.' He grinned. 'Walking the dog, my arse.'

They came to the village and turned right across the bridge. John let another car come between them as he followed her past a cemetery, through another roundabout and then for a further three miles. He lost her briefly then caught up and did his best to hang back as he drove along the twisty road, but when they took another right and then another onto a road not much bigger than a lane, he had no option but to drop right back to a crawl.

'Where the hell is it you're going?' he said as he pulled in to wait for Carmel to get ahead again. He climbed out of the car, grabbed his binoculars and watched her progress over the top of a hedge. He was glad to see her brake, then stop outside a set of gates about half a mile down the road.

'Gotcha.' John climbed back into his car and drove on. He pulled up in a lay-by twenty metres past the gates and grabbed his camera out of the glove compartment.

'Okay, sit, stay and don't chew anything.' He locked the Fiesta on a disbelieving Sumo.

He jogged back up the road, trying to skip over puddles. The light rain was heavier now and beat at him as he approached the locked gates. He checked for a camera and when he had assured himself that there was none, he tried to peer through the tiny gaps. He could see grass and a gravel drive, but nothing else.

He stepped back and looked around. A whitewashed wall enclosed the property on all sides. The house – if there was one – must be set back from the road.

John wiped rain off his face and considered the situation. There was a line of trees running along the other side of the wall. If he dropped down there, he would have cover.

He put his camera in his pocket and used the grass verge to boost himself up onto the wall. Seconds later, he dropped with a thud onto the pine-covered earth inside the property.

He crouched down and peered through the trees. He was looking out onto a long oval lawn, stables and two large red sheds. A grass-rutted lane ran between the stables and the sheds and in the distance, over the roofs, he could see the chimney stacks of a house.

Using the trees as cover, he made his way round the perimeter of the lawn and managed to get within twenty feet of the sheds. Here he had no choice but to come into the open and run for it.

He sprinted across the sodden grass and dived behind a pile of wooden pallets to work out his next move.

He edged round the shed and trotted alongside it until he came to the back of a garage. From there, he could see the Punto parked in a small courtyard to the right of a magnificent old Georgian house. There was no sign of either Carmel or Trigger.

John scanned the windows of the house. The upper ones had curtains and the bottom ones wooden shutters, all open except for the one nearest the porch.

He'd have to risk it.

John sidled forward, doing his best to keep close to the garage and then the stone wall that ran to the side of the house. At the porch, he took a deep breath, then began to crawl along the wet flowerbed, cutting his hands on the heavily pruned roses. Finally, he was beneath the window. He could hear music from inside the room and high-pitched laughter.

John got onto his knees and peeped over the window ledge into the study with wall-to-wall bookshelves and a roaring fire in the hearth. Trigger lay in front of it gnawing a bone.

Carmel Granger had a glass of what looked like Scotch in her hand, and her legs lay on the lap of a grey-haired man who was, by John's estimation, at least eighty. She was giggling and flicking her hair flirtatiously. It looked put on to John, but clearly not to her paramour, because moments later she had put down the glass and was playing tonsil hockey with the old man.

John got out his camera and snapped off a few shots. He changed the focus and wiped rain from the lens. He aimed again and had taken one of Carmel shedding her blouse when he heard a sound behind him.

'Hey, you there! You! What do you think you're doing?'

John whirled around. An elderly man wearing a green cap and overalls stood there with a wheelbarrow filled with filthy straw. A shovel rested on top and a wicked-looking collie hunched low to the ground beside it, eyes fixed on John.

John raised his hands. 'Sorry, I'm lost and I—'

The gardener clocked the camera. He looked to the window just as a scream rang out.

'Ya dirty fuckin' pervert!' he roared.

'No, wait!'

The man picked up his shovel. It looked like he meant business.

John glanced behind him just in time to see Carmel Granger's 'friend' heading for the window. He also noticed that Carmel was trying to put on her shirt as she ran out of the room.

The man tugged up the sash window and glared out. 'What the blazes is going on? Charlie?'

'This sicko was taking photos of you!'

'Photos?'

'Aye, through the window! He's a pervert!'

The man in the study flushed. He put his foot out of the window. 'Come here!' he bellowed. 'I'm going to shove that fucking camera up your hole.'

John decided he'd seen enough. He did the only thing he could. He bolted.

The man with the wheelbarrow yelled, 'Fly, go on boy, ssssiik siiik!'

John ran for the sheds – legs pumping, lungs screaming. Behind him, he could hear loud barking. Shit! He'd never make it back to the road in one piece. His only hope was a cluster of trees and brambles a few yards to the left of the path. Maybe he could climb—

He spun off the path and sprinted for them. The collie was on his heels and he felt it nip him on the back of the calf.

'Owww. Shit!'

He put on an extra spurt, vaulted a fallen tree and tore into the undergrowth. He hadn't gone three strides before he tripped over a half-buried wire fence and went flying. Fortunately, a slimy duckpond broke his fall.

'Argh!' He swallowed a mouthful of fetid water and struggled to his feet, managing somehow to keep the camera aloft. The bottom of the pond was mud and silt, and he sank into it until the water came up to his chest. He flailed, coughed, gagged and spluttered. A family of ducks flapped away from him.

He splashed his way to the opposite bank and dragged himself out. The water was freezing and his teeth chattered uncontrollably with the shock of the cold and his fall. When he was halfway out, the collie broke through into the clearing. It skidded to a halt and barked furiously. John wiped his eyes and glared at it. He picked up a rotten branch and flung it at the animal. '*Fuck off!*'

To his amazement, it stopped barking, sat down on the bank and watched as John – holding the camera aloft – hacked up and spat slime onto the ground. He staggered into the bushes and continued to make his way to the road.

He fumbled in his pocket for his mobile, took it out and tried to turn it on. Nothing. It was saturated. Cursing, he shoved it back into his pocket and made his way back to where he had left the Fiesta. He glanced behind him – the collie was watching him, its tongue lolling out of its mouth.

6

By four o'clock, Sarah was starving. She darted across the road to the supermarket, where she bought a hot chicken pie and a copy of the *Herald*, then she skipped back through the stalled traffic to the office. No sign of John and no word either. She had tried his mobile a few times but it had gone straight to voicemail.

She wasn't exactly worried. John marched to the beat of his own drum and it was likely that he'd got pissed off with tailing Carmel Granger and gone off for a bite and a pint.

Actually, he'd been trying to change his ways recently – he was shouldering more responsibility and had taken up the slack – *her* slack, Sarah thought, if she was being fair.

The QuicK Investigations office was housed on the top floor of a dilapidated old building on Wexford Street, and was also home to a run-down grocery on the ground floor. Freak FM, a pirate radio station owned by Mike Brannigan, a local hustler, took up the first floor, and Rodney Mitchell, an alcoholic solicitor, ran his practice – such as it was – from the second.

She was just about to push open the street door when she spotted John making his way down the road. He was a filthy, muddy mess and passers-by were giving him a wide berth. 'What the hell happened to you?' she gasped. 'What's that smell?'

'Pond scum.' John picked a piece of moss off his sleeve and flicked it onto the pavement.

'*Pond scum?*'

'More than I ever want to see again, that's for sure.' John sniffed his sleeve and pulled a face. 'I got chased by a dog.'

'Did he catch you? You're soaked through.'

'I'm aware of that.'

'It smells like sewage.'

'Tell me about it. I had to drive the whole way here with all the windows open.'

'Oh no, not my car.'

'Yup, sorry, it stinks to high heaven.' He held up his hand. 'And before you start, you were the one who insisted I take it.'

'That's because the Manta sticks out like a sore thumb. Are you telling me—'

'Excuse me.' A tall man stopped beside Sarah. He was in his early thirties, about six foot two, the same height as John, and handsome, like a young Robert Redford. He had pale blond hair, cornflower blue eyes and an intense expression on his face. He wore a well-cut suit, a slate-grey overcoat and highly polished black shoes. He had a sheet of paper in his left hand, nice watch, no rings.

'Sorry.' Sarah stepped aside but he didn't go past. He glanced at the piece of paper and at the filthy aluminium and tinted glass door of their building. He frowned.

John sighed impatiently. 'We help ya there, Bud?'

The man glanced at him and his eyes widened. 'I think I'm lost, I'm … I was looking for QuicK Investigations. It should be … I'm not sure if I have the right address.'

'This is QuicK Investigations.' Sarah gestured towards the tiny name on the doorbell.

'*We* are Quick Investigations,' John said.

The man looked at them. Whatever he had been expecting, it was clear that they had fallen far short of it.

'I'm Sarah Kenny and this is my partner, John Quigley.' Sarah held out her hand. 'You'll have to excuse his appearance. He's been on a stakeout most of the day.' There was green slime on John's cheek, plus feathers, muck and bits of … well, whatever it was, it was all over him. The smell was getting stronger. 'It's been a difficult assignment. Underwater.'

The man arched an eyebrow. 'I'm sorry?'

'I think she means 'undercover',' John said.

'What did I say?'

'Under water.'

'Oh.'

'I see.' The man nodded uncertainly. 'Maybe this is a bad time—'

'No, no, please.' Sarah knew if they let him go he'd never come back. She pushed open the door with her foot and ushered him inside. 'Please go in. We're on the top floor. I'll be with you in a moment.'

The man hesitated. He glanced once more at John, who beamed at him. 'If I were you, I'd make the most of it. I don't always look this good.'

'Top floor?'

Sarah nodded.

'All right then.' The man stepped inside.

When he was out of sight, Sarah said, 'Did Carmel Granger see you?'

'She might have done.'

'I promised our client discretion.'

'Yeah, well, shit happens.'

Sarah sighed. She reached out and wiped some dirt from his cheek. 'Gangrene smells better. You'd better head home and shower.'

'You want to come, do my back?' John winked lasciviously.

Sarah's dark eyes flashed. 'What girl could refuse such an offer?'

'Hey, plenty wouldn't. Be lucky I even asked.'

'Oh, I'm thanking my stars right this minute.'

John grinned at her and handed her his camera. 'I managed to keep it fairly dry. Pictures probably aren't the best quality, but my mobile's done in.'

'We'll charge it to the client's expenses.' Sarah took the camera from him gingerly. 'Did you get what we needed?'

John pulled a soggy box of cigarettes from his pocket and looked at it sadly. 'Christ, I hope so.'

'I'll get them developed. Catch you later.'

They stood looking at each other for a beat too long. Then Sarah pushed open the door and left him to squelch up the street and home.

On the opposite side of the street, the man sitting in the window of Eddie Rockets Diner put down his coffee cup. He had observed John and Sarah's interaction with barely contained fury. He had watched as she laughed, studied the way her eyes crinkled with amusement. When she had wiped John's cheek, he had tasted something sharp and bitter, and realised he had bitten the inside of his cheek hard enough to draw blood.

He remembered that look. He remembered her touch, the coolness of her skin, how her shotgun bark of a laugh had once made his heart rush.

Sarah.

He had been watching her for almost three weeks now, her habits, her routines, yet he always got a jolt when he saw her, a burning sensation that started deep in his belly. One night he had followed her almost to her front door. He had stood behind a withered hydrangea in the overgrown garden and watched as she had removed her coat and lain on the sofa in her mother's house, her long dark hair fanned out behind her. He fancied he could smell her perfume, lingering in the cool night air. It had been all he could do not to kick the door clean off its hinges and go to her, scoop her up, run his hands through her hair, cup her head in his hands and kiss her long and deep. To see the look in her eyes when she recognised him.

Sarah.

No. He had waited for his revenge, hungered for it. It had kept him company through the nights when he had lain awake listening to the howling around him. It had sustained him. He wouldn't blow everything now by acting hastily.

But it was hard. He longed to make his presence known. Sometimes he half expected her to feel him and glance up, for their eyes to lock. He almost wanted her to see him, to know he was there.

And yet he remained hidden. He had grown a beard and wore a cap low on his head. He was enjoying his secrets, the sense of power it afforded him.

Sometimes, like today, when he saw her with John, his hands trembled so badly he was forced to clasp them together to gain control of himself.

Sarah.

He watched John trudge up the street. John Quigley, her first love, the man whose name she had muttered in her sleep. A muscle jumped in his jaw. He wanted to rip the man's head clean off his shoulders. He wanted to crush him, rip out his eyes and stamp on them. He had seen the way John looked at Sarah. He loved her. Why wouldn't he?

Sarah's easy intimacy with John, however, had been a surprise.

Fools! They were in love, even if neither of them realised it.

He knew little about their early relationship because, no matter how hard he had pushed, she had not told him anything. He knew John had hurt her, not because she had said so but because he had seen it in her face when she had first mentioned his name.

He had been surprised to see them together, but he shouldn't have been. Sarah was a masochist. She embraced hurt. She needed it.

'Can I get you another coffee?' The little Chinese waitress hovered nervously at his table.

He regarded her, his wall-eye glistening milky white and alien under the overhead lights. 'Did you hear me ask for another coffee?' When he spoke his voice seemed gravelly and unused. How long had it been since he had spoken to anyone properly?

'No.'

'Then I don't want one. If I do, sweetheart, I'll ask for it.'

'Okay.' She glanced down at his scarred hands.

'We clear?'

'Yes.'

'Stay pretty.'

'Okay.'

He turned, back to his vigil and the waitress bolted to the safety of the counter.

7

'Okay, Mr...?'

'Sam Jones. Call me Sam.'

'Sam.' Sarah sat behind her desk and waved him towards a chair. 'Please take a seat.' She waited until he was settled, then gave him her most professional smile. 'How can I help you?'

'What happened to your partner?'

'From what I can gather, he and a pond collided.'

Sam nodded, as if this was a perfectly reasonable explanation. 'I've read about your agency. You solved a murder earlier this year – it was in the papers.'

'Yes.' Sarah linked her fingers.

'Was it difficult to find out what had happened?'

'I can't discuss our cases with you.'

'I don't want you to.' He looked about him.

Sarah waited. He'd get round to talking eventually.

'I've never done anything like this before,' he said.

'Okay.'

'I'm not even sure I should be here.' He fell silent again.

Finally, Sarah had to kick the ball and start it rolling. 'Sam, I can't help you if you don't talk to me. You must have come to me for a reason, so what is it?'

'It's about my sister.' He hugged his briefcase to his chest.

41

'I – we need…' His face was suddenly the colour of wax. 'I want you to find out what happened to my sister.'

'Okay. Let's start at the beginning.' Sarah took a pen out of a jam jar, slid a notebook towards her and opened it at a fresh page. 'She's missing?'

'Yes … no.'

Sarah waited, her hand poised over the clean page.

Sam cleared his throat. 'She was missing, and now she's in a coma.'

'I'm sorry to hear that. Was she in an accident?'

'She … there was a shooting. She shot herself, but she didn't die.' He snapped the locks on his briefcase, reached in and extracted a newspaper. He passed it to her. 'Please, read that.'

Sarah glanced down. An article had been circled in red ink. 'I remember reading something about this over the weekend,' she said. 'The shooter is your sister?'

'Yes.'

'I don't understand.' Sarah frowned. 'What is it you need our firm for?'

'It's complicated. There's something the papers don't know yet … Katie had been missing for years. We thought she was dead, and then she turned up and …' He rubbed his forehead. 'I – we just want to know what happened to her. We've had this journalist sniffing and we … I just want to know where my sister was before the press does.'

'But the gardaí—'

'They've had this since Thursday and they've done nothing.'

'That's not very long. Who's in charge of the case?'

'Detective Sergeant Dennis McBride at Pearse Street.'

Sarah wrote down the name.

'They're not interested in her,' he said bitterly. 'To them she's just a nut. If she'd succeeded in killing herself they wouldn't even be vaguely interested.'

'What's her name? Katie?'

'Yes.'

'And how old is she?'

'Twenty-eight.'

42

'How long was she missing?'

'Twenty-six years.'

Sarah put down her pen and looked at Sam Jones carefully to see if he was taking the mickey. 'Twenty-six *years*?'

'Yes, but it's … well.' Sam flushed. 'Maybe I should start at the beginning.'

'I think you should.'

So Sam Jones told Sarah about the sunny day when his world had been torn apart. She listened, and understood the torment he and his family had endured. Eventually the words stopped but emotion saturated the air.

'Sam, twenty-six years is a long time to—'

'She sent a locket to my mother at our old house in Ringsend. We got it on Friday, the day after she shot that man – and herself. She had a notebook, and my mother's address was in it, that and the man she shot. She had my mother's address. She knew where we were, she knew how to find us, but she didn't.'

Sarah leaned back in her chair. 'Okay, so she sent a locket to your mum's house. How is that—'

He reached into his pocket and passed Sarah the locket. She opened it. On one side there was a grainy photo of a little blonde girl and on the other a picture of a dark-haired boy of about three. 'I don't know who the boy is, but that's Katie. My mother took that photo a few weeks before Katie disappeared. There used to be a photo of me in the other side. Katie was wearing *that* locket the day she went missing. My question is, why did she send it? Why didn't she come to us? Why didn't she let us know she was alive? *Why*? And why would she send it and then kill herself?'

Sarah closed the locket and put it on her desk. 'So, why do you need us?'

'I told you! The gardaí aren't doing anything. They're not interested in finding out what happened to my sister. Their only interest is in her waking up so that they can charge her with murder.'

Sarah tapped the newspaper. 'She did shoot that man.'

'She must have had a reason.'

'The gardaí haven't found any connection?'

'Not so far. They haven't even found an address for her. The one she gave the hotel was false.'

Sarah frowned. 'Did she know Walter Hogan? '

'I've no idea.' He shrugged helplessly. 'I don't know anything. He's not married and has no children. His sister says she never heard him mention Katie. She says he was retired and looking forward to going on holiday to Rome to meet the Pope.' He lowered his head. 'Poor woman – she's devastated.'

'Of course.' Sarah twisted a strand of hair through her fingers. Twenty-six years was a hell of a long time … 'I'm not sure if we can—'

'I didn't believe it was her until I saw her lying in the hospital. I should have been watching her that day. I thought she was behind me, I was bringing water back to a sandcastle I was building and she was collecting shells for the ramparts. I should have been watching her, but I wasn't. I'd got caught up in what I was doing and she … I turned round and she was gone.'

'But twenty-six years ago … what age were you?'

'Eight.'

'You were only a child.'

He spread his hands. 'I should have been watching her.'

'It wasn't your fault.'

'She was my sister. I should have protected her. I let her be taken.'

'Trust me, I've dealt with enough bad people in the world to know that, sometimes, there's nothing you can do. You can't protect yourself from … from bad people.'

But Sam Jones wasn't listening, he was reliving his private misery. 'It destroyed my parents. Mam never forgave herself for nodding off. Dad never forgave her either. They split up the following year. Dad moved over to England a couple of years ago. You should see him, he's a broken man. He's never recovered from what happened that day. None of us have.'

He balled his hands into fists.

'They never said it, not out loud, but I could see it in their eyes. I should have watched her and I didn't and now she's in a coma. Something must have happened to her. Someone had her all these years, maybe the person who took her away. You have to help us.

44

If there's even a small chance, I need to know what happened to her. I need to know where she was. I need to know why she shot that man. I need to know why she shot *herself*.'

Sarah glanced at the page in front of her.

'I need to know why she felt she couldn't come to us for help,' he muttered. 'I need answers.'

8

Sarah was loading the film John had taken of Carmel Granger onto her computer when he returned in fresh jeans and a pale blue denim shirt. He was carrying a bag of chips from the chipper up the street.

'Well?'

'You got some great shots. I particularly like the one where they're trying to reach each other's tonsils.'

'Good. I'm glad you're happy. At least now when I'm dying from the dreaded lurgy I can be content in the knowledge that you're happy.'

'The dreaded *lurgy*?'

John flopped into his chair. 'What's the story with that other guy?'

'Have a look at the newspaper on your desk. The story on page two.'

John read it and glanced up quizzically.

'The shooter is his sister and, get this, she's been missing for twenty-six years,' Sarah said.

'Let's hear it.'

Sarah related the story to him.

'Who's the guy?'

'His name is Walter Hogan, and he's a retired GP.'

'How'd they manage to keep it out of the papers – about her being missing and stuff?'

'Sam says his solicitor was all over it from the get-go. And the gardaí are happy enough to keep a lid on some of the details too – at least until they can get the girl to talk. Thing is, the taxi driver who was witness to the shootings is kicking up. Sam reckons he's itching to sell his story and her being missing is part of it.'

'Sam?'

'That's the man's name.'

'Are we taking it?'

'I said we would.'

John stuffed a chip into his mouth. They looked greasy, but the smell was making Sarah feel hungry. 'Twenty-six years is a hell of a long time.'

'I know,' she said, and enlarged one of the photos. She switched on the printer.

'Cops probably have a handle on it.'

'I know that too. I rang the detective handling the investigation, one McBride at Pearse Street. He reckons we're interfering. Truth is, I don't think we'll be able to do much with a twenty-six-year-old case.'

'So why did you tell him we'd take it?'

'Money,' Sarah said, but that wasn't true. The look in Sam Jones's eyes had swayed her. He had given her such a look of sheer desperation.

While the photos scanned she yawned. It was almost half-past six. She needed to get her skates on if she was to relieve Belinda at seven.

If anyone had told her a year ago that she'd be running her schedule like this, she would have laughed. But now, between her job and her mother's Alzheimer's, she had no option but to organise her life with military precision.

'What's our plan of action?'

'Start at the beginning, I suppose,' Sarah said. 'Tomorrow I'll check with the taxi driver while you go talk to the hotel. I'll take a look at her possessions too. It might be an idea to go to Brittas, do a resweep of the area.'

'What's the point in that?'

'I don't know, but we've got to start somewhere.'

47

'All right.' John scrunched up the greasy paper and tossed it into his wastepaper basket. 'Come on, Sarah, it's late. Let's call it a day.'

'I've still got to print out those photos for Mr Granger.'

'I'll do it. You head on home.'

'Speaking of photos, we'll also need a picture of Katie Jones.'

'I can get one this evening.'

'You sure?'

'Might as well. It's not like I have much else on.'

'Thanks, John.' She smiled at him, pleased he was so enthusiastic. 'Where's the car?'

'Round the corner on Pleasant Street.' He tossed her the keys and she caught them mid-air. 'And don't worry, I sprayed the interior so it should be fine. It's Ocean Mistastic.'

Sarah whirled the keys around her finger and dropped them into her pocket. She jerked her head towards the photos. 'I can't believe a woman of her age carrying on with an old boy like that. Can't believe he's even up to it.'

'He's a man. If he's got a pulse, he's got a chance of rising to the occasion.'

Sarah shook her head wryly. 'I suppose so.'

'All it takes is one stiff breeze and the sail goes up.'

Sarah clicked through the photos, pausing at the one of Carmel Granger sucking the face off her buddy, her blouse half undone. 'I'm not sure I'd describe Carmel as a breeze.'

'No,' John agreed. 'I think my sail would curl up and die if she blew anywhere near it.'

'John Quigley!'

Sarah left the office and hurried to Pleasant Street. She reached the Fiesta and swore. There was glass all over the street.

Someone had put a brick through the windscreen. It was the second time in two weeks.

She pulled out her mobile and dialled the office.

''Lo?'

'Call the garage, will you? Someone's busted the bloody windscreen.'

'Again?'

'Yes, again.' She walked round the car. 'Dammit – and the back window!'

She glanced around, hoping for a witness, but the street was deserted.

'I'll be there in a minute.'

'I can't wait, John. I'll leave the keys under the passenger seat and grab a cab.'

'I'll take care of it. Do you need a lift?'

'I haven't time to wait around.'

She hung up and unlocked the car door, grimacing at the glass-covered seats. Yep, there it was. A bloody brick from the building site round the corner. Someone had gone to the trouble of carrying it here – not exactly random.

She slammed the door and stormed back towards Camden Street. She couldn't find a taxi, which meant she'd probably be late and Belinda would do that snort she did or, worse, say nothing at all but manage to look annoyed, put-upon and disappointed all in one.

And who could blame her? Belinda had a life of her own, after all. At this rate, they'd be lucky to hang on to her.

A fat splat of rain hit her shoulder, followed by another and then the sky opened again. Sarah began to run.

Gloria Bradshaw fixed her hair for the fifth time and checked her lipstick in the bathroom mirror. Gloria would turn fifty in less than a week and she'd never been so depressed before a birthday. She had always taken pride in her looks (everyone at work thought she was in her early forties), but lately she'd started to suspect she was fighting a losing battle against gravity.

She pushed back the skin of her jaw and watched as her neck smoothed out. Then she released it and watched it sag back into place. She'd go to Brussels and get the whole lot tightened up. Not for her the ageing-gracefully nonsense her elder sister went on about. If Alison wanted to look like a dried-up old prune, that was her business. Being an estate agent was tough, cut-throat. Image was everything.

Energy was everything. *Youth* was everything. And damn it, if she didn't have all of those things any more, she could fake it.

She patted her highlighted hair and straightened a hand towel. She didn't normally work this late but she was doing a favour for a friend. Helen Kenny had asked her to handle the sale, and Landon had been delighted to have another client.

At least Sarah kept her flat clean, not like some of the places that Landon had given her to shift lately. Oh, it had been so different in Landon Senior's day. Landon Senior was a gentleman, old-school. He would never have offloaded a mass of one-bedroom shit-holes into her portfolio and expected her to whisk a buyer out of her Marks & Sparks control-panel knickers.

She checked her watch. The viewer was late. Typical.

That was the problem with everyone these days – no respect, no consideration for anyone else. Of course, Landon would probably give her a hard time about this one too, as if somehow the—

The buzzer rang. Gloria checked her reflection, practised her most charming, non-threatening smile, then hurried to let in the viewer.

'Hello there. I'm—' Her smile faltered as the man seemed to fill the hallway with his bulk. 'I'm Gloria Bradshaw, and you must be—'

'John Quigley,' the man said.

'John, of course. We spoke earlier.' Gloria held out her hand and watched as it was swallowed in his. The backs of his hands were criss-crossed with white scars.

'Is it just yourself, John?'

He held her hand for a beat too long, then released it. 'Yeah. My girlfriend couldn't make it. Problems with her car.'

Gloria clutched her clipboard to her chest. 'This is an ideal investment property or, if you were looking for a pied-à-terre, it's in an exceptional location, a mere stone's throw from Dame Street and with a great selection of local shops, video stores and—' She was babbling and she knew it. Gloria Bradshaw was a good reader of people and something about this man was making her gut tighten. It was the way he looked at her with his freaky white eye.

'You gonna show me around?'

'Of course.' Gloria smiled tightly. 'Well, obviously, this is the entrance hall. It's small, I know, but it holds a good-sized hot press.' She opened a wood-slat door and waited for him to look inside. He didn't. 'To our right is the bathroom.' She switched on the light and waved a hand inside. 'As you can see, it's well maintained, white suite and tiled floor to ceiling. Very practical, especially if you were thinking investment.'

The man said nothing.

'And on my right here is the bedroom, a nice-sized double room. The wardrobe is built in. Of course, you can change that if you wish.'

The man walked in, stood in the centre of the room and breathed in deeply.

'Of course the rental from this type of apartment is excellent and it's surprisingly easy to find tenants.' Gloria watched him from the door. *Was he sniffing the air?* 'With Thomas Street so close, the College of Art and Design is '

'Show me the rest,' he said, turning towards her.

'Of course. Follow me.' Gloria led him into the sitting room. It was a pretty room, painted bright yellow, and the major selling point of the apartment. The man stopped in the doorway, trapping Gloria inside.

'There's a balcony overlooking the street and a small kitchen through here that the owner has lovingly updated. Although it's small, as you can see, there's room for a table and bench, a nice little breakfast area.'

The big man smiled, which did nothing to ease Gloria's anxiety. For the first time in her career, she realised how vulnerable she was alone. The truth rattled her down to her Manolos. 'So what do you think?'

'Interesting.' He nodded, more to himself than to her.

'What is it you do, Mr Quigley?'

'I'm a private detective.'

'*Really*? How exciting.'

'It can be.' He smiled again, and this time Gloria took an involuntary step backwards.

'Well, John, would you care to have a look round by yourself?' She glanced at her watch. 'I have another viewing shortly.'

'Yeah?'

He cocked an eyebrow and Gloria knew he didn't believe her.

'Yes,' she squeaked. 'Married couple, young, first-time buyers, and this is an excellent first home. Great, er … amenities and close to schools …'

He stepped close, towering over her. Gloria cringed.

'I've seen enough, but thanks for your time,' he said, then leaned in and kissed her cheek. Gloria did all she could not to flinch.

'You've been a great help to me. Stay pretty.'

When Gloria opened her eyes, he was gone. A second later, she heard the latch of the front door click.

Her legs buckled and she slid into the leather armchair behind her. She took a very deep and shaky breath. 'Jesus Christ.'

She didn't notice that the man had taken Sarah Kenny's address book with him. Truth be told, even if she had, she wouldn't have tried to stop him.

John walked along the hospital corridors, wrinkling his nose at the smell. It never seemed to matter which one he was in, they all smelled the same. Why was it? he wondered. Was it the cleaning products, the air conditioning, sickness?

He came to room fifteen and tapped softly on the door. There was no answer.

He pushed it open and walked in.

Katie Jones lay in the bed, hooked up to a monitor and a drip. One side of her scalp had been shaved and John could see the stitches where the surgeons had opened her up to repair the damage she had inflicted on herself. Apart from that, though, she looked like a sleeping child.

John moved closer. He had raised the camera to take her photo when he heard the door open behind him. '*You goddamned vulture*! Get out of here and leave us alone. Go on, get out! *Nurse*!'

John spun round. A woman stood in the door with a plastic cup of coffee. She was in her late fifties, maybe early sixties, small and dark-haired, going grey at the temples, and her eyes were clouded with fury. '*Nurse!*'

John lowered the camera and took a step towards her. He stopped when she made to throw the cup at him. He'd been wet once today and that was enough. 'I'm John Quigley, a private detective.'

She glared at him. 'What are you doing in here?'

'Can I ask who you are?'

'I'm Charlotte Jones.'

'Katie's mother?'

'That's right.' Her nostrils flared, but her eyes lost some of their fury. 'Now, are you going to tell me what you're doing here?'

'Your son, Sam, spoke to my partner earlier today.' John held out his hand. After a brief hesitation, she shook it. 'We've been hired to look into your daughter's ... whereabouts.'

A little more of the anger left her eyes. 'I didn't know he'd hired someone already.'

'You want to call him to confirm?'

'No.' She gestured at the camera. 'I'm so sorry. I thought you were a reporter. A man was here earlier, snooping about.'

'That's okay, I've been called worse.' John smiled and was relieved to see Charlotte offer a tight one in return. 'Look, I'm sorry,' he went on, 'I didn't want to disturb anyone, but we really need a photo of Katie if we're going to investigate. If you'd rather I came back ...'

'No, no.' Charlotte walked slowly to the head of the bed. She looked down at her daughter's prone form and ran the back of her hand over her cheek.

'This must be a difficult time for you.'

'It is. I don't know what to make of it all.' She sat down in a plastic chair and picked up Katie's hand. 'All these years ... I wanted to believe more than anything that she was alive. I refused to accept that she was dead. I waited that summer, you see – I waited months for her body to come ashore. I walked that beach for days. And nothing.'

'It must have been terrible.'

'It was,' she said simply. 'You're not supposed to lose a child.

They're yours, your flesh and bones. You ache for them, yearn for them. I looked into the face of every blonde girl I saw for years, imagining what Katie would look like as time passed. I never stopped searching. I couldn't.'

John nodded.

'It took a toll, not just on me, on everyone – my husband, my son. Everyone. And now here she is. My little girl has come back to me.' She brushed a lock of Katie's hair from her forehead. 'She looks so peaceful, doesn't she?'

'Yes, she does.'

'What could have driven such a beautiful girl to such an unspeakable act?'

John had no answer to that.

'What did they do to her?' She touched the soft curls, a lone tear running down the side of her nose. 'She was such a sweet-natured child. What happened to my baby to make her like this?'

John remembered the feeling of a man falling onto his chest after the top of his scalp had been blown away, the blood and brain matter on his own face. He could smell cordite, he could see Sarah's shocked eyes and the smoking gun in her hands. 'Fear,' he said softly. 'Fear can drive a person to kill another.'

'He was an unarmed old man.'

'Okay,.' John shrugged. 'But she may have had all sorts of reasons.'

'You really think so?' Charlotte's eyes searched his face.

'Sure.'

'I don't believe any reason is good enough to take a life.' She dried her tears. 'I need to know what happened to my baby. I need to know how'– she waved her hand over the room wildly – 'this happened.' She turned to him again. 'Take your picture, Mr Quigley. Find out what happened to my girl. I want to understand why she came back, why she tried to kill herself.'

John laid a hand on her shoulder. 'I promise I'll do my best.'

9

'Come in.' Sam Jones opened the door of his penthouse apartment and smiled. 'Your pungent partner isn't with you today?'

'He's checking out the hotel your sister was staying at.'

'Oh.'

He looked relieved, Sarah noticed. Sometimes John had that effect on other men.

'Will I do?' she asked.

'Of course. Please come in. I believe he was very kind to my mother last night.'

'He has a way with the ladies.'

'Does he indeed?'

'He seems to think so.'

She followed Sam down a long white hall and into a large airy split-level living room with a panoramic view of Bushy Park. A sliding door led on to a wooden-floored balcony. The walls were painted chalky white, highlighting the beautiful silk etchings that adorned them. The furniture was minimal, but dark and masculine. There were recessed bookshelves in almost black wood and a matching coffee table. The envelope and the cheap canvas sports bag on it looked out of place.

'You have a lovely home,' Sarah said. She sank into a soft suede armchair and caressed the arms.

'Thank you. I designed it myself.' Sam fidgeted with his cuffs. 'Em, can I get you a drink?'

'Coffee would be fine.'

'Milk and sugar?'

'Just milk.'

'Sweet enough.'

'I'm sorry?'

'Old joke. That's how I take my coffee too.' Sam looked like he might say something else, but he didn't. Instead he slid open a Japanese screen door and stepped into a galley kitchen. From what Sarah could see, it was obvious he didn't do much cooking at home.

'Everything I could get from the gardaí is on the table,' Sam said as he filled the kettle, 'and her clothes are in that bag.' He came back into the room.

Sarah opened the envelope and emptied it out. There was a watch, a cheap silver ring, a set of keys and a cigarette lighter.

'There was no passport, no identification. The only thing she had on her was our address and the address of … the man,' he added.

'The man she shot – the GP?'

'Yes.'

'What's the story with him? I assume the gardaí have looked for a link.'

'Yes, but they can't find a thing on him.' Sam shrugged tiredly. 'He was a retired GP, a member of the local historical society and a keen bridge player. There's nothing to suggest anything untoward in his life and as far as the gardaí are concerned, his shooting was the random act of a mad woman.'

'What makes them think she was crazy?'

'Well, normal women don't exactly go around shooting people, do they?'

'I don't know about that.'

'Look, I'm confused. My mother … is so sure there has to be a reason for all this. But I don't know …'

'You don't know what?' Sarah picked up the watch. It was small, silver, with a purple face. She turned it over. A rose was stamped on the back and, underneath, a faint engraving. She wiped it with her thumb: 'To Katie, my heart always.'

56

'Somebody loved her.'

'Katie? Yes, I saw that. She booked into the room at the hotel under the name "Todd", so I'm assuming it was a name she used. Katie Todd.'

'Or was given,' Sarah said.

'Right.' Sam looked away. 'I'll go and see to the coffee.'

Sarah put down the watch and picked up the ring. It was big and tacky with a dolphin on it. So, Sarah thought, an expensive dress watch and a cheap ring. Interesting combination. 'Katie,' she said softly, 'what the hell happened to you?'

She put the ring with the watch and opened the bag. Immediately, she jerked her head back, struck by the bad smell. 'Phew.'

'They're pretty rancid,' Sam called from the kitchen. 'I should have warned you.'

'It's smells like cat wee.'

'I think there's ammonia on the jacket and jeans.'

'Jesus.' Sarah tipped the bag onto the floor.

The clothes were banal, to say the least. A fitted red jacket, two grubby granddad shirts, one white, the other blue, a cashmere jumper, two pairs of jeans, socks and underwear, all cotton, threadbare but clean, and a pair of runners. Size four.

She put them down and turned her attention to the jacket. She flattened it on the table and shook her head at the damage the ammonia had done to the wool. 'This jacket seems a little out of place.'

'You think so?'

Sarah fingered it. It was exquisitely made; the collar was velvet, the lining silk and the buttons were probably real ebony. 'Well, compared to the rest of the clothing she has with her it is. What about the clothes she was wearing on … the day?'

'The gardaí kept them.' Sam handed Sarah her coffee and sat stiffly on the sofa opposite. 'They're evidence. I gather she had on a long dress and boots.'

Sarah searched through the clothes carefully, examining labels and checking pockets. She found nothing but bits of lint and a button. 'Did she have any identification on her?'

'No, no wallet, nothing.'

'That's strange.'

'She was carrying five hundred in cash.'

Sarah looked at the clothes again. 'Pounds or euros?'

'Euros.'

Sarah looked at the tags on the granddad shirts. 'Thornton's, same make as the coat. A boutique, probably.'

'I've never heard of it.'

'Me neither, but I'm going to check where they might have come from. At least they're not some generic brand.'

'Right. So then we can—' His mobile rang suddenly. He lifted it and pulled a face as he read the number.

'Will you excuse me a second?'

'Sure.'

He went out to the balcony, closing the door behind him.

Sarah watched him pace up and down outside. Whoever was on the other end of the line really had him jazzed up. Even from where she sat, Sarah could see the cords standing out on his neck as he spoke. Moments later, he snapped the phone shut and came back inside. He looked troubled.

'You okay?' she asked.

'A reporter.'

'Ah.'

'So, do you think the clothes might help?'

'Everything helps. It's just a matter of tracking back over what we have now.'

Sam swallowed. 'The gardaí say your company's irresponsible.'

'But good at what we do.'

'Right.'

Sarah raised an eyebrow. 'I wouldn't worry too much about them. We've had a few crossed wires before. They'll get over it. Sam, can I ask you a question? I wanted to ask you yesterday, but ... it seems a bit stupid.'

'Go on.'

'Are you glad your sister's alive?'

He said nothing for the a long time, but finally he sighed.

'Of course I am. Look, Sarah, if I'm totally honest with you, I don't know what to feel about anything any more. It's all so complicated. You reach a period in your life where you can see where you're going, you decide to move on and then – you get slapped back into place.' His blue eyes gazed at her intently and Sarah felt sorry for him. 'Does that make me a monster?' he asked.

'No.'

'My sister, whom I assumed was dead, whom I mourned for all those years ... I find out she's alive and I don't feel gratitude, I don't feel joy. I don't ... I don't know what to feel.'

'Why should you?'

He blinked rapidly. 'What?'

'Why should you? You're not a robot. We're not programmed to know how to react to stressful situations. Sometimes people can't afford the luxury of emotion. We've just got to carry on.'

His eyes narrowed. 'It's self-preservation.'

'It's a necessity.'

'So,' he tilted his head, 'what are you hiding, Sarah?'

Sarah started. 'I'm not ... I mean, I'm not talking about me.'

Sam said, a twinkle in his eye, 'Right – you're just a naturally *empathic* person.'

'Right,' Sarah said. But she smiled back at him and, for a brief moment, they stood in each other's shoes. It was a good fit.

It was beginning to rain. John ran across the street and up the steps of the shabbiest-looking building on the street. This was the Hotel Erin, where Katie Jones had stayed for almost ten days before the shooting.

He passed two bored Nigerians, sitting on the steps passing a joint between them. Neither man looked at him, but he could feel them watching his every move, sizing him up.

'Morning fellas,' he said, pausing at the door.

They got up slowly and moved away up the street.

John pushed open a filthy swing door. A second door greeted him, plastered with a huge sign that read: 'No credit cards. No pets.

Patrons must be out by twelve midday.' The interior door was boarded at the bottom where someone – probably a punter – had kicked the glass in. Maybe not everyone liked to be told when they could come and go.

The lobby was dark. The walls were painted in hospital green and a brown couch sagged against the wall. It smelled of damp and stale cigarette smoke. A surprisingly vigorous-looking plant caught John's eye. Next to it, a small glass-covered hatch with speaking holes looked into a second room. A tarnished brass sign beside it said 'Reception'. John tapped on the glass with his knuckles.

It must once have been a small stock room but had been converted into the messiest office John had seen in years. Behind a desk a large man with a pitted face sat in an oversized swing chair, watching a soap opera and eating a greasy-looking sandwich. 'Help you there?' he asked, with barely a glance in John's direction.

John dug out his wallet and dropped a card in. 'I'm John Quigley, private detective.'

'Yeah?' He could not have looked less impressed by that statement.

'I'm looking for the owner of this fine establishment.'

'You found him.'

'Can I have your name?'

'Jim Buckley.'

'Well, Jim, I'm investigating a guest of yours.'

'I have a lot of guests, regular revolving door here.'

'She was here for a while. Katie Jones – she was booked in here as Katie Todd.' John pressed the photo he had taken the night before up against the glass.

Buckley barely glanced at it. 'She the kid the cops were asking about?'

'Yes.'

'Gave all her stuff to them.'

'Okay,' John said. He leaned on the counter and noticed the business end of a crow bar sticking out from under Buckley's chair. 'But is there anything you can tell me about her? Anything you might not have mentioned to the cops?'

'Like what?'

'I don't know – how she seemed? How did she pay? Was she always alone? Did she make any calls? Anything at all.'

Buckley raised one shoulder. 'She paid cash and minded her own business.'

'She have any visitors while she was staying?'

'What am I? Her mother?'

John grinned. 'If you are, she gets her looks from her father.'

'Look, I've told you everything I know.'

'That it?'

'That's it.'

'She here long?'

'Ten days.'

'What day did she arrive?'

Buckley regarded John as he might regard a piece of shit that wouldn't flush. Grumpily, he opened the ledger and ran a finger the size of a sausage down a page. 'Wednesday, the twelfth.'

John flipped open his notebook. 'She talk to you about anything during the time she was here?'

'No.'

'Call any taxis? Ask for a map? Directions to anywhere?'

Buckley finished his sandwich, belched and wiped his hands on the legs of his less-than-clean grey trousers. 'Look, I can't tell you nuthin' I didn't tell the cops already. They came in here, asked me where her room was and I got my porter, Jimmy, to show them. I didn't want no trouble. I told them she was a quiet woman and paid me upfront in cash. I didn't ask no questions and they didn't ask me nothing other than when she arrived and if I ever saw her with anyone. I didn't.'

'Did you ever hear her mention a name? Or—'

'Jesus.' Buckley scowled. 'No, she didn't talk to no one. I'm telling you, she wasn't the chatty kind.'

'How do you know that?'

'Huh?'

'How do you know she wasn't chatty if she didn't talk to anyone?'

'Jimmy tried cracking a joke with her one time and she gave him such a look, phew, could have curdled milk. No, she minded her own

61

business, that one, and I mind mine. That's how it works here.' Buckley raised the volume on the television.

'Is he working today?'

'Supposed to be. Don't know if I'd call it work.'

'Might as well talk to him now. Don't want to have to call back and disturb you again.'

Buckley jerked his head towards the hall. 'Down back, last door on the right.'

'Thanks.'

Buckley didn't reply.

John pushed through another pair of double doors and made his way towards the back of the hotel. If the reception area was shabby, the corridor was positively grimy. Threadbare carpet, cheap prints and strip lighting gave the place an almost funereal atmosphere. The place reeked of lost souls.

John pushed open the fire door and stepped out into a small courtyard filled with bottle crates and bins. A small, wiry youth was leaning against a cleaning cart, smoking a cigarette. At John's approach he stubbed it out under his heel and tucked his white shirt into his black trousers. There was something familiar about him.

'Be right with ya, Pete. Just having a quick smoke.'

'Take your time.'

The smoker turned and flicked his oily fringe off his forehead. When he saw John, he took a hasty step backwards and the fixed grin slid off his face. 'Ah, bollix.'

John beamed. 'Jimmy Dunne! Well, now, that's a stroke of luck. Long time no see.'

'Not fucking long enough,' Jimmy groaned. 'Did he send you to track me down?'

'Andy? Nah. I think if he knew where you were he'd want to pay a personal visit.'

'You're not gonna bleedin' tell him I work here, are ya? Look, John, come on, man, he'll fuckin' string me up if he catches a hold of me.'

'He'll do more than that from what I hear.'

Earlier in the year, Jimmy had worked for John's friend and pool-playing buddy Andy Cosgrove for six months. Andy had hired the lad as a favour to his wife's best friend after he had dropped out of school. He had spent every day since regretting it. Jimmy was seventeen and handsome in the same way that stoats are handsome – and just as trustworthy. He was also bone idle, a bare-faced spoofer and a chancer. Six months of turning up late, long lunch breaks, cigarette breaks, piss breaks, tea breaks and scooting off early. Six months of being asked for subs weekly and practically lighting a fire under the lad's arse to get him to move. It had driven Andy to distraction.

But the final straw had come when Andy Cosgrove's wife found some less than family-friendly photos of Becky, her fifteen-year-old, in her daughter's bedroom. Then, friend or no friend, Jimmy Dunne was a goner.

Jimmy had been mixing cement lethargically and considering how long he could stretch a fag break when Andy had slewed across the road and leaped from the Jeep with a bellow of rage so loud his throat had hurt for a week after. The other men confirmed that they hadn't thought the little bollix had it in him to move as fast as he had that day.

'You remember the woman who was staying here? Katie Todd? The cops were asking about her?'

'Yeah, I saw her.' Jimmy looked shifty.

'You talk to her much?'

'No.'

'No?' John cocked his head. 'Pretty woman like her, blonde, all alone? And you didn't try your patter? Guess it's harder with women who aren't so young and gullible.'

Jimmy picked at a spot on his cheek. 'Look, she wasn't exactly friendly, all right? I tried to crack a joke with her one day and she froze me out.'

'And?'

'And what?'

'What are you sweating about?'

'I'm not sweating.'

'You are.' John took a step closer. 'What are you not telling me?'

'Nothing!' Jimmy held up his hands in front of his chest.

'What the fuck?'

John stepped closer to him and Jimmy bumped into the cleaning cart, upsetting the bottles on it. John put out his hand and steadied it. 'Jimmy, if you don't talk to me I'm going to take out my phone and call Andy, and I'm going to sit on you until he—'

'She wasn't Irish.'

'What?'

'She'd an English accent.'

John smiled. 'Go on.'

'Yeah, man, I swear.' Jimmy licked his lips twice in quick succession. 'Real English, like in *EastEnders* or something.'

'Go on.'

'And that's it, I swear on me ma's life.'

John knew he was lying. It was as clear to him as the nose on Jimmy's face. He was tempted to ring Andy anyway, let the cards fall where they might.

Jimmy was watching him. 'Look, man, please, don't mess it up for me here. Come on, man, if there was anythin' I could tell ya, I would, but I swear I never said more than two words to her.'

John jabbed a finger into Jimmy's chest. 'I find out you've been lying to me, I'll personally hold you while Andy removes whatever piece of your body he'd like to barbecue.'

John made his way back to the reception area, his head buzzing. English. That was a real break. He'd—

His mobile rang.

'Well?' Sarah asked. 'How's it going your end?'

'Good. She spoke with an English accent – like *EastEnders*, apparently.' John patted his pockets for his cigarettes.

'Yeah, I spoke to the taxi driver. He mentioned it too. He also said "she was real stuck-up" about fifty times, in between telling me of his heroics.'

'Sounds thrilling. Anything else your end?'

'I looked through her belongings, but there's no identification, no nothing. And the weirdest thing – the front of her coat and jeans were destroyed with ammonia. Probably explains why she wasn't wearing a coat on the day she shot Hogan.'

'Ammonia?' John thought of the bottles of cleaning fluid that had been on Jimmy's cart.

'Yes, why?'

'That little prick.' John spun round and ran back the way he had come. But it was too late. The yard was empty and the back gate creaked in the breeze.

Jimmy Dunne had legged it.

10

'I knew the little bollix was lying through his teeth about something.' John slammed down the receiver. 'I should have wrung the truth out of him.'

'We'll find him.'

'She knows where he is – she's covering for him.' John jerked his head towards the phone. Jimmy's mother had refused to help in tracking down her son. The only thing she'd had to say was that he'd turned eighteen two weeks before and, as far as she was concerned, what he did now was his own business. She couldn't give John any address for him. The address Pete Buckley had was two months out of date, and the landlord there had asked John to give Jimmy a 'few digs' from him if he ever caught up to him. It seemed like Jimmy Dunne was fast running out of people to call friends.

'He's got to be staying somewhere.'

'So we'll find him,' Sarah repeated.

'I had the little bastard. And you can bet your last pair of clean knickers he knows much more than he's letting on about Katie Jones.'

This time, Sarah didn't bother to say anything. Instead, she switched on her computer and typed 'Thornton', 'clothing' and 'London' into Google and tapped return.

Bingo. Up it popped. Thornton and Son. She scanned the information and wrote down the phone and fax numbers.

Next she typed 'rose jewellery' and 'London', but this time she struck out. She tapped her pen on her teeth, frustrated. Maybe it wasn't a rose. She typed 'flower' and got two links She called them, but they didn't sell watches with insignias.

'I'm not getting a hit on the watch, but the jacket is definitely London,' she said to John.

'What?'

'Her clothes. Originally they came from a boutique in Camden.'

'Originally?'

'That jacket looks expensive and old-fashioned to me. I doubt Katie bought it new.'

'So, what now?'

'I guess one of us is going to London,' Sarah said, 'and by "us" I mean you.'

'What about Jimmy Dunne?'

'I'll find him, you can be sure of that.'

'How? The little shit's gone to ground.'

'What school does Andy's daughter go to?'

John thought about it. 'It's the one up in Terenure. The kids wear a blue uniform.'

'Presentation?'

'That's it.'

'Perfect.' She reached for her bag.

'She won't know where he is,' John said. Then his expression darkened. 'She'd better not know where he is.'

'Worth a try.' Sarah checked her watch. Ten minutes before lunchtime. She stood up and grabbed her coat. 'I'll see if I can have a chat while you get yourself a flight.'

'What about Sumo?'

'He'll be okay, I'll take him to Mum's house.'

John's scowl deepened. 'You know I hate flying.'

'It's not even an hour.'

'Plenty of time to crash.'

Sarah buttoned her coat and picked up the keys for the Manta from John's desk. 'It'll do you good to confront your fear, Johnny-boy.'

'Where the hell did you get that stupid idea?' John slapped open the phone book. '*Cosmopolitan*? *Oprah*? *Dr Phil*? Chinese fortune cookie?'

Becky Cosgrove was a stunner. She was blonde, fresh-faced and didn't look a day over fifteen. Or, rather, she didn't look a day over fifteen when her face was make-up-free and she was in uniform. Pop Becky into her street clothes and make-up and it was another matter.

Sarah watched her and her friends congregate and chatter noisily outside the convent's main gates, feeling a mild wave of nostalgia for the carefree days of her youth. Days before dead fathers, sick mothers, broken hearts and shot ankles. Days when everything was possible and life had yet to dig in its claws. Days when you didn't need to glance over your shoulder to make sure you were safe.

She climbed out of John's car. Those days were gone. She watched Becky wave goodbye to her friends and start for home. She crossed the road against the traffic and tapped her shoulder.

Becky spun around, a smile faltering on her lips. 'Yes?'

'Hi, Becky, remember me? I'm Sarah Kenny. You've probably seen me with my partner, John Quigley.'

'Dad's friend.' Becky nodded, and now a flush crept over her cheeks. Sarah almost laughed. John had that effect on girls. She dug out a card and handed it to her. 'Is there somewhere we can talk?'

'I'm on lunch—'

'I'll treat you to a sambo.'

'Uh-uh.' Beck looked a little worried. 'My mother will be expecting me.'

'I won't take up too much of your time, I promise.'

'Wait – why do you need to talk to me?'

'It's about Jimmy Dunne.'

'What about him?' She tried to look disinterested, but a tell-tale blush crept up her cheeks.

'I'm looking for him. He's done a runner and I need to talk to him. I'm hoping you might help me find him.'

Becky stopped walking. 'I don't know anything about him any more.'

Sarah smiled kindly. 'You don't keep in touch at all? You're going to stand there and tell me you don't even send each other the odd text message?'

'We don't, I *swear*!' Becky said, so guiltily it was all Sarah could do not to laugh.

'Come on, Becky. Don't try to feed me that bull. I'm not going to mention anything to either John or your dad, I promise. I just need to talk to him. He's a witness in a case I'm working on.'

'I wouldn't know where to find him. We haven't spoken since Dad went after him. His mother might—'

'She's a bit pissed off with him at the moment and I gather she doesn't know where he is.'

Becky's brow furrowed and Sarah saw immediately that she knew this wasn't true and that Jimmy's mother had lied to John. She was protecting her boy.

'What about a phone number?' she asked

'I—'

'John and I would really appreciate it,' Sarah added.

'Well ...' Becky was a good kid and Sarah could see she was struggling.

'Okay,' she said in a rush. 'I don't know his mobile number any more, I really don't – he lost it – but ... I know where his flat is. But not because I've been there or anything.'

'Becky, I won't tell if you have or haven't.'

Becky chewed her lip. 'Dad would kill me if he thought I had. He's really mad with Jimmy.'

'I won't tell him.'

'Or John?'

'Or John.'

She nodded. 'Okay, it's Flat G, 24 Lower Rathmines Road. It's in the basement. But the doorbell doesn't work. You have to knock on the window.'

'How long has the bell been broken?'

'Since last mo—' Becky flushed deep red.

'You sure you've never been there?' Sarah said, smiling. She wrote the address down in her notebook.

Becky looked at her with huge eyes. 'Is Jimmy in trouble?'

'No,' Sarah said. 'We just want to talk to him. That's all.'

'Please don't tell Dad. Jimmy's not a bad person, you know,' Becky said shyly. 'Everyone's got the wrong idea of him. If you knew him you'd see he's really great.'

'Oh, honey.' Sarah slipped her notebook back into her pocket. 'I'm sure he's a prince.'

11

Sarah parked in front of the army barracks and walked down the Lower Rathmines Road. She paused outside number twenty-four. It was one of many once-magnificent Edwardian buildings that had been divided into flats. It was also one of the most run-down.

She walked up the cracked pathway and checked the doorbells. Becky was right, of course, G was the basement and the bell was missing. She went down the metal steps and had a look at the door – three panels of bubble glass in a rotten frame. She could have opened it if she'd wanted to, but no. She wasn't John.

She trotted back up the steps, crossed the road to the Centra shop and bought a large A4 envelope. She wrote Jimmy's address on the front.

She returned to his front door and rapped hard.

After a minute or two the grimy curtain twitched. Sarah made a big production of looking at the envelope and knocked again.

Jimmy pushed aside the curtain and Sarah got a good look at him.

He was young, shirtless. His black hair was mussed and he eyed her warily through the glass. He had the kind of looks that whithered with age, but Sarah could see how Becky might be taken with him. He glanced to the right, and Sarah had the impression he was not alone. 'Yeah?' he shouted.

Sarah gave him her friendliest smile. 'Jimmy Dunne?'

'Yeah?'

'I've got a package for you.'

'Just leave it there.'

'No can do. You have to sign for it.'

Jimmy cursed and let the curtain fall. Seconds later, Sarah heard a rusty key turn in the lock.

'Here, give it.' He put out his hand. Sarah handed him the envelope and took her phone out of her pocket. Jimmy stared into the envelope. 'It's empty.'

'Really?' Sarah said, dialling a number.

Jimmy's shifty eyes narrowed. 'What's the story?'

'Story is, I'm about to call my good friend John Quigley and he's going to call his good friend Andy Cosgrove. You and I are going to wait here until they arrive and then I'll head off and you can talk to them instead of me. How's about that, then?'

'How did—'

'So, what's it to be?' Sarah turned her phone and let him see the screen. 'Will I press call or are you going to be a good boy and ask me in?'

'This is blackmail.'

'I guess it is.'

'Look, can we do this another time?'

Sarah laughed. 'So you can scarper again? Don't think so, Jimmy. So, what's it to be?'

'It's just, I've got a bit of company right now.'

'So? I won't bite.'

Jimmy flicked back his hair. 'Jesus, you're a real fucking ball-breaker.'

'All right, forget it. I'll call John. I don't know, you try to do a good thing—'

'*All right*!' Jimmy said. He opened the door and waved her in. 'Fuck me.'

Sarah went into a tiny under-the-stairs kitchen, which consisted of a hotplate, a sink, two shelves and a fridge. It was the second kitchen she had seen that day in which little cooking was done.

She followed Jimmy into a dark sitting room, sparsely furnished with bare walls and an uncovered lightbulb dangling from the ceiling. The only pieces of furniture were a mouldy sofa, a beanbag and a TV that sat on a table made of blocks. A door to what must have been the bedroom stood ajar and through it Sarah could see a bare foot at the end of a rumpled bed.

'Nice digs,' she said.

Jimmy coughed and dropped into the beanbag. He began to roll a cigarette. 'I've lost me job cause of that other fuck.'

'Why did you run?'

'Thought he was going to call Andy. Seems that's what you lot like to do.' He gave her a filthy look.

'You shouldn't have messed with his daughter. She's only a kid.'

'She don't act like one.'

Jimmy smiled in such a lascivious way that Sarah felt her hand twitch with the urge to slap him. 'She's underage, you bloody shit.'

'Yeah, well, I doubt her old lad wants to go to court.'

Sarah watched him as he licked the papers and pressed them together. He searched in his jeans pocket for a lighter.

'How did Katie Todd end up with ammonia all over her clothes?'

He glanced up. 'Dunno. Ask her.'

For a lad of eighteen, Sarah thought, he had remarkably old eyes. And they were regarding her with fierce concentration. Clearly, despite her threat to phone John, she did not trouble him in the slightest. She knew she was going to get nowhere with him until she showed him who was boss.

She marched over to the bedroom door and booted it open. There was a startled shriek.

'Hey!' Jimmy yelled, but Sarah held up a hand and he shrank back.

'Hello, there. Don't mind me,' she said to the huddled form of the girl who had dived beneath the covers. Then her eyes rested on the uniform tossed over the chair. 'St Luke's School this time. My, my, Jimmy. Do you leave flyers in all the lunch rooms?'

'You can't do this! This is an invasion of privacy! It's *harassment*!' Jimmy said, but he had lost his cockiness.

'See, Jimmy, here's how it works. You talk to me or, by God, you'd better hope Miss Shy under the covers here is seventeen. Because you, Jimmy – according to your own mother – are eighteen, and that makes you a man in the eyes of the law. Forget Andy. I might just phone a cop friend of mine right this second. I bet this would come in as statutory rape.'

'*Rape?*' Jimmy's voice wobbled. 'I didn't rape no one. Tell her, Siobhan!'

There was a muffled sob in reply.

'*Siobhan!*'

'Don't worry, Siobhan. Jimmy here is going to do the right thing. Aren't you, Jimmy?'

Jimmy gulped and two jets of smoke shot from his nostrils.

'Siobhan, I'm going to close this door, but you need to put your clothes on and get your arse back to school. Understand? Jimmy's going to make me a cup of coffee. I suggest you're out of here before I've drunk it.'

Sarah closed the door and sat on the sofa.

Jimmy looked at her with a mix of pure loathing and new-found respect. 'And I thought John was a bollix.'

'I take it white, Jimmy, no sugar.' Sarah undid her jacket and took out her notebook. 'I'm sweet enough, apparently.'

12

John flung two clean pairs of underpants and some socks into a sports bag, then tried to decide which pair of tattered Levis looked least like it belonged in a bin.

Sumo lay on the rug under the window and watched his every move. He was pretending not to be interested in what John was doing, but John saw that the dog's eyes were following him as he moved about. 'You'll be fine. It's only two days,' he said to him. 'No kennels this time – not that they'd take you after last time.' He remembered the hard look the woman had given him when he had collected Sumo after a weekend away with the lads. 'You'll be staying with Sarah. You like her.'

He threw in two shirts and a pair of runners. If he was going to be doing a lot of walking, he might as well be comfortable. 'And you better be good for her. She's got a lot on her plate right now.'

He went to the bathroom and packed his toiletries. 'No barking, no biting and no pulling her around like she's made of candy-floss. She has a weak ankle – remember that.'

John zipped up the bag and sat on the end of the bed. Sumo stood up, came to him and put his massive head on John's lap. He gave a half-wag with his tail.

'Mind her,' John said softly and patted the dog's wiry head. 'Make sure nothing bad happens to her. Okay? You do that and I'll let you keep those balls of yours for another year.'

Sumo sighed heavily and, not for the first time, John suspected his dog understood a whole lot more English than he gave him credit for.

His mobile rang. ''Lo?'

'It's Sarah.'

'Hey. Where are you?'

'At the office. You?'

'Packing a bag. I managed to get on a flight tonight.'

'Okay, but come here first.'

'Why?'

'I think I have an idea where Katie got the gun.' Sarah sounded very pleased with herself.

'*What?*'

'I said, I think I might know where she got the gun.'

'How the hell did you manage that?'

'Well, it wasn't charm. Are you coming in before you head to the airport?'

'I'll be right there.' John hung up and leaped off the bed. 'What did I tell you, Sumo? She's special!'

Sumo had done all the tail-wagging he was going to do that day. He lay down on the rug and closed his eyes. John waved at him and grabbed his bag. 'Be good. I'll see you in a few days.'

John looked at the piece of paper again. On it were the names of a man and bar. The man was Willie Staunton and the bar, John wasn't surprised to see, was Nesbitts, a rough-and-tumble dive on James' Street.

'How did you get this again?' he asked.

'Jimmy Dunne. Talkative chap when he gets going.'

'He just volunteered this information?'

'Sure.' Sarah tucked her hair behind her ear. 'Well, it was either that or explain to the cop why he knew where her wallet had gone.'

'Let me get this straight. Jimmy Dunne – who you happened to meet on the street – suddenly gets a conscience and says, "Hey there, Sarah, I've been thinking. That girl your partner was talking about, well, I was trying to rob her, she caught me and there was a fight.

Ammonia somehow got spilled over her clothes, but she said she wouldn't get me fired or arrested if I helped her, so I gave her the number of a guy who might or might not be able to hook her up with a gun. Then, when she shot someone and herself, I – being a gentleman – thought, Well, that's me in the clear, and I should have told John all this but he scared me, and now I've had a complete change of heart." Is that what you're telling me?'

'I think he felt it was weighing him down a bit.'

John raised an eyebrow sceptically. 'I don't buy it. What have you got on him?'

'Nothing.'

'Where is he?'

'I can't say.'

'You can't *say*?'

'I told him I wouldn't.'

'You told him—' John glared at her in disbelief. 'Did Becky tell you how to find him?'

'She didn't know where he lived.'

'So how did you find out what he looked like?'

'I've seen him before, John. He was with Andy in the Jeep one time.'

'And you happened to remember him? I don't believe that. You're full of it.'

'Why would I lie?'

That was a good point. John studied her face. She was almost impossible to read, damn her inscrutable chops. 'I will find him, you know.'

'Fine by me,' Sarah said, returning to her desk. 'And if you track him down, it had nothing to do with me. Maybe you'll get lucky and run into him, too.'

'What are you going to do? You can't just wander over to Nesbitts and ask if anyone knows a guy called Willie who sells guns.'

'I know that.'

'Well?'

'I'll think of something.'

'Do not do anything until I get back.'

Sarah's head snapped his way. 'What?'

'I want you to wait until I get back.'

'Why?'

'That place is rough as fuck. It's not safe.'

'I can look after myself, John.'

'No one's saying you can't.'

'You are.'

'I'm just asking you to hang on for a day or two. What's wrong with that?'

'Nothing. But I don't take orders from you.'

'Fine.' John sat down and folded his arms. 'Then you'd better get on the phone and organise a flight for yourself because I'm not going to England after all.'

'Are you blackmailing me?' Sarah said incredulously.

'Yes.'

'Do you need a lift to the airport?'

'I'm getting a taxi, and don't change the subject.'

'I'm not a baby, John.' Her dark eyes flashed.

'Nobody's saying you are.'

Sarah said nothing for a moment. 'All right. I'll wait until you get back. We can go together.'

'Good.'

'So, what's the plan?' she asked.

'I'm meeting with Jeremy Thornton in the morning. It was his father who started the business and he reckons the shirts are off the rack, but the jacket might be our link. Each one was tailored to very specific measurements. So if he can match it to when it was made, he might be able to trace who it was made for. Anything turn up on the watch?'

'Not so far, but I'll keep trying.'

'Okay.' John rubbed his hands over his scalp. 'Oh, while you were out, Geoff Granger called in for his photos. I apologised for the quality, but I guess he's not the waiting kind either.'

'Yeah, all right.' Sarah sat forward. 'What did he say?'

'Not a whole lot. He stood there staring at them, poor git. Guess who the other guy fiddling with Mrs Granger's sail turned out to be?'

'Who?'

'The owner of the local hotel where they've been dancing every Friday night since the day they got married.'

'Jesus.' Sarah shook her head in wonder. 'What's he going to do?'

'Take her to dinner there tonight and confront them with the photos. He took off out of here like a bat out of hell.'

'Not nice.'

'I think he knew she was diddling someone else. But what I can't understand is why that old fella. I mean, Geoff's not bad looking, rather like Roger Moore, I'd say. And the wife is no great shakes.'

Sarah sat back in her seat and linked her hands behind her head. 'I know what you mean. Why do they do it? He's a nice man and they've been married so long, why muck it all up for a bit of how's-yer-father with someone else – especially a lesser someone else?'

'Excitement, risk, stupidity,' John told her. 'Everyone's entitled to make a mistake.'

'John, you know I didn't mean you.' It was true, but that didn't change the fact that John Quigley had once broken her heart by cheating on her.

He stood up abruptly. 'Well, I've got to make tracks. Security in the airport's so tight these days. Keep the car until I get back, right?'

Sarah was a little surprised. John's pristine silver '85 Opel Manta Berlinetta was his pride and joy. It guzzled petrol and cost a fortune to keep on the road, but he wouldn't hear of selling it. Other than Sumo, it was his most prized possession. That he had offered it to her touched her.

'I really appreciate it.'

'Never mind that. Say, "I won't crash your car, John."'

'I won't crash your car, John.'

'And Sumo will need a walk this evening, at least a mile. As I've discovered many times, an energetic Sumo is not necessarily a good Sumo.'

Sarah stood up and came round the table. 'I'll take good care of him, I promise.'

He moved in to hug at the exact time she did. They bumped hips clumsily.

Sarah laughed and John rolled his eyes. 'To think I was always so smooth.'

'Yeah, right.' Sarah's eyes twinkled with mischief. 'Left or right?'

'I'll go left.'

But he didn't. He leaned in, cupped her face and kissed her lips.

Sarah caught her breath. Her cheeks were flushed. 'Give me a ring when you get to the hotel, won't you?' she said.

'Sure.' He was gazing into her eyes.

'Well, have a good trip.' She turned away and began to arrange the papers on her desk.

John waited for another moment, but it was clear she had nothing more to say to him. He flung his bag over his shoulder and left.

Sarah slumped into her chair and stared into space for a long time, listening to her heartbeat. He had kissed her. She should have been angry – she should probably have slapped him. There was no place for that in their relationship, no way! That ship had sailed.

Hadn't it?

So why the hell was she sitting there, grinning like a fool?

Across town, the man watched Jackie Kenny help Sarah's mother into her car. He noted that she made sure she was strapped in securely before she pulled out of the drive, just as he had noted the time the carer had left. He watched them go. He knew this was Sarah's evening off. He had found Jackie's address in the book he had taken from Sarah's apartment. And he wanted to scope the house. Without her car, he knew Sarah would be late back, so he had plenty of time.

He pulled on a pair of latex gloves and waited for the shadows to lengthen. The dark was his friend.

13

It was almost dark when Sarah picked up Sumo from John's house and made her way across town to Clontarf. As she pulled up outside her mother's home, Sarah was struck once again by the circle of her life. Here she was, back at her childhood home, thinking of John Quigley. Thinking of kissing him.

It was as if she had never been away.

'Come on in,' she said to the big dog as she pushed open the front door. 'Now I'm sure you're used to the lap of luxury at John's, but around here there's no getting up on the furniture or anything like that. And no chewing things you shouldn't.'

Sumo gave her a half-wag and trotted off to explore his new digs. Sarah let him go. He had been in the house before, with John, so she had decided to let him settle down as he thought best.

She carried her groceries into the kitchen and plonked them on the worktop. She had the best part of three hours to herself before Jackie brought their mother back, and she intended to make the most of them. She put away the food and made a cup of tea. Sumo came into the kitchen and progressed into the living room. She heard him moving about, sniffing and growling softly. Funny dog – ever since John had rescued him as a pup he had been a champion growler. John said he growled in his sleep.

'I'll get changed and then I'll take you out. Sumo?'

He came back into view, an ear raised.

Sarah drank some of her tea, tossed the rest into the sink, grabbed her bag and went upstairs. Sumo followed her, still growling softly.

'I haven't decided where you're sleeping yet, but I *suppose* you can share with me.' She opened her bedroom door and switched on the light.

'Hey—'

Sumo barrelled past her into the room, hackles raised. His growl now meant business. Sarah watched him stalk the room stiff-legged. He did a full circuit before he jumped onto her bed and snarled at Barney, the purple teddy bear.

'Sumo! Off!' She grabbed his collar and hauled him onto the floor. 'Sit!'

Sumo sat, but then he whined softly. Sarah ignored him. She put Barney up on a shelf, then reached under the bed for her runners.

'Two days, Sumo, that's all. I know this is strange for you, but come on, old lad, it won't be that bad.' She sat on the end of the bed and pulled off her boots. 'Look, you can sleep up here with me. I know what I said about furniture, but come on...' She patted the top of his massive head and he licked her hand. 'Don't worry, he'll be home soon.'

Sarah stood up and took a lightweight jacket from the chair by her dressing table. 'A tired Sumo is a good Sumo, right? So, let's go get you good and tired.'

She trotted downstairs, Sumo following reluctantly. At the bottom while she looked for his lead, Sumo growled again. As she clipped it to his collar, she noticed his hackles had risen. What was wrong with him? Overprotective in a strange house, she guessed.

'Come on, mutt, let's hit the road.'

A few seconds after the front door had closed, the man in the attic dropped quietly onto the landing. The dog had fucked things up royally. His plan had been to wait until she was in the shower, then surprise her. He could hardly do that with a fucking *dog* roaming the house.

He walked into Sarah's bedroom and watched her disappear down the road with the animal. Christ, it was huge – and a smart fucker, too. It had known he was there. He plucked Barney off the shelf and held the bear tight to his chest while he rethought his options.

He could kill the dog, but while he dealt with it, Sarah might get away. No, he'd have to enjoy his revenge in more creative ways.

Of course, with John out of the way, he had time to be inventive.

Helen was sitting at the kitchen table in Jackie's Rathgar house, her dark hair gleaming under the lights. She had removed her suit jacket and was as close to relaxed as she ever got. Jackie was cooking pasta and sipping a glass of red wine. She regarded her sister over the top of her glass.

'What are we supposed to do, Jackie? She sounded very put out when I spoke to her.' Helen tore a chunk off a bread roll and popped it into her mouth. 'She's right, of course. She finishes at seven and that's that. She's got a family of her own to look after.'

'Of course she has,' Jackie said.

'And if we lose Belinda it won't be easy to find a replacement. Good carers don't grow on trees.'

'No.'

'And Mum hates her, which, of course, doesn't help.'

'True.'

'Why Sarah can't get home on time is beyond me.' Helen shook her head. 'It's typical of her to be so undisciplined.'

'Well, in fairness, she had a good reason to be late. Her car had been smashed to smithereens.'

'Yes, and that's another thing,' Helen said, jabbing a finger at her. 'Why *was* her car smashed up? What trouble is she in now? It's the second time in a month. Is that normal?' She took a gulp of wine. 'I swear, John Quigley won't be happy until he's put her in the ground.'

'Helen—'

'What? She was shot last year. Now her car's being vandalised. Are you telling me you think that's normal? Would she have been shot if she'd worked in a shop?'

'No, but—'

'Exactly! Don't try to tell me you never worry about her.'

'Of course, but—'

'She's so flighty – I wish she'd just settle down.'

'Sarah's a grown woman, and she makes her own decisions, Helen. We have to respect that.'

'Decisions? That girl never made a decision in her life. It's stumble from one disaster to the next. Who knows half of what she gets into? She's so bloody secretive.'

Jackie put her glass down and stirred the sauce.

Helen rubbed her eyes. She was exhausted and the irate phone call from Belinda had done nothing to brighten her mood.

'She's trying, Helen, she really is. It can't be easy for her either. Anyway, she's great with Mum.'

'I know that,' Helen said with a sigh, 'and I love her for trying, God help me I do, but sometimes she drives me up the wall. And you and I both know she's only prolonging the inevitable. I mean, Mum can't—'

'Can't what?'

Helen froze.

'Mum can't what?' Deirdre Kenny repeated.

'Mum, I—'

'Where's that woman?'

'Belinda?'

'Yes.'

'She's gone home for the evening.'

Deirdre nodded. 'Right. What are you talking about, Helen?'

Helen smiled. 'Nothing, Mum.'

'It didn't sound like nothing to me.' Deirdre regarded her eldest child with keen interest. 'You look tired, love. Not getting enough sleep? Worrying, no doubt. You always were a worrier.' She began to leave the kitchen, then stopped. 'Jackie, that smells lovely, whatever it is.'

'Good.' Jackie took another sip of wine. 'It'll be ready shortly.'

'It's weird, isn't it?' Helen said softly when their mother had gone. 'The way she can drop back in.'

'Pockets of lucidity, was what the doctor called it.'

But the pockets were becoming rarer and rarer. At any minute, their mother might come back in and forget what she was doing there or, worse, ask Jackie what time their dead father had said he'd be back.

'Mum's right, you know, Helen. You do look very tired.' Jackie hesitated. 'Is everything all right?'

Helen played with the stem of her glass. 'I'm fine. Just work and Paul, you know?'

'He won't go to counselling?'

'The great surgeon doesn't need counselling. Hah!' Helen laughed bitterly. 'Paul thinks it's perfectly *normal* not to see his wife for more than twenty minutes a day.'

'Everything will be okay, darling, you'll see.'

'Sanguine as ever, Jackie. The carriage is never a pumpkin in your world.'

Jackie poured herself another glass of wine.

'You shouldn't drink that,' Helen said. 'You're driving Mum home after dinner.'

Jackie stared wistfully at her glass and poured it back into the bottle. It was going to be a long night.

14

The flight was as bad as John had expected. Although there was hardly any turbulence, he felt sick and claustrophobic. Also, he was stuck beside the only person on the flight more nervous than he was about flying. The woman grabbed his arm and said 'Sweet Jesus', every time the plane so much as dipped. By the time he reached Gatwick, he had a headache and was bathed in sweat.

He made his way through the airport, taken aback as always by the sheer scale and the masses of people. He caught a train to Victoria Station, then took a cab to Kensington. By the time he reached his hotel, he was tired and famished.

He checked in, had a quick shower and called Sarah's mobile.

'I'm here.'

'How's the hotel?'

'Basic. No soap in the bathroom and no remote for the TV – oh, and if I'm murdered in my sleep, any one of the other guests could have done it.'

'Good flight?'

He detected stiffness in her tone. 'Not bad. How's Sumo?'

'A bit unsettled, but he'll be okay. I took him for a long walk down by the strand and he's lying here under my feet now. Do you want to talk to him?'

'Nah, you're okay. I'm going to head out for a bite to eat. I'll call you tomorrow when I've spoken to Thornton.'

'Night, John.'

He tried to think of something else to say. Do you feel the same way about me as I do about you?

'Night.' Sarah repeated softly and hung up.

John cursed. He closed his phone and looked round the room. Suddenly he felt like a fish out of water. Sam Jones was picking up the tab for the trip, and he supposed he could go anywhere he wanted, but right now, he would have given a lot of Sam Jones's money to be sitting by Sarah Kenny. He touched his thumb to his lips, remembering the feel of hers. She hadn't pulled away. He smiled. He hadn't imagined it. There was a chance.

Feeling inexplicably nervous, but pleased with himself, he picked up his hotel key and went in search of some food.

The next morning he was up bright and early. He had some coffee and a croissant in a café opposite the hotel, then made his way to the Tube. He got off at West Kensington and went out into the street. Although it was early, it bustled with people. He passed designer shops, side-stepped a crusty playing a harmonica and, after a good ten-minute walk, found himself outside a rather old-fashioned shop. The brass sign outside read, 'Thornton and Son, Fine Clothing'.

John rang the bell and was admitted by a bald man with the build and movements of a boxer. He had a hooked nose and hooded eyes and reminded John a little of Telly Savalas. He wore a sharp, grey-pinstripe suit with a cerise shirt. John put him at about forty-five, but he might have been younger.

'Good morning, sir.' His voice was deep and the accent could have cut glass.

'Morning.'

'And how may we be of service today?'

'My name is John Quigley and I—'

'You're the detective. I spoke with your partner yesterday. I'm Jeremy Thornton.'

They shook hands. Despite his athletic build, Thornton's hands, John noticed, were rough and arthritic.

'I don't know how much I can help you. Your partner mentioned this was in regard to a case you're working on?'

'A shooting.'

'And some of our clothing was found at the scene?'

'The shooter had a jacket and some shirts. We're trying to find out more about her and we're hoping you might be able to help.'

Thornton inclined his head, as though he was sizing John up. Finally, he nodded.

'You have the jacket?'

'Right here. I brought the shirts too.' John slipped the sports bag out of his own and opened it. He removed a plastic bag and handed it over. 'You might not want to open that in here. The jacket's ruined and stinks of ammonia.'

'Ah. Perhaps we should go through to the back.' He called over his shoulder. 'Fred? Could you mind the front of the shop, please?'

An ancient man, tiny, white-haired and wearing thick bifocals, stepped into view and took up residence behind the counter. John clocked him at eighty if he was a day.

Thornton led him into the back of the shop. They passed through a windowless room stacked from floor to ceiling with fabric on wooden rolls, then went into a brightly lit studio to the rear of the building. Here, two more old-timers were working, bent almost double over a large table. One was cutting fabric with what looked to John like a pair of shears, while the other took the pieces and pinned them to large sheets of tissue paper. Neither man took the slightest interest in him.

'Would you care for some tea?' Thornton asked as he opened the glass door to a tiny office. 'I have English Breakfast and Earl Grey.'

'No, thanks.' John pulled a photo out of his pocket. It was the one he had taken of Katie Jones as she lay unconscious in her hospital bed. He passed it to Thornton. 'Do you recognise her?'

Thornton took it and studied it carefully, tilting it towards the light.

'She's beautiful, but I don't recognise her,' he said. 'What happened to her? She's injured?'

'She's in a coma.

'Ah.'

'The clothes were with her.'

'Then perhaps I should look at them.'

Thornton took a seat and cleared his cluttered desk. He opened the bag, his nose wrinkling at the smell. John folded his arms and leaned against the wall.

Thornton removed the clothing and examined each item, his gnarled fingers moving with surprising speed and dexterity. After a while, he sat back and tapped his index finger against his upper lip. 'The clothes are ours, but the jacket is perhaps thirty or thirty-five years old.'

'Really?' John said. 'It's in pretty good nick.'

Thornton smiled. 'Good clothes are made to last. This is bespoke.'

'I don't suppose there's any way you could find out who they were originally made for?'

'The shirts, no. I'm afraid they're off the peg. The jacket, however, I can help you with.'

'That would be great.'

'May I ask you what all this is in connection with?'

'The girl who wore that jacket shot a man last week, then she turned the gun on herself. He's dead, she's in a coma. We're trying to find out where she came from, and so far that's our only lead.'

'I see.' Thornton's nostrils flared, but that was the only sign he gave of shock. 'Well, we should have the measurements of the client for whom we made this, but they won't be on our computer system. It might take me some time to find them. Are you staying in London?'

'I'm at the Lillie Hotel. Do you know it?'

'I know of it.' He smiled and John guessed he was not the sort of man the Lillie would attract. 'I'll look through the archives.' He touched the jacket again. 'Cashmere with shell buttons – that'll narrow the field a bit.'

'Thanks.'

'Will the girl live?'

'I don't know,' John said truthfully. 'They can't say for sure.'

'So tragic,' Thornton said sadly, 'when a thing of beauty is destroyed.'

'It sure is.'

For the life of him John couldn't work out if Thornton meant Katie Jones or the jacket.

15

Sarah, too, was up and about early. She had slept poorly and needed no excuse to take Sumo out onto Dollymount Strand. She walked briskly, although her ankle ached from the damp, her breath fogging in the freezing air. The beach was deserted so she unclipped him to run free. She laughed as he chased seagulls, which flew leisurely away when he was almost upon then, squawking and tormenting him.

After an hour they headed for home. She fed him and tried to talk Belinda into letting him stay at the house, but the carer was having none of it. 'Sarah, I can't do my job right with that wolf skulking round the house.'

'He can stay in the back garden.'

'No,' Belinda said and folded her arms across her chest. 'I'm not taking any chances of getting bitten.'

'He doesn't bite.'

'Huh. That's what they *all* say.'

'But Belinda, I've got to go down the country today. I need to talk to a witness and—'

'You'll have company on your journey, then.' Belinda cocked an eyebrow. 'I don't like dogs and they don't like me. That thing either goes with you or you can stay here with your mother and I'll go home to catch up with my housework.'

Arguing with Belinda, Sarah had learned, was a waste of time. 'Okay, okay.'

'Now, tell your mother to come down for her breakfast.'

'Yes, ma'am.'

Sarah found Deirdre sitting at her dressing table in her nightdress, brushing her hair absent-mindedly.

'Hello, Mum. Where's your dressing gown? You'll freeze to death like that.'

Her mother put the brush down. 'Is it time to go already?'

'Go where, Mum?'

'School.'

'I'm not going to school, Mum. I'm going to work.'

'I know *that*.' Deirdre snapped. She picked up the brush again and began to sweep it furiously through her hair. 'That's what I meant, Sarah, you know that.' She paused. 'Is that woman here?'

'Belinda's downstairs.'

'I don't want her. I can look after myself.'

'Mum, I—'

Suddenly Deirdre's face crumpled. She dropped the brush and buried her head in her hands. 'Don't leave me with her, Sarah. *Please* don't. I don't like her – I don't like the way she talks to me. She treats me as if I was a child.'

Sarah composed her face. Her mother was right, of course, but these crying jags were becoming more frequent. The doctor had warned them it would happen and they should try to ignore them. But it killed Sarah to see her mother cry. 'Now, Mum, come on. Belinda's nice, she—'

She ducked as her mother flung a bottle of Clinique Happy at her head. It smashed against the door behind her, saturating the room with heady perfume.

'She is *not*! I'm not staying here with her! I don't want her!'

Sarah stared at her mother. She wiped her cheek. There was blood on her hand where a tiny sliver of glass had cut it.

Deirdre opened her mouth to say something, but nothing came out. She glowered at Sarah, her eyes dark and furious, yet she looked trapped, frightened.

'Belinda is a nice woman, Mum,' Sarah said stiffly. 'I'll get the dustpan and brush. Stay there in case you cut your feet on the glass.'

She walked downstairs to where Belinda was buttering toast and listening to the news.

'What was the crash?' Belinda wiped her hands on a teacloth and popped two eggs into boiling water.

'Perfume. She threw a bottle at me. It broke,' Sarah said dully. She opened the press under the sink and got out the dustpan and brush.

'She doesn't mean it, Sarah. She's confused and angry.'

'I know.'

'You're bleeding.' Belinda took a step towards her. 'Let me clean that.'

'I can do it myself.' Sarah tore a couple of sheets of kitchen towel from the roll and got the Savlon from under the sink. She poured it onto the paper and dabbed at the cut. 'But if you could clear up the glass, I'd be grateful.'

'Are you okay?'

'Dandy.'

Later that morning, Sarah pulled up outside a house on the coast road. She had already walked along the beach, with Sumo charging ahead, and taken photographs of where Sam and his family had been that day. It was smaller now due to erosion, but the high reeds and steep dunes would have made it easy for anyone to disappear.

The cottage was double-fronted, small and picturesque, set back from the road in an overgrown garden. Even though it was late in the year, it was still beautiful. A woman with her back to Sarah was chopping logs with an axe. Two fat Jack Russells lay near her feet, their eyes on Sarah.

Sumo growled softly.

'You're staying here.' Sarah climbed out and closed the door firmly.

'Hello there.' The moment she put her hand on the gate, the two terriers sprang up and raced down the path, barking furiously. Sumo barked back, scrabbling at the car window with his paws. The dogs heard him and threw their little bodies at the gate with such ferocity that Sarah took a hasty step backwards. 'Jesus.'

At the commotion, the woman had straightened. She was in her forties, red-faced with long dark blonde hair that was greying at the temples and tied in an untidy bun at the nape of her neck. 'Hey, stop that!'

'And I thought it was the big ones I had to watch out for!' Sarah called to her over the noise.

'What's that?'

'Are you Mrs Lynch?'

'That depends,' she said, but there was a twinkle of amusement in her eyes.

'My name is Sarah Kenny and I'm a private investigator. I'm looking into the disappearance of a little girl. Could I have a word with you?'

The woman put down the axe and wiped her hands on her trousers. She whistled to the dogs. They ignored her. 'Go on now – go on with you.' She clapped her hands and finally, reluctantly, the dogs trotted back to the logs.

'That's a fine big fella you have there.' She nodded to Sumo, whose nose was pressed into the two-inch gap Sarah had left for him in the window. He was gallantly trying to fit his whole body through it. 'My two would make a fine snack for him – not that they think so. As far as they're concerned, they're giants of dogs. What breed is he?'

'Wolfhound–German shepherd mix, I believe.'

'He must be a handful.'

'He has his moments.'

'I'd say so,' the woman said with a laugh. 'Yes, I'm Mrs Lynch, but call me Bernie. Mrs Lynch makes me sound old. Private investigator, did you say?'

'Here you go.' Sarah handed over her card, and Bernie read it carefully.

'Well, now, I don't know who sent you this way, but I haven't heard anything about a missing child.'

'It's not recent. Your father used to own the ice-cream van in the Brittas car park. I'm investigating the disappearance of Katie Jones. She went missing from the—'

94

'Oh, Lord save us and bless us, I know *that* name. *That* little girl. You're investigating that now? But sure, it must be near enough twenty-five years or so?'

'Twenty-six,' Sarah said. 'And you still remember her?'

'Oh, I do.' She patted Sarah's arm. 'Sure, how could I forget. The screams of the poor mother that day – I swear to God, some nights I wake up and I can still hear her. And that poor little mite, and him sobbing to beat the band.'

Sarah was used to people waffling, but Bernie's distress was genuine. She took out her notebook and pen. 'Can you tell me what you remember about that day?'

Bernie folded her arms and rested a hip against the gatepost. 'I was eighteen that summer. I was down on the shore when I saw the little lad in an awful state. Sam was his name. He was running up and down the beach calling for his sister. Next thing I knew, he turned and ran straight into the sea. If I hadn't gone after him, he would have kept going. I had such a job holding on to him.'

'That was you?' Sarah said. Sam had told her about the woman, but not her name.

'Yes.' Bernie nodded. 'I was working in the van with Daddy that day. It was fierce hot and we'd been run off our feet all morning, but in the late afternoon when it got quiet I always went down to the water for a dip. I couldn't swim, but I used to like to get in for a splash around.'

'Did you see the little girl?'

'No. That's what was so queer about it. I don't remember seeing her go out into the water, but her bucket was there and one of those water-wings you see the little ones wear. Oh, if I'd seen her I'd have kept an eye on her. Only two, poor little thing, and the poor little lad.' She shook her head sadly. 'I have kids of my own, all grown now, of course, but my God, if anything happened to them ...' She took a breath and composed herself. 'Can I ask why you're investigating this now?'

'The little girl turned up,' Sarah said.

'*What?*'

'Katie Jones turned up last week.'

95

Bernie Lynch couldn't have looked more astonished. 'She wasn't drowned?'

'Nope.'

'Oh my—' She put her hand on Sarah's shoulder and gripped it tightly. 'He was right.'

'Who was right?'

'Daddy. He was right all along.'

'What about?'

'Daddy used to say there was no way that little one's body wouldn't have washed up at some point if she'd drowned, like they said. He knows the waters of the bay. He told the gardaí at the time, but sure, they didn't take a bit of notice. And then there was the man ...' She bit her lip, as though she was speaking out of turn. 'Maybe I shouldn't mention this.'

'Mention away.'

'A man. Daddy said he saw him when he was changing the gas out the back of the van. He was walking behind the toilets over to where the picnic area is now and he was carrying a child. Daddy said the little one was roaring crying, but he didn't think anything of it. Lots of kids bawl their eyes out when they have to leave the beach. And, anyway, he said there was a woman with him so he never ... But he did mention it to one of the guards at the time, and that he thought they were driving an odd sort of car for a family.'

'Can your father give me a description of the man?'

'Not today.' Bernie Lynch shook her head. 'My father's not a well man. He goes up to Rathdrum for a few days' respite care during the week. But he'll be back tomorrow. He had a stroke a few years ago, he's ... Well, he's not himself these days. Oh, it was so long ago ... All I remember Daddy saying was that he had shaggy dark hair, and a longish moustache – but sure, everyone looked like that. It was the fashion then, I suppose.'

'Age?'

'Twenties, thirties, I don't really remember,' she said slowly. 'It was so long ago.'

Sarah wrote it down. 'What about the car? Did he mention anything else about it?'

'No, no, I don't really remember. See, it was so busy that day. Packed on account of the heat. It was so hot, up into the thirties.' She pressed a hand to her chest. 'I couldn't tell you what make of car he said it was, only that it was blue and he did say to the gardaí that it was one of them sporty-looking numbers. That's why he remembered it.'

'Sporty-looking?'

'That's what he said. Now, back then that wasn't the norm. These days, they have all sorts of contraptions on their cars, but not then.'

Sarah scribbled furiously.

'Everyone said she'd drowned, even the gardaí didn't seem that interested. I mean, a man and a woman ... but now ... it could have been her, couldn't it?'

'Or it could have been a tired kid kicking up about going home,' Sarah said.

'I wish I'd been paying more attention that day. But it was so hot, a real scorcher, I'd been run off me feet all day, and all I wanted to do was have a dip and head off home. That's when I heard this godawful screaming and I found the little fella trying to wade out to sea, swinging his arms like he was trying to part it.' She wiped at a tear.

'It's not your fault. You probably saved Sam Jones from drowning,' Sarah told her.

'Poor little fellow. They say you never get over losing a child. I'd say it's just as hard if you lose a sibling.'

'I have two sisters,' Sarah said, 'and I know if anything happened to them I'd be devastated.'

'Tell you what, you come back tomorrow evening if you can, talk to Daddy. You don't know how much this would mean to him.'

'Are you sure?'

'Oh, yes,' Bernie said, her eyes shining. 'This would set his mind at ease.'

16

John was in McDonald's eating a Big Mac when Thornton called. 'I believe I've located the original order.'

'Be right there.' John wolfed the rest of his food, then hurried back to the shop.

One of the oldies let him in and waved him towards the office where Thornton waited, a massive ledger before him.

'So you've found him?'

'Not him, her.' Thornton opened the ledger, turned it to John and pointed at a set of numbers and a yellowing receipt. 'The jacket was ordered by Lady Hall.'

John squinted at the faded and almost illegible handwriting.

'I remember her, you know. She was my father's client. Fred, do you remember Marisa, Lady Hall?'

Fred had appeared at John's elbow. 'Lady 'all? Yes.'

'Have a look at this, would you?' Thornton turned the ledger round and John waited, somewhat impatiently, as Fred peered myopically at the print. Finally, he nodded his grey head. 'Yes, that's her. Lord 'all, great big fellow he were before the accident.'

'Lord Hall?'

Fred nodded. ''E was in a car crash, turned 'is car over one winter. Oh, I don't remember now what year it was … but 'e done his spine in. Paraplegic 'e is now, very sad.'

'I see,' John said, his mind racing. Maybe the Halls had had Katie all along? Maybe they had adopted her.

'I can ring Lady Hall if you wish,' Thornton said. 'Perhaps she would know how that poor girl came by the jacket.'

'I'd really appreciate it,' said John.

'Of course, I'd be delighted to talk to her ladyship anyway and it's nice to have a genuine reason for calling. Excuse me.'

Thornton retired to his office and closed the door as he made his call. John watched him through the glass and marvelled at the range of expressions he worked through in just a few minutes.

'Seatbelts,' Fred said suddenly.

'What?'

'Seatbelts. It weren't the done thing to wear 'em back then. Nowadays, everyone wears one, don't they?'

'I guess so.'

'Well, there you go, then.' Fred gave him an irritated glance and crept off I to do whatever he did.

Ten minutes later, Thornton emerged, flushed and triumphant. 'Remarkable woman.'

'Did she tell you how Katie Jones ended up with the jacket?'

'Lord Hall died last year, and a few months ago she donated his clothes to charity with some of her own.'

Score one Sarah, John thought.

'Do you know where she sent them?'

'Yes. To a remarkable charity shop called Le Chá, it raises money for retired greyhounds.'

John blinked at him. 'Greyhounds?'

'Lord and Lady Hall were well-known aficionados.'

'I don't suppose you have the address of the shop.'

Thornton went back into his office and pulled out the *Yellow Pages*. He flicked through it. 'Here we are, 22 Cambed Lott Place.'

John scribbled it down. 'Mr Thornton, you're a diamond.'

'Yes,' Thornton said with a chuckle, 'so everybody tells me.'

'I promise you, if I ever have enough money to buy one of your suits, I will.'

'If I could eat goodwill, I'd be a very round man.'

They shook hands and John left the shop and made his way west.

Less than an hour later, he was standing outside the glittery window of Le Chá. He rang an old-fashioned silver bell and presently a tiny woman with pale blue hair opened the door and peered up at him. 'Yeth?'

John felt like Gulliver. 'Hello there. My name is—'

'Oh, you're Irith. I do love the acthent.' She patted his arm. 'Come in, pleathe. We're juth back from our lunch.'

Tickled by her lisp, John followed her into the shop. It was small, not much more than a counter with some rails and shelves. But what rails and shelves! Stuffed chock-a-block to the ceiling with a stagger-ing array of clothes. Sequined gowns, dress coats, tails, glittery shoes, furs, hats, gloves. A glass display case was filled with tiaras, drop earrings, huge pendants and cameo brooches.

The air was rank with money and mothballs.

John handed her his card. 'My name is John Quigley. I'm a private investigator.'

'Tilly Hyde-Dunwoody.'

They shook hands.

'What can I do for you, John?' She took up residence on a stool and eyed him a little warily.

He lifted a top hat off a mannequin and twirled it. 'Wow, you've got some selection of gear here.'

'We're very well known and people are kind.'

'And all of this goes in aid of greyhounds?'

'Don't be so amazed.' She pointed over his shoulder. John turned and saw the fattest greyhound he'd ever clapped eyes on, sprawled asleep on a moth-eaten sofa. 'In her youth, Clara was one of the very betht two-year-olds in the country. Then, when the poor darling hit three and … lotht form, her owner threw her away. I've had her for nearly a decade now and, believe me, the greyhound can make a wonderful companion dog. It's vile what people do to it in the name of entertainment.'

John glanced at the fur coats and thought that people did vile things to lots of animals. Tilly noticed his expression and her mouth pulled into a thin defensive line. 'You think it's foolith? Do you have a dog?'

'Yes.'

'What kind?'

'He's part German Shepherd, part wolfhound.'

'My, quite a handful.'

'He is.'

She nodded, seemingly much happier to talk to him now that he had risen to the rank of dog owner. 'You claim you're a detective. Well, what can I help you detect? Did you want to talk about anything in particular?'

'I'm here about some clothing that was donated to you by Lady Hall.'

'Oh!' She clapped her hands in delight. 'Why didn't you mention that? Lady Hall's a wonderful lady.'

'So everyone keeps telling me. She donated her late husband's and her own clothes to you recently, and a few items – a jacket in particular – ended up on the back of a girl I'm investigating.'

'How exciting. I remember the donation, of courthe. High quality, naturally.'

John pulled the photo of Katie from his bag. 'Could I show you a picture?'

'The girl you're enquiring about?' Now she was as eager as a kitten with a butterfly between its paws.

'Yes.' He passed her the photo and waited while she searched a handbag the size of Wales for her reading glasses.

Eventually, she located them, put them on and studied the photo. After a while she gave a disappointed sigh. 'I don't believe I know her.'

'No?'

'No.' She shook her head and returned the photo. 'I have a very good memory for people.'

John sighed too. 'Oh well, it was worth a try.'

'Do you have the jacket?'

'Sure.'

'Might I view it?'

John opened the bag. 'It's a bit pungent.'

'I won't mind. Tho ith Clara,' Tilly Hyde-Dunwoody said with a throaty laugh, and John felt a wave of affection for her.

He took out the coat and spread it on the counter. She examined it as carefully as Thornton had, running her hands over the lapels and buttons.

'I remember now. A man bought thith. A young man, I would thay twenty-five to twenty-nine.'

'So late twenties. You remember anything else about him?'

'I do. Very jumpy, he was.' She scowled. 'Impathient, kept looking back out out of the window. Wouldn't let me wrap it or give him information on cleaning. Important, you know. Tat material needth care. And as you can thee,' she rubbed the bleach stains with her thumb, 'he didn't care for it at all.'

'I don't think that was down to him. I don't supposed he paid for it with a credit card, did he?' John asked hopefully.

'He did not, I'm afraid.'

'Can you remember what he looked like?'

'I'm sure I've encountered him about the area, you know.' She removed her glasses and closed her eyes. 'About your height, but very thin and he had bleached hair, yellow. Oh, and he wore it in one of those …' She flattened her perm to the sides of her head, '… you know, when they cut it at the thideth.'

'A mullet?'

'Ith that what they call it? Well, one of thothe. Oh, and he had … bratheth.'

'Braces?'

'On the teeth. And an anti-war badge here,' she pointed to her right breast, 'on the pocket of his denim jacket. The jacket was black, in keeping with the retht of his apparel.' She opened her eyes. 'Will that do?'

'You really do have a gift.' John grinned. 'If only every witness was as sharp as you, my job would be so much easier.'

'Oh you Irith, charmerth to a man.'

John thanked her for her time and she offered to call him if she recalled anything else.

He left and walked up the street, wondering about the connection between the rude young man and Katie Jones. He put a cigarette between his lips and was patting his jacket, looking for his lighter, when he stopped so suddenly that a woman texting on her mobile walked straight into him.

'Ow,' she said.

'Sorry.'

'Watch where you're going.'

'Yeah, right.' John didn't even look at her. He opened the bag and removed the watch Sarah had given him from a brown envelope. He turned it over, raised his head and smiled.

The rose on it was an exact match for the one he was looking at on a sign that swung in the breeze outside a trendy jewellers. 'La vie en' was printed over it. 'A rose by any other name would smell just as nice,' John muttered, murdering Shakespeare.

Sarah had been on the phone to Sergeant Frank Duffy, retired, the man who had been in charge of the case at the time of Katie's disappearance. Despite her best effort at charm, he had been reluctant to talk to her until he had checked her out, then reluctant to talk to her after he had confirmed who she was. But he had eventually admitted that Tom Kelly, Bernie's father, 'might have mentioned a car', but that no one else had reported anything untoward so that had been that. He had become angry with her when she tried to push him further. In the end, she had simply thanked him for his time and hung up.

She could ring Detective McBride and pass on the information, she supposed, but she didn't want to make that call until John was back. It wasn't as if the gardaí were ever willing to pass on information to them. Anyway, all they had to do was drive for an hour, as she had, and they could find the information for themselves.

She pressed her fingers to her cheek. She needed to keep busy. When she was busy, she could forget about the look on her mother's face that morning. She did not question whether she was – as Helen never tired of hinting – making a royal cock of caring for their mother.

She picked up the phone. 'Gloria, hi. It's Sarah Kenny here.'

'Oh, Sarah, yes. Hello.'

'Any more interest in the apartment? How did the viewing go last night?'

'Strange man, but just another looker, I'm afraid. If a buyer does commit, I'm sure someone will be in touch.'

'Someone? I thought *you* were handling the sale. You told Helen you'd handle it personally.'

Gloria sort of clucked.

'Gloria?'

'Well, Sarah, I know what I said, and, really, it was more as a favour to your sister ... but I don't have time to take on more clients at the moment. Ruth Kelly will be—'

'Ruth? But didn't you tell me she's only been at your office three months? Gloria, I told you I needed a quick sale on that apartment, and you're the best seller there is—'

'Sarah, that's very kind of you, but Ruth is a perfectly competent agent and I really have to go now. I'm about to meet a prospective client.'

'I thought I was a bloody client!'

'Give Ruth a call if you want, but you shouldn't worry. She's a fine girl. Talk soon. Ciao.'

Sarah slammed the phone down. Her hand hovered over the numbers for Landon's office, but she didn't dial. Instead, she rested her elbow on the desk, propped her head on her hand and stared at the ceiling. This was turning out to be quite the shit week. Her car was smashed, her mother was getting worse, and now Gloria had dropped her. Good job she didn't believe in curses or she'd be sacrificing chickens in no time.

She was in that position a moment later when Sam Jones knocked softly and popped his head in. 'Hello, I was—'

That was as far as he got before Sumo launched himself at the door, barking furiously.

Sam slammed it shut just in time to avoid disaster.

'Oh my God! Sumo!' Sarah leaped up and ran round the desk. She grabbed his collar and wrenched open the door to find Sam clutching his briefcase, his face ashen.

'I'm so sorry,' Sarah said, trying to keep the dog from making a second attempt at mauling her client to shreds.

'What's *that*?'

'He's John's. I'm minding him while John's in London.'

'Minding him? From what? I imagine he's at the top of the food chain.'

'I'm so sorry. I didn't know you were coming.'

Sam lowered his bag. 'He's a monster.'

'Well, he can be a little protective.'

'It's my fault, I suppose,' he said. 'I should have buzzed, but the door downstairs was open, so I thought I'd just pop on up.'

'Right.' Sarah shifted her weight. Her arm was tiring from holding Sumo back.

'Look, I wanted to talk to you about the case ... would you like to go for a coffee or something to eat?'

'Sure. Just give me a second to grab my keys and I'll be with you.'

'Okay.' Sam looked a little worried. 'You're not bringing him, are you?' He pointed at Sumo, who bared his teeth.

'I can if you'd like.'

'Oh, no, no, thank you.'

Sarah laughed and closed the door over. Moments later, she had her jacket on and they went down together.

'Have you heard from John?' Sam asked as they reached the bottom of the stairs.

'I spoke to him last night,' Sarah said, eyeing the empty boxes in the hall and making a mental note to complain. No matter how many times the old cow who owned the grocery was warned that leaving them there was a fire hazard, she still did it every chance she got. 'He was going to see the makers of the jacket this morning. I'm sure as soon as he has anything, he'll contact me.'

Sam held the door open for her.

'Thank you.'

'So, what do you fancy? We could go to the Westbury Hotel – they do a lovely lunch.'

'I'd better stick close to the office. I can't leave Sumo alone too long. You should see what he can do when he gets bored.'

'Maybe some other time then, when you're not dog-sitting.'

He was smiling but Sarah couldn't read his expression.

'I'll hold you to that,' she said. 'There's a café up the road. It's not quite the Westbury, but they serve good coffee.'

'Lead on.' Sam slipped his hands into his pockets. 'My mother seems to think Katie can hear when she speaks to her.'

'Maybe she can. I've read about things like that – people remember snatches of conversation and songs from when they were in a coma.'

'Do you think we'll ever find out what happened to her?'

'Maybe.' Sarah filled him in on what she had learned since they'd last met as they walked. When they took their seats, she had more or less finished.

Sam was particularly upset that his sister had asked for and been given information on how to get a gun.

'That's not good. Shows that was premeditated, doesn't it?'

'We don't know that she bought the gun specifically to shoot anyone. Maybe she just wanted to protect herself.'

'That's not how the gardaí will see it. And this car, is this Kelly man sure of what he saw?'

'I don't know. I have yet to speak to him personally,' she said. 'What do you want me to do? I can give this to the gardaí.'

He tapped his fingers on the table as Sarah drained her coffee. 'Aren't you obliged to tell them?'

'I don't work for them, I work for you.'

'It might be best if we hold off on it for the moment.'

'I thought so too.'

'What now?'

'Now we try to find whoever Katie spoke to and if he was the one who supplied her with the gun. Which, of course, will be next to impossible, as he's hardly likely to say, "Sure, lady, it was me." But I have a friend who might help me with that one.'

'I still can't believe any of this.' Sam shook his head. 'I can't believe she's alive. After all these years …'

'I'm sure it's hard, but we'll get to the bottom of it.' Sarah patted his hand.

'I don't know how you can do this job.'

'Me neither.'

'How did you come to pick this line of work? If you don't mind my saying so, you're not at all the sort of person I'd imagined I'd encounter.'

'I don't know that I did pick it. In fact, it sort of picked me.'

'John's not how I'd imagined a detective either.' He laughed. 'I mean, when I saw him standing there covered in whatever the hell it was, I almost turned on my heel and ran.'

Sarah forced a smile.

'My mother said he was lovely to her at the hospital. I guess he's a diamond in the rough.'

She remembered John, the night Patrick York had shot her. He was injured, carrying her through the mud. John, who had held her tight when she wept over her mother. John, who had given her his car. John, who laughed easily and cared deeply – no matter how hard he tried to hide it.

'Thanks for the coffee, Sam. I'd better be getting back.'

'I'm sorry, I didn't mean ...' Plainly he knew he'd crossed the line. 'He's your friend. I'm sorry.'

'John Quigley is a lot of things, Sam,' Sarah said, putting her coat on, 'and you're right, he's a little rough around the edges, scruffy, impatient and he likes to bend things to suit himself. He's also loyal, trustworthy and worth twice any man in this room.'

'Of course. I really didn't mean anything by what I said.'

'I'll be sure to call you as soon as we have a lead on anything. Now, if you'll excuse me, I have to get back to the office.'

17

John pushed open the door and walked into a brightly lit room, decorated with geometric wallpaper, lava lamps and plastic sixties furniture. The Stones played on a record player on the counter and a large Teddy-boy poster took pride of place behind it.

'Groovy,' John said.

'Most of it's authentic, too.' A woman with a jet-black beehive hairstyle, wearing a black and white mini-dress and patent knee boots, climbed down from a ladder. She smiled at him. Or, rather, her mouth did – her-kohl rimmed eyes were as cold as the Atlantic on a January morning. 'Can I help you?' she asked.

'I hope so. My name is John Quigley and I'm a private detective.'

'Yolanda Vaughn.'

'Hello, Yolanda. I noticed your sign out front – the rose?'

She smiled, genuinely this time. 'Ah, yes, my grandmother's idea. 'La Vie en Rose' was one of her favourite songs.' She waved a bangled wrist. 'This was one of the first jewellers my grandfather opened when they settled here after the war. It's the smallest now, but of great sentimental value to us.'

'I see.' John approached the counter and laid the watch on the glass top. 'Can you tell me if this came from here?'

She picked it up and examined it. 'It looks like one of ours. I can—' She turned it over, and her eyes narrowed.

John put his hands on the counter. 'What is it?'

'Where did you get this?'

'From a girl.'

'What girl?'

'Katie Jones.'

'Who?'

John took the photograph from his bag and passed it to her. She took it and gasped. Her hand flew to her mouth. 'You recognise her?'

'I— Yes, of course I do! That's Katie. But where is she? What happened to her? Why does she look like that?'

'She's in a coma. How do you know her?'

'Oh, my ... Wait, why did you call her Katie Jones?'

'That's her name.'

'I don't understand.' Yolanda returned to the photo. 'The girl in this picture isn't called Katie Jones. Her name is Todd, Katie Todd.'

'Katie Todd *is* Katie Jones – or at least she was a very long time ago.' John held out his hand and Yolanda reluctantly handed back the watch and the photo. 'How do you know her?'

'Through Drake.'

'Drake?'

'Drake Vaughn, my brother. He owns this shop. She's a friend of his.'

'A friend?'

She regarded John with sudden suspicion. 'Look, who are you? And what's happened to Katie? Where is she?'

'When was the last time you saw her?'

'I don't know – about a fortnight ago.'

'What about your brother?'

'I don't know.'

'Were they close?'

She made a noncommittal gesture, but her eyes were wary.

'Does your brother have bleached hair, with braces on his teeth?'

That shook her. 'How do you know? What's going on? Why won't you tell me what's happened to Katie?'

John pulled out his notebook. 'I've been hired by Katie's brother to find out where his sister has been these last few years.'

Yolanda was stunned. She opened her mouth but no words came out.

'Obviously this has come as a shock to you, but what can you tell me about her?'

'Well, not much, really. She's from Kilburn and she works at an old folks' home in Knightsbridge. That's how she and my brother met. Our grandmother passed away last year and Katie cared for her.'

'She's a nurse?'

'Yes.'

John asked for the address of the home and Yolanda wrote it down. 'What about family?'

'She has her father and a brother, but they don't see each other much. Her mother died a few years back – oh … I don't know if that's true or not now, do I?'

'How long has Katie known your brother?'

'Since New Year's Eve.'

'They get on okay? I mean, are they close?'

'Why are you asking?' She glared at John. 'I hope you don't think Drake had anything to do with this! He's the sweetest thing on earth.'

'I'm sure he is. I'd like to talk to him. Does he work here too?'

'No.'

'I'm sure you can get in touch with him, though? Got a number for him?'

'I can't give it to you.'

'Why not?'

'Look, my brother … he's not – I mean, he's an incredibly intelligent and gifted man, but he's not always good under pressure. Being asked questions … when he finds out Katie's in a coma, he'll freak out.'

'I'm sure he'll handle it,' John assured her. 'Either way, I'll need to talk to him.'

'I can give you any information you might need. There's no need to involve him.'

'Are you kidding me?'

'Can't it wait until later, then?'

Why was she stalling him? John wondered. All he wanted to do was talk to her brother. 'I'm on the clock here, Yolanda, I don't have time to wait around. Now, is there some reason you don't want me to talk to your brother? Something you're hiding?'

'No.'

'How old is he?'

'Thirty.'

'You act like you're trying to protect him.'

'It's nothing like that.'

'Then what?'

'I don't want my brother upset. He's very vulnerable.'

'I promise I'll be gentle.'

Her eyes darkened. 'You don't understand. Drake is gifted – he's an artist.'

'Tell you what,' John said, 'gifted or not, you call him and tell him I've dragged my arse all the way from Dublin and I don't like to fly, then tell him I want to talk to him or I'll just give his name to the police and they can talk to him instead.'

Yolanda reached under the counter and came up with a pad and some paper. 'Okay. There's no need to call anyone. I'll give you our address.'

'He lives with you?'

'Yes. But wait until this evening to call. Drake works during the day and doesn't like to be disturbed. Leave it until, say, half past seven.' She wrote the address on a piece of headed paper and handed it to him. 'Will Katie be all right?'

'I don't know.' John took the paper, folded it and slipped it into his pocket.

'But a coma – how did it happen? Was there an accident?'

'No accident.'

Yolanda frowned. 'Then what happened to her?'

'Nice of you to ask. She shot herself.'

Every ounce of strength seemed to leave Yolanda's body. She sagged against the wall. 'Oh my God! Poor Drake will be devastated.'

'Yep,' John said. 'She's in a coma, having shot herself, but poor Drake.'

'You don't have any right to speak to me like that. You don't understand anything about me or my brother. My brother *worshipped* Katie.'

'Did you or your brother file a missing persons report with the police when you couldn't contact her?'

A small muscle in Yolanda's jaw bunched. 'No, we didn't see any reason to involve them.'

John frowned. 'So, according to you, your brother's much-worshipped friend goes missing for two weeks and neither of you files a police report?'

'I don't have to explain myself to you. I don't even *know* you.'

'No, you don't, and I'm just asking. Seems kind of strange to me, that's all.'

'We thought she might have gone to visit her father or something.'

John could see she was lying and she wasn't very good at it. For whatever reason, she was very rattled. 'So, seven, half seven, then?'

'Yes.'

'Okay, I'm gone.'

When John left, Yolanda picked up the phone. She dialled a number with shaking hands and pressed her forehead to the wall. All of a sudden, she had a splitting headache.

'Harry! This is the fifth message I've left for you and I'm getting fed up waiting.' She went to the window and watched John cross the street. She pressed the heel of her hand to her forehead. 'I want you to call me as soon as you get this. I mean it, Harry. I need to talk to you.'

18

John had no intention of hanging about for Yolanda until half past seven. As soon as he left the shop, he headed for the address she had given him.

By the time he had made his way back across the city to Kensington and found the house, darkness had begun to fall and a bitter wind was making his ears ache. It was turning into a filthy evening and, as he struggled to zip up his jacket against the rain, he was struck by a wave of homesickness.

Jesus, what was he like? He hadn't even been out of Ireland twenty-four hours. What the hell was wrong with him?

He found Ongar Street and was pleasantly surprised to notice it wasn't a million miles from his hotel. The house, he was surprised to see, was a four-storey Edwardian affair. Okay, it was probably the shabbiest one on the street, but still, it must have cost a mint and Yolanda hadn't struck him as a multimillionaire.

He trotted up the steps to the front door, pausing only to whistle softly at the vintage pale blue Mercedes coupé parked haphazardly across the pavement, its nose crushing a privet hedge. He pressed the doorbell, which played a snatch of classical music at him that Sarah would probably have recognised.

Thinking of her made him feel homesick again.

After a moment, the door opened and John saw Tilly Hyde-Dunwoody had been right on the mark, God bless her. The man before him was in his late twenties, maybe more, but he was dressed as though he was a teenager. Stunted development, Sarah called it. A Knob Jockey, was John's take.

He was slender and moved in a series of jerks. He wore black skinny jeans, a Ramones T-shirt and Converse runners. His hair was shoulder length, peroxide blond and looked as if it had been cut with a bread knife. His left arm was covered from wrist to elbow in plastic and leather bangles. He had dark brown eyes that were ever so slightly crossed, and the fingers of his left hand were smudged with dark blue ink.

'Drake Vaughn?'

'I would surmise so.' He looked alarmed.

'I'm John Quigley.' He held out a card and waited an abnormally long time for the younger man to accept it.

'It says here you're a detective.'

'I know. I want to talk to you about Katie Todd.'

'Did he send you?'

'Who?'

Drake winked at him. 'Oh, yes, very good. That would be my way of doing it too.'

John was confused. 'Your sister sent me. She gave me your address.'

'Yolanda?' He seemed sceptical.

John located the piece of paper Yolanda had written on. He passed it to Drake, who read it. 'This is my sister's handwriting.'

'Can I come in? I'm freezing my nuts off out here.'

'Oh – yeah.' Drake looked past him onto the street, then grabbed John by the front of his jacket, yanked him into the hall and slammed the door.

'Whoa.' John was more than a little annoyed at being manhandled. 'Everything okay there, bud?'

'Oh, yeah,' Drake repeated, peering through the keyhole. 'Never be too careful, you know?'

'Careful about *what*?'

'People.' Drake glanced at him. 'Don't you know that?'

114

'Right,' John said, thinking this guy was nuttier than a Walnut Whip. No wonder his sister hadn't been keen on giving out his number.

The hall was filled with musty-smelling, old-fashioned furniture and tatty oil paintings. The floor was filthy and the tiles were cracked. Along one wall, a collection of Wellington boots mouldered, some of them covered with cobwebs. It was nearly as cold in the house as it was outside.

'Have you found Katie?' Drake jerked his head towards the back of the house to indicate they should walk that way. 'How is she? Will she be back soon?'

'I don't think so,' John said slowly. 'I'm afraid she's in a coma.'

'Oh? A coma? That's very bad.' He slapped his hands together twice, fast and loud, making John jump. 'Very bad news.'

'Yes, it is.' John wondered if he was taking the piss, but he seemed genuine enough. Maybe he was on some kind of drug.

'So, what would you surmise? She's going to be okay, right?'

'I don't know. I hope so.'

'Me too. Come on.'

Drake led him down a short flight of steps and into a huge kitchen divided by a long, cluttered breakfast counter. It was warm a massive wood-burning stove took up half of one wall. An easel had been set up under a skylight and around it were stacks of papers and a battered leather sofa covered with sheets and blankets. There were books everywhere. John figured Drake spent a lot of time in this room.

'Take a seat. You want some coffee?'

'Sure.' John rubbed his hands to warm them. He sat on a stool by the breakfast counter and watched as Drake scratched his head and glanced about in apparent confusion. What was wrong with the guy? He sniffed the air, but there was no smell of grass or hash, and he didn't seem stoned. 'Or whatever you have handy.'

'I don't know if we have coffee. I don't drink it, but Yolanda does so ...' He opened a press and peeped in hopefully. 'So ... well, I don't know where ... Oh, here's ... No.'

'It's okay,' John said. 'Water's good too.'

'Hold on.'

It was almost painful to watch. It took another five minutes of head-scratching and peering before Drake admitted defeat. 'What about tea?' he said finally.

John nodded. 'You know where it is, right?'

Drake flashed him a surprisingly disarming smile. 'Tea I can do.'

And tea he did. Five minutes later John was holding a steaming cup of very good tea indeed.

'So, Katie's in a coma, poor old thing.'

'Drake, Katie Todd, your friend. What do you know about her?'

'Oh, lots. She likes yellow and the countryside. She likes cats. I'm going to get her one as a wedding present. Probably a Burmese. I hear they're clever.'

'She's getting married?'

'Well, sure.'

'To whom?'

'Me.'

John put down his cup and took a deep breath. 'Drake, are you telling me that you and Katie Todd are engaged?'

'Since last month. Very romantic.'

'Your sister didn't mention it. She said you were friends.'

'Oh, well, *that*'s Yolanda.'

John took a sip of his tea and tried to think. Why hadn't Yolanda mentioned this? Was it true or was this guy's clearly wobbly brain making up a story? Either way, it was as confusing as hell. 'Drake, I don't know how to tell you, bud, but your fiancée is not who you think she is. Katie Todd's real name is Katie Jones.'

'Really?'

'She was taken – kidnapped, actually – when she was a toddler. She's not who she thought she was either, for that matter. Do you understand?'

Drake put his cup down and smiled at the ceiling. 'That's funny.'

'It is?'

'Uh-huh, that works. Katie, Katie. Right, I can see it. Very matched. But Katie always said she never fitted in, and this explains it. Easy to understand if you have the facts at your disposal, but then again, most things are, aren't they?'

'Okay. Did you know about it? Did Katie ever tell you about her name?'

'No.' Drake frowned. 'But is it important? We're getting married, you know, so I suppose her name will change again soon anyway, right?'

Drake wasn't completely *compos mentis*, John mused, but it was difficult to grasp how unconnected from reality he was. Especially as what he said made a kind of sense. 'Er ... right. It is kind of important, though. Katie's blood family want to know why she was called Katie Todd. Your sister Yolanda mentioned she has a father.'

'Everyone does, don't they?'

John had to agree that yes, they did.

'My father died, you know. Mother too. Katie doesn't like hers, not a good person, I would surmise.'

'Who?'

'Her father. Her mother's dead. That's why she understands, you see. Shared experience, very important.'

'Right. What makes you say that? I mean, about not liking her father.'

'Well?' Drake shrugged a bony shoulder. 'She didn't want him coming to the wedding.'

'No?'

'No. None of her family was to be asked.'

'Does she have brothers and sisters?'

'One brother.'

'They don't get along either?'

'I would surmise not. He's younger, but I don't know him.'

'Drake, how did you meet Katie?'

'Well, she cared for Gamma. Very well, I would surmise.' He waved a wrist. Yolanda had made the same gesture, John recalled. 'Top-notch. Very caring person.'

'Your grandmother?'

'Dead now, too, I'm afraid. Heart attack. Very sad, but quite normal at her age, I would surmise. Poor Katie, she was most upset. Yolanda, too.'

John took a sip of his tea as he tried to make sense of everything he was hearing. 'What is it you do, Drake?'

'Oh, I write and draw.'

'What do you draw?'

'Comics mostly, and the jewellery. Very interesting. Do you find people say that? Interesssting. Yolanda says "*in*teresting", but when she does, it means she doesn't like something.'

'Your sister says you own the jewellery shop?'

'Yes.'

'You *and* your sister?'

'Just me.'

'But you don't work there?'

'Mmm.' Drake looked away, and John could see he was uncomfortable talking about it.

'Do you know where Katie's father lives?'

'Frank? Here.'

'Here?'

'London. Kilburn.' Drake took a sip of tea and began to hum. He stopped. 'You will need an address, I would surmise.'

'You surmise correctly.'

Drake beamed at him. 'Come on, we'll have to go upstairs to Katie's room.'

'She lives here?'

'Yes, as of recently.'

That bloody Yolanda! What the hell had she been playing at?

John followed Drake up two flights of stairs to the top floor. As they climbed, the state of the house astounded him. The walls were full of damp, as were the stairs. Judging by the creaks and groans of the wood, some of the steps were rotten beneath the ancient carpet. Window panes were missing, the spaces covered with plastic sheeting. In one case, one entire glass panel had been replaced with a soggy piece of cardboard, held with blue masking tape. The wood around it had splintered, as though someone had used a crowbar to force it.

'What happened there?' John nodded to it.

'Somebody tried to gain access. A thief, I would surmise.'

'Looks pretty recent.'

'Mmm.'

'Did they get anything?'

'No, I scared him off.'

'Yeah?' John was impressed. 'When did it happen?'

'Hard to say. Two weeks ago, perhaps?'

'Was Katie here?'

'Yes.'

'Did you call the police?'

'No, Yolanda said not to bother. Come on, we're here.'

They had reached a small landing with two doors. Drake pointed at the one to John's right. 'That's Katie's room and the bathroom is the other door. Self-contained, really. Very important. Katie likes her privacy.'

'Don't you sleep up here too?'

Drake tutted. 'No. I have a room off the kitchen. Too cold for me. Katie said she didn't mind. It's good to have an understanding.' He tapped the side of his nose. 'Very important.'

'What about Yolanda?'

'Oh, she has the first floor. Used to be Gamma's.'

'Ah. This was your grandmother's house.'

Drake smiled. 'Yes, everything was Gamma's, and now it's mine.'

'Yolanda's too?'

'Well. Not really, but don't worry. That's our understanding. She's my sister.'

John nodded. It was beginning to make sense. In a funny way, everything Drake said – though a bit fuzzy – stemmed from sense. Obviously, the grandmother had left everything to him, but he clearly couldn't run things alone, so Yolanda took care of things. It was good to have an understanding in a relationship. But John wondered how this charming but slightly batty young man managed to hook himself someone like Katie Jones, or how Katie put up with this vast, freezing house and his idiosyncrasies. He wondered how Katie got on with Yolanda. He wondered how much Drake Vaughn was worth, on paper at any rate.

Drake was watching him, a worried look on his face.

'What?'

'I rather think Katie won't approve of us tramping about her room.'

'She's in a coma.'

'You mentioned that.'

'Look, you want to protect her privacy. If you'd go in and get her old man's address for me, I can wait here.'

Drake bit his lip and gazed at the door. 'I wouldn't know where it might be. I don't go in there much.'

'Look, Drake, I came all the way from Ireland to find out what happened to your fiancée. I really need her father's address. Don't you think Katie would want you to let him know she'd been hurt? Don't you think he has a right to know?'

'Ah!' Drake held up an ink-stained finger. 'Now, that's *our* understanding. We're to be married, yes, but we should inform him.'

'Right.' John stuck his hands into his pockets and rocked back on his heels. 'So, will we go in? You're practically her husband anyway. I'm sure she wouldn't mind her husband having a look through her things.'

Drake beamed at him. 'Logically, that's sound.'

He opened the door and they went inside.

'Holy crap!' John said, gazing around him in awe. He had walked into a bucolic wonderland. Every square inch of the walls had been hand-painted in pastoral scenes. It was the countryside as only an artist could render it, downy trees, a softly glowing sunset behind the headboard, fields of corn so lifelike that he wanted to run his hands through them, and by the window a magnificent oak reached into the ceiling, its branches stretching as a canopy to the bed.

'Did you do this?' he asked.

Drake nodded happily. 'Katie said she liked the country, so I thought I'd provide it.'

'It's beautiful.'

'Like Katie.' Drake flopped down on the end of the bed. John couldn't help but laugh. 'You're really smitten.'

'I would surmise so.'

'Come on, let's get this address.'

John watched Drake search the room. It was a relatively simple task as, apart from some clothes and cosmetics, Katie Jones had few personal effects.

'There doesn't appear to be an address book,' Drake said finally, after a look through a small cardboard box containing payslips, a bank book and some photos of a house he claimed he didn't recognise.

'What about before she lived here?' John said, trying to conceal his frustration. 'Did she—'

'Hey, you!' an angry voice interrupted.

Drake jumped up so fast he spilled the contents of the box onto the floor. 'Yolanda! You scared me. Don't shout like that.'

'You said you'd wait.' Yolanda marched into the room and jabbed her finger into John's chest.

'Put that away,' John said mildly. 'You could have somebody's eyes out.'

'Yolanda,' Drake said, 'Katie's in a coma.'

Yolanda looked as if she was going to thump John. 'You told him?'

'He's her fiancé. He's got a right to know.'

She flinched, but recovered quickly. 'You've no right to be here. I asked you to wait before you spoke to my brother.'

'Drake didn't mind talking to me. Did ya, Drake?'

'No,' Drake said, but he looked anxious.

'Get the hell out of here.' Yolanda tugged at John's arm.

John let her drag him to the door. 'Drake, nice meeting you, man. Katie's in Beaumont Hospital in Dublin. If you can, you should go to her, it might—'

'*Get out!*'

Yolanda shoved him out onto the landing and slammed the door. 'I told you—'

'A pack of lies,' John interrupted. 'Let go of my arm. Show's over.'

She released him and took a deep breath. 'He's not really engaged.'

'No? I suppose she doesn't really live here either.'

'I—'

'You're a liar, and I'm wondering what you're covering up.'

'Nothing.'

'Right.' John trotted down the stairs. 'I suppose you don't know anything.'

'Maybe the gold-digging tramp was afraid people would see through her fucking act!' Yolanda spat.

John stopped. 'You're a real piece of work, Yolanda.'

'Get out of my house.'

'Yours, is it? Or your brother's?'

She went back into Katie's beautiful room and slammed the door.

19

Sarah was listlessly eating a tub of natural yoghurt when John called.

'Hey you,' she said. 'I was getting worried. Why's your phone off?'

'I forgot to bring the charger with me so I'm trying to save the battery.'

'Everything okay?'

'I found where Katie was living.'

'Wow! Well done! How did you manage that?'

'The watch. I found the jewellery shop it came from and it led me to her home. Well, her most recent home. Still no address for her. But I got a name – Frank Todd. She's got a brother here too. Oh, and she worked at a nursing home.'

'Where are you now?'

'Just leaving her fiancé's place.'

'She was engaged?'

'I would surmise so.'

'What?'

'Nothing. How are things your end?'

'Okay. Did a check with the witness the day she went missing. Her name's Bernadette Lynch and she and her father were the chip-van owners. Bernie said her father remembers a car, but I can't question him until tomorrow. Nice woman, still feels bad after all these years.'

'Give us the details on the car.'

'Blue and sporty-looking. She said he remembers it because it seemed an odd choice for a family. Bernie's going to ask some of her father's friends if he ever mentioned anything to them about it, but there's not too many of them left these days, so we won't hold our breath on that one.'

'Any word on the reg?'

'Nope.'

'Damn. Description of the guy?'

'Youngish, with dark hair and a moustache. She thinks there was a woman with him.'

'That it?'

'That's it, and there might not be anything to it other than a tired kid not wanting to go home.'

'Is that what you think?'

'To be honest, no,' Sarah said. 'When she was telling me I got a sort of tingling in my gut.'

'Funny you should say that. Do you want to hear something weird?'

'Go on.'

'I got the exact same feeling when I saw the jewellery shop today.'

'You know something, John, maybe we're getting … I don't know, it sounds sort of corny, but maybe we're getting a feel for this business.'

'Maybe we are.'

'I've been thinking. I want to go check out this Willie Staunton guy.'

'Sarah—'

'I'll be discreet. I just want a face to put to the name.'

'I asked you to stay away from that bar until I got back.'

'I can look after myself.'

'I'm not saying you can't. But I'll be back tomorrow and we can check it out together.'

'Okay, okay.' Sarah dropped the yoghurt into the bin by her desk. 'You okay? You sound tired.'

She heard him sigh. 'I'm all right. Look, I'm going to switch this off now, there's bugger-all signal in the Tube anyway. I'll head on over to the nursing home where Katie worked, see if they can help me out with an address for her.'

'Well, give me a shout if you hear anything.'

'Will do. I'm telling you, Sarah, stay away from that bar and Willie Staunton.'

'Right. Bye, John.'

Sarah hung up and dialled another number. *I'm telling you?*

'Hello?'

'Jackie? Look, I know it's an imposition, but can I ask you a huge favour?'

'Oh, Sarah, I'm just sitting down to—'

'I wouldn't ask if it wasn't important.'

'What is it?'

'Can you take Mum for a few hours tonight?'

'I – oh, I'm not that long back in, you know, and I—'

'It's just for an hour or two. I've got something to check out.'

'Well, all right. I suppose I can. I'll give Belinda a call.'

'Thanks, Jack, you're a star.'

Sarah winked at Sumo. 'Come on, mutt. We're going for a ride.'

Jackie drove to her mother's house and let herself in. 'Hello?' she called.

Belinda came out of the sitting room carrying a tray with a half-eaten bowl of soup on it. 'Hello, Jackie.'

'Everything all right?'

'She's okay. A bit restless today.'

'Oh?'

'Did Sarah mention what happened this morning?'

Jackie brushed a strand of hair off her forehead. She was tired. She'd had a glass or two of wine before Sarah called, but hadn't the heart to refuse her younger sister's request. 'No, she just asked me to watch Mum for an hour or two until she got back.'

'She's probably upset.' Belinda went into the kitchen and began to wrap up the bread and clean the worktops before she left. 'Your mother threw a bottle of perfume at her head this morning. Glass everywhere.'

'Oh dear,' Jackie sighed. 'Poor Sarah. No wonder she wanted an hour or two to herself.'

'It's not easy when they're angry and confused. It's hard on everyone,' Belinda said. 'Lord knows, I watched my own father turn into something he never was a day in his life.'

'Is that why Mum's restless?'

'I don't know, Jackie. Truth is, she's been acting more and more unruly these last few weeks.'

'Well thank you, Belinda. Whenever you want, you can head off.'

Belinda held her gaze. 'You might need to speak with your sister. Your mother's a lovely lady, but there will come a time when she needs more than I can provide.'

'I'll talk to her.'

Jackie went into the sitting room. 'Hi, Mum.'

Her mother was sitting in her favourite chair watching *National Geographic*. Belinda had somehow managed to get her into some clothes today, including shoes. Jackie lowered herself on the couch. 'What are you watching?'

'Emperor penguins,' her mother said softly. 'Amazing how they look after their chicks in those conditions. So cold.'

'Yes,' Jackie replied. 'It *is* amazing, but that's family for you.'

She settled back among the cushions and watched Emperor penguins with her mother.

Sarah parked the car opposite Nesbitts and turned off the engine. At this time, Thomas Street was slowing down, the traders and businesses shutting up for the evening.

'You stay here and try not to get me into trouble,' she said to Sumo, who was standing up in the back seat watching every passer-by with suspicion. 'Stay. Mind the car.'

She climbed out and locked the door. Seconds later, she was pushing her way into the gloomy pub. It was deserted, save for an old boy seated at the bar. He was wearing a faded nylon jacket and a plaid hat pulled low over his forehead. Sarah sat on a stool not far from him and looked around. It was an old-fashioned place, full of scored dark wood and rickety furniture. A highly punctured dart-board occupied one wall and a cigarette machine the other.

A fat barman in a sweat-stained Italia '90 T-shirt was watching American horse racing on a telly bolted to the wall at the far end of the room. He left Sarah to wait for a good minute and a half before he deigned to come her way. 'Whatcanigetcha?'

'I'll have a Sprite, please,' Sarah said cheerily, ignoring his rudeness. She nodded to the old man, who smiled toothily.

'Not a bad day out there.'

'Ah, sure, it could be worse.'

'That it could.'

The barman got her drink and plonked it on the counter.

'Two seventy.'

She handed him a ten-euro note. 'I'll need a receipt.'

He grunted.

Sarah opened her handbag and took out the photo of Katie. When the barman came back, she slid it across the counter to him. 'Can you take a look at this for me?'

He barely glanced at it. 'Who is it?'

'Her name's Katie Jones. I believe she was in here a few weeks ago. She might have been with a man, a regular of yours, by the name of Willie Staunton.'

'Who's asking?'

Sarah passed him a business card.

He read it with the same enthusiasm he had put into serving her. 'Never heard of her and never heard of him neither.'

'No?' Sarah raised an eyebrow. 'That's weird. I was told he drank in here a lot.'

'Lot of people do.'

'I can see that.' Sarah glanced round the empty room.

The barman picked up a damp cloth and flung it over his shoulder. 'You need anything else?'

'Nope, this is fine.'

'PJ, keep an eye on the bar for a minute 'till I change the barrel.'

The old man raised his pint in response. The barman gave Sarah one last look, then walked to the end of the bar and disappeared down a trapdoor.

'What about you?' Sarah asked quietly when he was gone.

'You notice a little blonde in here recently? She would have had an English accent.'

The old man folded his arms. 'Don't be askin' me now. I don't want to be gettin' involved with any trouble.'

'What makes you think there's trouble?'

'You're askin' 'bout Willie Staunton, aren't ya?' He gave her a half-smile. 'Where there's one there's the other right behind.'

'If you could just take a look at—'

Sarah tried to slide the photo over to him, but he shook his head. 'Don't be botherin' an old man. I can't help you.'

Sarah put it back into her bag. 'All right, thanks anyway.'

The old man regarded her. He spoke again, so softly Sarah strained to hear him. 'You seem like a nice sort of a young one, so here's somethin' I can tell ya. Stay away from Willie Staunton. He's not the sort of fella that likes people messin' with him. He's not right.' He made a swirling gesture towards his temple.

'No?'

'No.'

'I'll keep that in mind.' Sarah patted his arm.

She left the rest of her drink on the bar and pocketed her change with the receipt.

She had to find out more about Willie Staunton, which meant one thing: it was probably about time Sergeant Steve Magher got another of the calls he loved so much.

Willie Staunton was sitting on the floor of his flat in Crumlin. He was playing Pro Evolution Soccer with his mate Martin Butler when his mobile rang. He prodded Martin's back with his shoe. 'Press pause.'

Martin, about to cross in a wicked ball, said, 'Ah, man, come on—'

Willie prodded him again, only this time it was more of a kick. The younger man sighed and did as he was told. Willie didn't like repeating himself: it made him angry. And Willie angry was not good. He was a big man, outweighing Martin by at least fifty pounds, most of it running to fat. He was twenty-eight, hot-tempered and quick with his fists. Even though they were mates, Martin knew little good came of antagonising him.

Willie took out his phone, listened and said, 'A what?', his face expressionless.

'Say again?' His voice was steady, but Martin knew his friend was upset from the way he twirled the stud in his right eyebrow and his grey eyes focused somewhere off in the distance.

'Is she there now? Don't worry about it, fuck her. I'll be over in a couple of hours … Yeah, yeah, thanks.'

He hung up and slipped the phone back into his breast pocket.

'Everything all right, Willie?'

'Grand. Turn this shit back on.'

Martin pressed play and they resumed their game, but neither man's heart was in it.

'I'm going to need to borrow your car for a while.'

'Okay, Willie.'

Everything wasn't grand with Willie Staunton. And he needed to find that little rat-fuck Jimmy Dunne to find out why some bitch had been in his local bar asking questions about him, and how she had connected his name to Katie Jones.

Two hours later, Willie Staunton watched Jimmy Dunne admire himself in every window he passed. The kid was dickied up six ways from Sunday as usual and, as he bippity-bopped his way down the road towards the car, Willie's lip twitched. The little git really thought he was something, all right.

Willie waited for Jimmy to draw abreast with the back door before he sprung out of the passenger side. 'Jimmy-boy.'

Jimmy Dunne faltered. For a moment, he looked like he was about to bolt, but then his shoulders slumped. 'Hey, Willie, how you doing?'

'Good. You?' Willie indicated that he should get into the passenger seat. Jimmy blanched but did as he was bade. Willie closed the door, walked round to the driver's side and climbed in. He snapped the central locking.

Jimmy was trapped.

'Hey, how you doing, Willie?' His voice was too high, girlie almost. 'Been a while, how's it going with you? How's that phone I got for you? It going good? If you need any more I can—'

'There was a woman in Nesbitts asking for me earlier. You know anything about that?'

'A woman?'

'A private detective. She was asking about the blonde girl you hooked me up with.'

'Yeah?'

'You're sweating, Jimmy.'

'It's hot in here, Willie.'

'You told me I wouldn't regret getting you that piece. You promised me you'd make sure I was kept out of any shit.'

'Willie, I swear. I don't know anything about any girl.'

Willie took a cigarette from the pack in his pocket. 'Got a light, Jimmy?'

Jimmy patted himself down. 'Nah, I must have left it in—'

'No matter.' Willie pushed in the cigarette lighter on the dashboard. 'So, you don't know anything about her, huh?'

'I don't know, I don't know why—'

'I keep a very low profile, Jimmy. I've been inside, and once was enough. I didn't like it.'

'I know, man. I totally understand.'

'So I'm not real happy about this detective. I'm not real happy about her sniffing around my bar.'

'Jimmy, listen, I *swear* I don't know nothing about her. She must have found something in the girl's room.'

'Yeah? I thought you swept that when she shot herself.'

The lighter popped. Willie took it out, blew on its red-hot coils and lit his smoke.

'I did, but—' Jimmy was babbling, his hands slapping frantically in front of his face. 'Maybe she kept something.'

Willie's free hand snaked round Jimmy's neck and tightened. With the other, he rammed the glowing lighter into the soft skin under Jimmy's right eye.

Jimmy's scream was long and high.

'You'd better start talking, Jimmy. I gotta be somewhere in half an hour,' Willie said, snapping the kid's face against the window.

The car would reek of singed flesh for days.

A short while later, the man in Eddie Rocket's Diner watched the silver Toyota cruise past the building. This was the second time it had gone by and he was pretty sure the driver wasn't looking for the pirate radio station or the piss-artist solicitor. The big man took a keen interest in the car's occupant, noting his body language and the expression on his face.

This man was trouble. He recognised trouble when he saw it.

20

John stepped into the porch and rang the bell. While he waited for the porter to let him in, he rubbed his eyes. He was tired, and the travelling was catching up with him. He glanced at his watch. Twenty past seven.

A large black man wearing a grey uniform opened the door and peered down at him.

'Visiting hours are over. It's tea-time.'

'I'm not here to visit. I'm here to see Sister Carol.'

'She expecting you?'

'Should be. I called her earlier.'

'Name?'

'John Quigley.'

'Okay, wait there.'

He closed the door and John lit a cigarette. He had smoked it to the butt before the security guard returned. 'Come with me.'

John followed him through the overly warm corridors of the nursing home. Something about the smells and sounds, the murmurs and the squeak of rubber-soled shoes on tiles spun him back to the last few weeks of his father's life.

'You can wait here.' The guard showed him into a yellow-painted room. John sat on a blue couch and picked up a magazine. He was about to leaf through it when he noticed the guard hadn't left, but was now standing alert by the door. John got the distinct impression he was waiting for trouble. Everything about him was watchful.

After a short time, a woman bustled in. She was about forty-five and had freckles and curly strawberry-blonde hair tied into a thick ponytail. She wore a dazzling white uniform and oozed practicality.

'Sister Carol?'

'You must be the detective.' Her eyes were hazel and, while not exactly friendly, interested at least. 'You wanted to talk to me about Katie Todd?'

'Yes.'

'I called Yolanda Vaughn after we spoke,' she said sharply. 'Is it true Katie's in a coma?'

'Yes.'

'I see.' John could see the news had upset her deeply. 'Can you tell me what happened?'

'She shot herself.'

Sister Carol closed her eyes and whispered, 'Dear God.'

'Did Yolanda tell you anything else about why I'm here?'

She opened her eyes and glanced behind her at the guard. 'I thought you might be here to talk about the man who's been bothering her.'

'What man?'

'An older man, with a moustache. He approached Katie ... oh, about three weeks ago now and upset her terribly. I think she was frightened of him.'

'I haven't heard anything about him.' John sat forward to the edge of his seat. 'Sister Carol, the girl you know as Katie Todd is actually Katie Jones and she was kidnapped from a beach in Ireland twenty-six years ago. I came here to ask you if you can supply me with an address for her before she moved in with Drake Vaughn.'

She was stunned. Behind her, the guard had stiffened. John could see that his hand now rested on the shaft of his nightstick. What the hell was going on here?

'Do you have identification, Mr Quigley?'

John passed her a card and his ID. She studied them carefully but remained silent. The wall clock behind them ticked loudly in the quiet. Finally, John could bear it no longer. 'Look, I'm not trying to be difficult, but is something hinky going on here?' he demanded.

Her head snapped up. 'What do you mean?'

'I mean, what's with the beefed-up dude standing guard? What's with the twitchiness?'

She looked at his ID again. 'Like I said, you're not the first person to come here for Katie, and the last person who did became very *insistent* that we tell him where she was.'

'The man with the moustache?'

'No, a much younger man.'

'What do you mean by insistent?'

'He threatened to break my face for me. If it hadn't been for Jamal here, I believe he would have done so.'

John took out his notebook. 'Can you describe this guy for me?'

'Of course. He was perhaps twenty, slim but powerfully built. He wore a baseball cap, but he had very odd eyes, almost yellow, like a cat's.'

'Yellow?'

'That's how I'd describe them.'

'And the man with the moustache?'

'He was older, about fifty or fifty-five.'

John wrote it all down. 'Did you call the police when the younger man threatened you?'

'No.'

'Why not?'

She hesitated. 'Because Katie asked me not to.'

'Why? And, more importantly, why did you agree to that if this man threatened you with violence?'

'I … clearly she was very upset by this man being here. He was someone she was definitely trying to avoid. I didn't want to cause her any trouble. Katie Todd was the sweetest person I ever had the pleasure of working with. As it was, she resigned two days after the incident and I was very sorry to see her go. I tried to talk her out if it, but she wouldn't be persuaded. I knew it was because of that man coming here. I could see it in her face when I told her about him.

She looked, absolutely crushed.' She handed John his ID.

'How long did Katie work here?'

'Three years.'

'You must have an address for her.'

'Of course.'

'Can you give it to me?'

'Is it true that Katie isn't … really Katie?'

'Yes. She was kidnapped when she was just two.'

'Poor girl, she can't have known. She was always so kind to everyone here. The older ladies loved her, always so patient. I can't believe that she'd shoot herself. It's so utterly out of character.'

'Sister Carol, did Katie ever mention her family to you?'

'Her mother is dead and, as far as I know, she didn't discuss the rest of them. She was a private person. An absolute sweetheart, but very private. It was lovely when she and Drake Vaughn got together. Oh, that man adored her and she him.'

'That's right – he did say he met her here. She looked after his grandmother.'

'The old lady doted on her.'

'Drake's quite a character, isn't he?'

'He's very gifted. I have an etching he did of me one day – a very talented man.'

'You should see the painting he did for Katie,' John told her. 'Did she ever say anything else to you about the young man who came here looking for her?'

Her smile faded and she looked John straight in the eye. 'No, but she was frightened, Mr Quigley, that much I was sure of.' She glanced at the watch pinned to her lapel. 'I'll go and find that address for you.'

John checked his watch, twenty to nine. He was in Paddington, outside the last known address of Katie Todd. A light rain fell and, although the wind had died down, the cold was seeping into his bones. He yawned.

He climbed some well-worn steps, opened the gate and walked up the weedy path to the door of a run-down Victorian semi.

The house was divided into flats and there were four doorbells. John scanned them. Only two had names printed on them, strips of papers slipped into plastic casing. John sighed. He had hoped, despite her digs at Drake's not so humble home, that Katie had kept on the flat. If not, he had nothing else to go on.

First things first, which flat was it?

He rang the first unmarked bell and waited. *Nada.*

'Okay,' he said to himself, and kicked the door.

He rang the second bell and a grouchy man answered. The ensuing conversation did little to improve John's situation except to clarify that, no, he didn't speak Urdu.

He rang the next bell. No one home. He rang the last and, again, no one answered.

'Fuck.' He rested his head against the door, trying to decide what he should do next.

'What are you doing there? You! What are you doing, hiding in the shadows? Come out of there before I call the police.'

John turned. At the gate stood a very old woman with a shopping trolley nearly as big as herself. She was hunched over so far that her chest was almost horizontal with the pavement. She waved a walking stick at him.

John stepped into the light and held up his hands. 'Sorry if I startled you.'

'What do you want?'

'Here, let me help you with that.' He went to her and brought the trolley up the path for her.

'Thank you. Nice that some people have manners even if they use foul language.'

John's lips twitched. 'Sorry about that. I've had a long day.'

'No excuse for that kind of talk.' She squinted up at him. 'You're Irish, aren't you?'

'Yep.'

'Thought so. Who are you looking for?'

'Katie Todd, blonde woman about—'

'I know her. She lives across the hall from me. I haven't seen her in a while, mind, but I wouldn't be surprised about that. No one stays here long. She's a lovely girl, that one, took my blood pressure for me. Nice as you like. Woman below me keeps leaving her bin bags out in the hall. Stinks the whole place up.'

She jabbed her stick at the window to the right of the door and John was certain he saw the curtain move.

'He pretends he can't speak English, but he can, you know, I hear him.'

'When was the last time you saw Katie?'

'About three weeks ago. She dropped in and asked me to hang on to her mail for her.' She eyed John suspiciously. 'Here! Why you asking all these questions? Who are you?'

'I'm a friend of hers from the nursing home.'

'Oh? I never heard her mention any *friend*.'

'She's not exactly chatty, our Katie.'

'That's true enough,' said the old lady. 'She minds her own business, that's for sure. Not like *some people*!' The last part was directed at the front window.

John edged away. 'Well, I—'

'Can't be too carefull. There was another fella here looking for her, but he weren't no friend, I knew that. I can tell trouble the moment I see it. And he was trouble.'

She had John's attention now. 'This guy, was he short, grey-haired, about fifty with a moustache?'

'Oh, you know him, do you?'

'No, but he was at Katie's work recently and she wasn't too pleased to see him,' John said, mingling lies with the truth.

'No, I shouldn't think she was. He got in here somehow, started knocking on the door of her flat. Well, I know who let him in, of course.' She shot the window another filthy look. 'Don't mean nothing to anyone if an old lady gets robbed.'

'So what happened?'

'Happened?' The corner of her lip curled. 'Nothing. I said Katie wasn't at home and if he didn't get out I was calling the police. I told Katie and, next thing, she's asking me to look after her mail and she's gone.'

'She didn't give you a forwarding address?'

But John had pushed it too far.

'You ask a lot of questions for a *friend*.'

'I'm worried about her, that's all.'

'I thought you said you worked with her?' she said slyly. 'Can't you see her there?'

'She hasn't been at work for a few weeks. That's why I'm worried.'

'Maybe you are, maybe you aren't.'

'Well, if you do see her, will you tell her John called?'

'All right.'

'Thanks.' John winked at her. 'You okay getting that trolley upstairs?'

'I'll be fine. I'm used to it,' she said.

'Bye then.' John walked back across the street and slipped into a littered playground where he waited for the old lady to go inside. Minutes later, a light came on in the left side of the building.

Okay, John thought. That means Katie's room was to the right. He'd give it another hour to get dark and then it would be time for a little B and E. He thought of Sarah and pulled a face. She didn't approve of such behaviour. What she didn't know would never hurt her.

21

It was after eight when Sarah got home. Sumo bounded out of the car and trotted up the path to the front door, pausing only to saturate a bedraggled-looking rosebush. 'Nice.' Sarah said.

A little further down the street a silver Toyota pulled in and parked behind another car. Willie switched off the engine, typed the address into his phone and flipped it shut.

So, this was where she lived. He sat there for a while, thinking. He hated this kind of shit and he'd been a bloody fool to sell a gun to that girl, but the money had been too good to pass up.

He ground his teeth in annoyance. Was it too much to ask that he could do a bit of business, get paid and be done with it? He wasn't doing any harm, just providing a service – nothing more, nothing less. He couldn't risk going back inside. He wasn't tough, not really. Oh, he could boss Martin around, but his twelve-year-old sister could do that. The last time he'd gone inside he'd had a rough time. Guys like him were a snack to some of the more hardened criminals and he didn't have the wit or the resources to keep out of trouble.

His hands tightened around the steering wheel. He wouldn't go back inside. And he needed to make sure no one could point the finger at him.

On the other hand, that was a very big dog.

He started the engine and did a U-turn. Moments later, he drove back down the street.

* * *

The man sitting in his van watched Willie turn out of the road and was curious about this turn of events. He could see the driver of the Toyota was casing the house and it troubled him.

He didn't like the idea of competition. And if the fool in the Toyota thought he could rob him of his pleasure, he was very much mistaken.

He settled back to wait, perturbed. The sister would be heading home soon. Then he would decide.

Unaware of the forces at play, Sarah had taken off her coat and was making tea. She was relieved that her mother had retired for the night. 'I can't believe she's asleep already,' she said.

Jackie was seated at the small pine table, which had been there for as long as either woman could remember. 'Belinda gave her a mild sedative. She said she'd had an unsettled day.'

Sarah didn't like the idea of Belinda drugging their mother.

'Did you get done what you needed to do?' Jackie asked.

'Kind of. You know the case I'm working on, right?'

'The girl in the coma.'

'We've got a name for the guy who might have sold her the gun, and he drinks in the bar I was checking out this evening. But the barman's face when I asked about him – *whoo*! He was lying, Jackie. I mean as clear as day. He's there saying he's never heard of him and I'm thinking it must be something if the barman won't even admit to knowing him. So I'm waiting for Stevie Magher to get back to me with some background.'

Jackie twisted her engagement ring around her finger. 'You're not going to do anything stupid, are you?'

'Jesus! Why do people keep saying that?' Sarah put the kettle on the gas ring and lit it. 'I'm not a bloody idiot, Jackie. I just want to know more about him. That way, if Katie Jones ever comes out of her coma, we'll have two sources of confirmation.'

'Well, be careful. These people you deal with—'

'Jackie, I'll be careful. I'm only asking a few questions.'

* * *

Jackie eyed Sumo nervously. The dog was watching her, she was sure. He was terrifying. Why did her little sister always surround herself with freaks and oddballs? Why was it so hard to get through to her? It was a pattern now: Sarah was like a moth to a flame, never happy unless she was in danger of getting burned.

Even this thing with their mother struck Jackie as typical Sarah. Rather than face up to their mother's illness, she was refusing to compromise. It was exhausting, upsetting. It was … well, it was Sarah.

'I read about that girl, the one in the coma. She murdered that poor man in cold blood.'

'I know.'

'You're okay with working for a murderer?'

'I'm working for her brother and he's an architect. Pass *that* on to Helen, would you? I'm sure she'll feel better for knowing,' Sarah said, somewhat sarcastically. She poured boiling water into the teapot and set the whole lot in front of her sister. 'I assume you're asking all these question under orders?'

'I'm *asking* because I'm worried. Helen's got enough on her plate at the moment.'

'Oh, sure. Must be exhausting bossing people about the phone company all day, then returning to her pristine mansion.' Sarah rolled her eyes. 'Oh, and you can tell her that that Gloria Bradshaw she hooked me up with was a total washout. She's fobbed the flat off on a newbie.'

'Gloria did that?' Jackie was flummoxed. 'I can't imagine her doing any such thing. She and Helen go way back – she was Helen's bridesmaid.'

'Well, she has.'

'I'll check into it. Or, better, why don't you ring Helen?'

'I don't think so.'

'Oh!' Jackie ran her hands through her hair. 'You and her – two peas in a pod. Just apologise, Sarah, and end this stupid row.'

Sarah jabbed her chest with her thumb. 'Me?'

'Yes, you! Why not? You called her a bitch.'

'She was acting like one.'

'So were you, darling.'

'You always take her side.'

'There is no *side*, Sarah,' Jackie said, keeping her voice calm as Sarah's rose. 'You were angry, she was angry.'

'She's always trying to tell me how to live my life.'

'She just wants you to be happy.'

'I am happy.'

'She wants you to be safe.'

'I am safe.'

'Safe people don't go around asking about gun dealers. Safe people don't get shot. Safe people don't investigate murders—'

'The gardaí do,' Sarah said. She knew it was a childish retort, but if her sisters treated her like a kid, what else could they expect?

'You're not in the gardaí. And then there's John—'

'Hah! I knew it would come back to John bloody Quigley.'

'Darling, I know how you feel about him—'

'Do you indeed?' Sarah's nostrils flared. 'So, tell me, how do I feel about him?'

'You don't fool me, Sarah. You think I can't see what's going on?'

'*On?*'

'You and him.'

'I don't have a clue what you're talking about.'

'You could have anyone you want, but you don't want anyone. That's why you're single, and that's why you're sitting here minding this' – she jerked her head towards Sumo – 'this dog.'

'He's my partner.'

'He didn't have to be.'

'It was my choice.'

'Yes,' Jackie said, 'and I wonder why.'

'You've got it all wrong. We're just friends.'

'Fine. Pretend.' Jackie put out her hands, palm up. 'But Helen's not the bad guy you think she is. She's worried about you, that's all. She doesn't want to see you get hurt again.'

'I seem to have said this a lot recently, but let me try it once more. I can look after myself. I'm a grown woman.'

'All right, all right.' Jackie poured some tea into her cup and added milk. Sarah did the same. The clock ticked. Sumo sighed, lay on his side and closed his eyes. 'Belinda says there was a little altercation this morning.'

'Mm?'

'This morning, with Mum.'

Sarah got up and put the milk into the fridge. 'It was nothing.'

'What happened?'

'Really, Jackie, it was nothing.'

'Maybe Dr Heffernan could—'

'Could what?' Sarah whirled round. 'Maybe he could do what? Maybe he could miraculously find a cure for the fog that's taking over our mother's mind? Maybe he could ... I don't know, say "Alakazam", and turn back time? Maybe he could inject her with something and make her Mum again?'

Jackie gazed steadily at her. 'I thought perhaps he could check Mum's medication. These snaps are becoming more frequent.'

'It was nothing, Jackie. She got angry. She doesn't like Belinda being here. She used to get angry in the old days too.'

'True. It runs in the family.' Jackie raised an eyebrow.

Suddenly, Sarah felt ashamed of herself. Jackie, her sister, her greatest ally, was here in the kitchen because Sarah had asked her for a favour, darling, lovely Jackie, Jackie with the soft eyes and kind smile, Jackie who was most like their mother, and Sarah was giving her a hard time.

She rushed across the kitchen and wrapped her arms round her sister's neck, burying her nose in her hair, which smelled of paint and turpentine. 'I'm sorry, Jackie, I really am.'

'It's all right,' Jackie said, startled by the display of affection. 'It's all right, I know you're doing your best.'

Sarah hugged her harder.

'But, darling,' Jackie pulled away from her, 'see how easy it is to say sorry? Why don't you try it with Helen?'

'Oh, Jackie,' Sarah said and kissed her sister's cheek. 'For you I will.'

22

John slid down the back wall as quietly as possible, but it was higher than he'd thought and he landed awkwardly, pitching forward onto his hands and knees into a bog of wet cardboard, leaf mulch and Christ knew what else. It reeked.

'Shit.' He climbed over the mess and wiped his hands on the wall. He was filthy.

He waited to see if a security light would come on at the back of the house, but nothing stirred and no one glanced out. He moved along the wall and saw a dodgy-looking fire escape running up the side of the building with a slender branch to the second floor. He could get to Katie's window but he'd have to go past the old lady's apartment.

He wiped his hands again, on the legs of his jeans this time, and crept to the bottom rung of the ladder. He gave it a gentle tug.

The metal screeched and he was sprinkled with rust particles. He dived into the shadows and behind a bin, scattering a nest of rats that had been watching his progress ever since he had dropped into the yard.

'Yeeeee,' he squealed. He knocked over the bin and tried in vain to catch it, but the clatter of metal on concrete was deafening. He watched as a rat skittered across his shoe.

A light went on upstairs.

Great! The old bat had heard him – although considering the amount of noise he had made, he'd be surprised if the people in the next county hadn't. Above him, a window opened and, seconds later, a bucket of freezing water was dumped over him.

'Get out of it, you cats, go on. *Scat*!'

John bit on his lip to stop himself from screaming. He was saturated. This had been one masterful idea.

The window slammed down and all was darkness again.

After a moment or two, he eased himself out of his hiding place. In the space of a few minutes, he had gone from normal to filthy and was now soaking wet.

He wiped his face and looked up. There was no other way to get to Katie's window other than by the fire escape, and old Bat Ears would hear him the moment he set foot on the ladder.

He made his way to the opposite side of the yard and tested the drainpipe. He gave it a bit of a tug. It was plastic, but seemed sturdy enough. He hooked his hands behind it and planted one foot on the wall, hoisting himself up, and heard a rip. Then he felt a stabbing pain in his upper thigh.

'Ow!' He dropped back to the ground. He had torn his favourite pair of jeans and a warm sticky liquid was flowing down his leg.

'Fuck!' he hissed and hobbled backwards. He felt along the wall until his fingers found a rusty bracket. Now he'd have to get an anti-tetanus jab.

'Shit!'

He limped back to the drainpipe and gazed up again. 'Okay.' He spat on his hands and rubbed them together. 'Second time's a charm.'

Ten minutes later, a dishevelled, wet and bloody John Quigley stood in the doorway of the Victorian semi.

'So, you see, I'm not a friend of hers after all and I really need to come in and see the inside of her flat,' he was saying to the tiny woman who was staring between him and the photo of Katie Jones in bemusement.

'I keep telling you I don't have a key.'

'I don't need one.'

145

'Was that you making all that racket out there?' An incredulous yet delightfully malicious gleam lit her beady eyes. John was too tired and sore to bother lying. His leg was beginning to throb. 'What were you trying to do? Break in?' He nodded.

'I should call the police, have you arrested.'

'You could, but it won't make any difference to her,' John said miserably. 'For what it's worth, I wouldn't blame you if you said no.'

She looked down at the photo of Katie and her mouth drew into a thin line. 'All right. She was a good girl, and if you think you can help her, you'd best come inside. How are you going to get in? You can't go breaking the door down.'

'I won't break anything, I promise.'

'Why didn't you just say all this in the first place? What a carry-on.' She opened the door and let him in.

'Thanks very much,' John said, mortified. He shuffled past her into the hall.

She wrinkled her nose at the smell emanating from his clothes. 'It's true what they say about you Irish, plenty of blather but not a brain between those two ears.'

In fairness, he was in no position to contradict her. John found he could do nothing but nod and pray to God he hadn't contracted some terrible disease from flailing about in the filth outside.

'Up the stairs, towards the back of the house,' the old lady said.

'Thanks very much.' John made his way slowly up the stairs. 'Do you think you could get me something for my leg – some disinfectant or something?'

'You think I'm going to let you snoop around alone? Oh, no – no matter who you say you are.' She climbed the stairs behind him, muttering under her breath, 'Knew he weren't working in no nursing home. Folk these days …'

John tried his level best to ignore her, and when he reached the door something else caught his attention. He knelt down painfully and looked closely at the lock. There were faint scratches in the wood. Someone else had jimmied it.

'Can you smell it?' the old lady asked.

'Smell what?'

'It's that lot downstairs, leaving their bags of rubbish in the hall. Place reeks and I sprayed this landing earlier on.'

'It's not that bad.' The lock was easy to pick. He got out his wallet and found his tools.

The old lady hovered behind him. 'If you get caught, I'll say I knew nothing about it. I'll tell them you broke in.'

As he worked, John was wondering which of the two men had tried to gain entry – the older man or the scary, aggressive younger one with the yellow eyes.

The lock sprang open.

John stood up and gripped the door handle.

'And don't think you can take anything,' the old lady said, fiercely. 'Look for her father's address and be done with it. Don't try anything funny. I'll be keeping a close eye on you.'

John opened the door and stepped inside. The air in the room was stale and he could smell rotting food. He hit the light switch inside the door.

The room had been destroyed. Furniture had been overturned, glass was broken, pictures hung askew.

'Oh, my!'

He turned. The old woman was right behind him, but now she wasn't so cantankerous. She looked stunned as her eyes took in the damage. She pressed her hand to her mouth. 'What *happened* here?'

'Did you hear anything? A fight, shouting?'

'Nothing at all.'

John peeped into the kitchenette. The smell was coming from here – the bin had been overturned and when he opened the fridge the stench was overpowering. Katie had obviously left in a hurry.

He came back into the living room, stepped over the coffee table, his feet crunching on pieces of glass, and picked up a photo in a broken frame. In it, Katie was holding a diploma flanked by two beaming people, whom he assumed to be Frank Todd and his wife.

He removed the photo, slipped it into his pocket and went towards a door at the back of the room. He opened the door and turned on the light. This room was as bad as the other. The wardrobes had been emptied, clothes strewn everywhere, and the

147

bedside locker stood open, its contents spilled across the floor.

'This doesn't look like a fight,' John said over his shoulder. 'It looks like someone was searching for something and got mad when he didn't find it.'

This time there was no argument or snide comment. He heard her hurry across the hall and slam the door. Who could blame her? She was probably on the phone to the police right this second.

He went back into the sitting room and lifted a black address book from the floor. He ran his hand down the alphabetical stubs at one side and found 'Dad'. He memorised the address and put back the book.

He walked across the floor and out of the door, pulling it closed behind him. Time to go.

Before he'd even put a foot on the stairs, the old lady opened her door. She had a swanky-looking cordless phone in her hand. 'That's right, Officer, he's here now.'

John winced and waved at her frantically, but to no avail. 'I'll put him on.' She passed the phone to him. 'They want to talk to you.'

John sighed, pressed the phone to his chest and then cleared his throat. 'Hello? … Yes, that's Quigley with a Q.'

23

Sarah tried John's number again, but it went straight to voicemail. She hung up and paced the sitting room. The carriage clock on the mantelpiece told her it was twenty to eleven. Surely, he'd be back at the hotel by now. Wouldn't he? Maybe he'd gone out for a drink.

She turned off the lights and went upstairs to bed, Sumo trailing in her wake.

But she couldn't sleep and, as the minutes clicked by, her anxiety grew. She tried his number again. This time it rang and a tired-sounding John answered, "Lo?'

'There you are!' Sarah sat up in bed and switched on the lamp. 'I've been trying to contact you all evening. Is everything okay?'

'Were you worried about me?'

'Of course I was.'

'Sorry. I was in a police station.'

'Are you all right?'

She heard him yawn and the click of his lighter. 'I've been better,' he said slowly.

'What happened?'

She listened incredulously as he told her about the apartment and how the police had hauled him to the station to make a statement. He neglected to mention about his attempts to gain entry to the building.

'This isn't looking good for Katie,' she answered.

'Nope. Everywhere she goes, trouble keeps popping up.'

'Did you call Sam?'

'I didn't need to. The cops rang him to confirm I was working for him.'

'Any idea what's going on?'

'Not yet, but the head nurse where she worked said she'd quit her job and that *two* men had been asking about her. She said Katie was scared, which explains why she left her apartment in such a hurry.'

'Scared of what, though?'

'I don't know.'

'So, what now?'

'I located the father's address. I'm going to see him tomorrow, try to find out how the hell he ended up with her.'

'Be careful. For all you know he's the one who kidnapped her.'

'I will. Look, Sarah, I've got to get some sleep. I'll call you tomorrow when I have something new.'

Sarah put the phone down on the bedside locker. Sumo, who had been sleeping on the floor by her bed, raised his head. 'That was your boss. He's fine.'

Sumo lay down. Sarah switched off her lamp and, within minutes, was asleep.

Less than an hour later, the phone woke her.

Groggily, she reached for it. 'John?'

A male voice said, 'Sarah?'

It was familiar but she couldn't place it. 'Yes?'

'Sarah, it's Paul.'

'Hello.' Helen's husband, the great surgeon.

'Sarah, I'm sorry to ring you so late, but I'm afraid there's been an accident.'

Sarah's heart lurched. 'What's happened to Helen?'

'It's not Helen. It's Jackie. Sarah, she was in a car crash and she's in the Mater Hospital.'

'What?'

'It happened earlier this evening, the fire brigade think about twenty past nine.'

Jackie had been on her way home then. 'Oh, Jesus, is she hurt? Please tell me she's okay.'

'I don't know the full extent, but she was talking at the scene, so at least she was conscious.'

'Oh my God.'

'Helen's already on her way there. What do—'

'Paul, call her and tell her we're on our way.' Sarah hung up and leaped out of bed. She dressed quickly and hurried into her mother's room. 'Mum, wake up.'

'What is it?' Her mother sounded confused.

'Jackie's been in an accident.'

'An accident?'

'Yes. Come on, we've got to go. Here, I'll help you.'

'Stop pulling me, Helen. You're hurting my arm.'

'*I'm Sarah!*' she screamed, frightening herself and her mother. 'I'm sorry, Mum, I'm so sorry.' She pushed her hair back and tried not to cry. 'But will you just work with me here? Come on.'

Her mother climbed out of bed and stood silently, head bowed, while Sarah dressed her quickly. Together they hurried downstairs and out into the freezing night, leaving an anxious Sumo standing guard in the hallway.

24

Sarah found Helen in the waiting room, flicking through a tattered magazine, her dark hair shiny and sleek under the harsh overhead lights. There were only three other people, a mother with a wheezy-looking toddler and a girl with a spider tattoo on her neck. She was chewing gum and her eyes were fixed on Helen's Hermès bag, which lay open on the floor beside Helen's chair.

'Helen.' Sarah rushed to her sister. 'What happened?' She felt a jolt of surprise to see her sister so shaken. She was pale and wore no make-up, and looked as if she'd been crying.

'Oh, Sarah.' She stood up and hugged her younger sister. Sarah hugged her back. As upset as she was, she was shocked to feel how thin Helen was.

'Mum?' Helen had noticed her suddenly behind Sarah.

'Helen.' Deirdre looked awkward.

'You brought Mum with you?' Helen said in a low, angry voice.

'What was I supposed to do? I didn't want her to wake up and be alone.'

'Of course.' Helen pressed her index fingers to her temples. 'I'm sorry.'

'Jackie, is she—'

'She's been moved out of A and E. She has a broken arm, cuts and bruises, and three broken ribs. They think that could have been from the airbag. They want to keep her in tonight for observation – she lost consciousness for a while on the way in and was a bit confused after.'

Sarah swept her hair over her shoulder. 'Do they know how it happened?'

'She was driving up from Harold's Cross and somewhere between the church and the little park her car went off the road and ploughed into a shop.'

'It went across the road?'

Helen nodded. 'Luckily there was nothing coming the other way, or …' She took a deep breath and grabbed Sarah's arm. 'They think she'd been drinking. We're waiting on the results of her blood test.'

'Oh, no! Surely not.'

Helen slumped back into her chair. 'I don't understand what happened. Jackie likes a drink, I know, but she wouldn't drink and drive – she knows better than that. What the hell was she thinking?'

'It's my fault.'

'What?'

'It was my fault.' Sarah said miserably. She sank onto the plastic chair beside her sister. 'She was watching Mum for me earlier.'

'But it wasn't her night.'

'I know, but I had this lead to follow up on and I asked—'

'*God damn it, Sarah*!'

The girl with the gum stopped chewing and the toddler gave a startled yelp.

'I'm sorry, Helen.'

'Sorry?' Helen's face was dark with fury. 'You could have called me, not Jackie! What was so important that it couldn't wait until tomorrow? I suppose it was—'

'Stop now.' Deirdre was growing agitated. 'Please.'

'—work. Why can't you conduct your bloody job on your own time? Why can't you get a normal bloody job?'

'Helen, I'm sorry.' Sarah tried to put her hand on her sister's arm, but Helen pulled away and leaped to her feet. Deirdre began to rock back and forth.

'If anything happens to her, Sarah, I swear to God we're finished. I've had as much as I can take and I can't do it any more.'

'I didn't mean for this to happen,' Sarah said, shocked by Helen's anger.

'And I'm sick of hearing that. It's always about you. Every conversation, every whim, we *bend* to your rules, no matter what, no matter who's right. What Sarah wants, Sarah goddamn well gets.'

'Don't say that!' Sarah cried, her own temper rising now. She dashed away her tears. 'It was an accident, Helen. An *accident*.'

'You're a fucking accident!' Helen yelled. 'A walking bloody disaster!'

'Shut up!'

'No, you shut up!'

'Excuse me, ladies,' a sharp voice said.

Helen and Sarah swung around.

A nurse stood behind them, lips pursed. 'Are you the family of Jacqueline Kenny?'

'Yes,' they said in unison and Deirdre nodded, looking confused and old.

'She's awake. She's asking for ...' she consulted a piece of paper in front of her, 'Sarah?'

'That's me.'

'I'm coming too,' Helen said angrily.

'I'm afraid only one is allowed in at a time. She's very groggy.'

'But I've been waiting for ages,' Helen said.

'She *asked* for Sarah.'

Sarah walked past Helen to the nurse. 'I'll tell her you're here, and you can go in after me. Mum, I'll be back in a few minutes, okay?'

Deirdre nodded. She seemed so small and frail under the stark lights of the waiting room that Sarah was reluctant to leave her. 'Helen, please—'

'Mum, sit down here,' Helen said, her voice tight.

Sarah waited to see Deirdre seated, then walked with the nurse down a yellow corridor. 'How is she? Is she in any pain?'

'Not at the moment. We've given her an analgesic.' The nurse glanced at Sarah. 'She'll probably sleep through the night, but she seemed anxious to speak to you.'

They walked the rest of the way in silence. Sarah couldn't get Helen's words out of her head. Was it her fault? Jackie wouldn't have been out at all if not for her ... They stopped at a door halfway down the corridor.

'She's on the trolley behind that curtain on the left. She's a bit banged up.'

Sarah nodded.

'And try not to agitate her.'

Sarah nodded again.

'Five minutes tops. We clear?'

'Thank you.' Sarah tiptoed over to the curtain and pulled it back a bit. 'Oh, Jackie.'

Jackie was pale and bloody. Her right arm was bound in a temporary cast and she had a drip in her left hand. Her forehead was cut to ribbons and her left eyebrow had gone. The skin under her eye was peppered with tiny cuts.

Sarah sat down in the plastic chair and took her sister's free hand. Her skin was cold, but she squeezed Sarah's hand and her eyes fluttered open. Her pupils were tiny pinpricks.

'Sarah.' Her voice was faint, barely above a whisper.

'Oh, Jackie.'

'Sarah ... listen, I told them ...' Jackie licked her chapped lips. There was dried blood on her chin. She closed her eyes again. 'A van, it hit the car.'

'Don't try to talk,' Sarah said. 'It's all right. Get some rest. Oh, Jackie, I'm so sorry.'

But Jackie opened her eyes again. She tightened her fingers round Sarah's as hard as she could. 'Listen to me. There was a van ... tell them ...'

'Jackie, you've had a knock, you're in—'

'There was a man, he came to the side of the car ... He hit me, he hit the car.' Jackie swallowed. She closed her eyes and, in seconds, her breathing was shallow and rapid as she slipped into a deep, drug-induced sleep.

Sarah sat and stared at her sister's sleeping face. What had she been talking about? What van? What man? It had to be the concussion talking.

Didn't it?

25

She was winded but still walking hard. A sleety rain was beating against her face, making her cheeks sting and her lips numb. She was freezing cold, her threadbare coat no match for the weather.

She was late, only ten minutes now, but she was sure she wasn't going to make it back before him.

Sid had held her up: it wasn't her fault this time. She tried not to think about it. It was only a few minutes. Maybe he'd understand, maybe – if she was really lucky – he wouldn't notice.

She tried to run again but the stitch was agony. Maybe she should get Sid to call him, explain – no, that was stupid. He wouldn't like it and maybe Sid would think she was more trouble than she was worth. Vic wouldn't be bothered if she lost her job, but the last thing she wanted was to rock the boat. She needed that job … it was all she had left to keep her sane.

She forced herself to run.

She made it to the house and her heart sank when she saw the light on in their flat.

He was home before her. She could see his massive bulk behind the curtain.

He was waiting for her.

Her feet climbed the stone steps to the door. Her teeth were chattering, but not from the cold. She fumbled her key, guiding it *slowly into the lock, and opened the door. She didn't call out, and from the shadows his face appeared. 'You're late,' he said, his voice flat and empty.*

Sarah forced herself to take another step. 'Sid called a meeting … There was nothing I could do.'

'Really?' Now he moved fast, his face morphing into something terrible.

'No!'

Sarah opened her eyes. She blinked against the sunlight streaming through the curtains and waited for the dread to subside, the fear to dissipate.

She turned her head to her alarm clock. Twenty to eight. She was exhausted. She had barely slept a wink.

Jackie.

She threw off the duvet, stepped over Sumo and padded to the bathroom for a quick shower.

Afterwards she went downstairs and put on the kettle. The house was cold and she shivered as she let Sumo out for a wee. She sipped her coffee.

A van, Jackie had said.

She pulled the phone book out of the press and traced her finger down a page. She found the number for the pound and picked up the phone. 'Hi there, I'm wondering if you can help me. My name is Sarah Kenny. My sister's car was brought in last night after a crash … that's right, a Volvo. Would you mind if I came down this morning to have a look at it? … Great, perfect, see you then.'

She hung up and finished her coffee just as Belinda arrived.

She filled her in on what had happened during the night and that her mother would probably stay late in bed.

'What about you?' Belinda asked. 'You look exhausted. Why don't you go back to bed for a while?'

Sarah put on her coat and slipped Sumo's collar round his neck. 'I'm fine, I've got something to check out. Come on, Sumo.'

She went out and closed the door.

* * *

Belinda watched her climb into the car. She wasn't a hard woman, despite what people thought of her. She was pragmatic and efficient – she had to be to do her job properly. Also, she was no fool and she knew people better than they knew themselves. And right at that second she knew that Sarah Kenny was hanging on by a thread.

'Where's Sarah?'

She turned round. 'Good morning, Mrs Kenny. She's left for work already.'

'Did she? Is it early?'

'Yes. Are you tired? I heard about Jackie's accident. I'm very sorry.'

'Yes. Helen was very upset.' Deirdre frowned. 'Where's Sarah?'

Belinda smiled. 'Why don't we make some toast and tea?'

Willie watched Sarah leave her house and drive away. He waited five minutes more, then got out of the car. He walked down the street to her house and tapped on the front door.

After a moment, a middle-aged woman opened it, a dishcloth in her hand.

'Can I help you?'

'Hi there, my name's Adam Irvine. I'm here about the Mini. Sorry I'm early, but I've got to get to work.'

'The what?' The woman's face crinkled up in bewilderment.

'The Mini? It was advertised in *Buy and Sell*. I spoke to someone about it this morning?'

'I think you have the wrong address. There is no Mini for sale here.'

'Who is it, Belinda?'

Belinda glanced behind her. 'It's all right, Mrs Kenny. It's a mistake.'

'Who *is* it, I asked?'

An older woman pushed her aside and opened the door fully. Willie noted her bare feet and the puzzled, vacant look in her dark eyes as she gazed at him.

'Yes?' she said.

'Good morning, I was just telling your daughter here I'm looking—'

'Huh, *she's not* my daughter. My daughter's not here. She left, she's gone to … where's she gone to?' She peered past him onto the street. 'Did she say?'

'Mrs Kenny, come in – you'll catch your death.' Belinda tried to remove her hand from the door and guide her back into the hall. 'Come on, now.'

'Let go of me, you! I don't want you pulling me about.'

Belinda released her. She turned to Willie, exasperated. 'You'll have to excuse us, but you have the wrong house.'

Willie bobbed his head. 'I'm so sorry, I didn't—'

'What does he want?'

'He's looking for a car.'

'A *car*? What car?'

'Goodbye.' She closed the door in his face.

Willie stepped back. There was no alarm that he could see, and the carpet in the hall had been dated. The sash windows were rotted in places, the garden overgrown and offering plenty of shelter. He'd bet a kidney it was just as bad out the back.

He paused at the gate, making a production of looking lost in case anyone was watching. The middle-aged woman had arrived and the young one had left … obviously, she was a nurse or housekeeper, which meant she went home in the evening.

Willie walked up the road to his car. A plan was forming in his mind, and it helped that the old woman was dotty – she'd be careless, forget to turn things off; she'd be a danger to herself and others, everyone knew that.

But the dog was a problem.

Willie smiled. He had ways of dealing with problem dogs.

Sarah squatted and rubbed her hands across the back bumper of Jackie's red Volvo. The paint was scarred in and the metal dented. She scraped off some flakes of black paint and stared at them.

She stood up slowly and walked around the car, taking in the damage. The windscreen had shattered, the front fender and wheel arch were crushed, the bumper was gone and the bonnet stoved in. If she hadn't been in something as solid as a Volvo, she might have been killed.

Jackie hadn't been concussed. Someone had hit the back of her car. Someone had run her off the road.

26

John woke up. He opened his eyes and rolled over. Then the pain hit.

'Ow! Son of a ' He eased himself upright and slid down the blankets gently. His leg was a mess. The cut was oozing pus and looked infected.

He swore some more and climbed gingerly out of bed. He took a half-hearted shower and got dressed, relieved he had packed a change of clothing.

He checked out of the hotel and limped down the street to a chemist, where he bought some Solpadeine. He gobbled two, then drank a bottle of water to wash them down while he waited for the Tube. He felt like shit and, from the way folk seemed to be giving him the surreptitious eye, he looked like it.

He caught the Tube to Kilburn and made his way painfully to street level. Todd lived at Dunster Gardens, so that was where John hoped to catch him.

It took him forty minutes and five passers-by before he found what he was looking for, a smart semi in a quiet cul-de-sac. He rang the bell and waited, wondering how long it would take the painkillers to kick in. If anything, his leg was throbbing more now than it had been earlier.

'He's not there, mate.'

John looked up. A grinning ginger monkey peered down from the upstairs window of the neighbouring house. No, not quite a monkey, but surely the missing link scientists had been hoping to locate and study.

The monkey had a ginger beard, ginger eyebrows and ears that stuck out so far they looked like the open doors on a car.

'Any idea where I can find him?'

'You the police?'

'Nope.'

'You a friend of his?'

'Nope.' John shook his head. 'I'm a private detective.' He had learned his lesson about lying over the last day or two.

'Oh, yeah? Like Mike Hammer?'

'The TV decetive? Sure. I left my fedora back in the office.'

'No need to get smart.' The monkey looked hurt.

'Sorry, mate, I'm having a rough morning. Look, do you have any idea where he might be? I'm working for his daughter, Katie.'

'Yeah? Ain't seen her in a while. She used to come here all the time. How's she doin'?'

'She's great.' Maybe the odd lie here and there wouldn't hurt.

The monkey mulled this over. 'Well, I ain't seen him in a while neither.'

'Does he work somewhere?'

'Irish Frank? Work? You're having a laugh, mate. He don't work no more, he's *retired*. Try down the social club. You ask me, that's where you'll find him.'

'The social club?'

'Big Irish one over on Quex Road, near the church.'

John looked at his watch. It was barely ten. 'At this hour?'

'At any hour, mate.'

'Okay, cheers.'

'Mention it.' The monkey grinned and slammed his window. John limped back the way he had come.

He wandered down Kilburn High Road and on to Quex Road. He found the church easily enough and, as luck would have it, the social club was next door.

A large truck was unloading at the kerb. A woman in high heels and a blonde wig was barking orders at two gormless-looking youths lugging kegs and crates of beer inside. 'Come on, put your back into it, Smithy. What are you afraid of? Breaking a nail? I haven't got all day and that bar won't stock itself, you know.'

John cleared his throat. She whipped round and gave him the once-over – so thorough he might have been hanging naked on a hook in a butcher's window.

She must have been sixty, but her face was tighter than a camel's arse in a snowstorm. Although it was only ten-thirty, she wore full make-up and her clothes wouldn't have been out of place on a Soho street corner. A pair of spectacles hung round her neck on a gold chain.

'You're late. Think I run a sloppy ship, do you? Well, I don't. You can hop it – go on, see if anyone else'll hire you after this. They won't, you know, not after I'm done. I told Fr Durran, no messin' about.'

'I think you're mixing me up with somebody else.'

She raised a crookedly drawn-on eyebrow. 'You're not from the centre, then?'

'No, I'm from Dublin.'

'Cheeky, I know that from the accent, don't I? I thought Fr Durran had sent you here for work.'

'Nope. My name's John Quigley and I'm a private detective.'

'Maura Spencer.'

They shook hands.

'Smithy, get on with it. I can feel ya slowin' down,' she yelled over her shoulder. 'Come on inside, John. It's right brass-monkey weather out here today. Let's put the kettle on. You fancy a cuppa?'

'Love one.' John followed her inside.

'What's the matter with your leg?'

John was surprised. 'You don't miss much, do you?'

'Been here thirty-five years – you don't run a place like this missing much.'

She led him past some stacked chairs into a small lounge. It was an old-fashioned place, shabby but comfortable, with low tables, chunky ashtrays and thick red and green carpets. The walls were decorated with posters of Irish pub doors, a pope and some GAA flags. A glass cabinet took up most of one wall. It held cups, medals and yellowing photos of sporting heroes. There were dusty bundles of plastic flowers everywhere.

'Sit down, take the load off.'

John pulled out a stool and sank onto it with a sigh of relief.

'So, what happened?' She disappeared from view and John heard the rattle of cups and saucers.

'I caught it on a nail.'

'Nasty. You get a shot?'

'Not yet.'

'Get the shot or you'll end up with lockjaw, septicaemia or something worse.'

'Yes, ma'am.'

She reappeared a few minutes later with a tray and set it down on the bar in front of John. 'Help yourself.'

John poured tea for them both and added his sugar and milk to his mug. 'Cheers.'

'Bottoms up.' She took a gulp and eyed him over the rim.

John sipped his tea and spluttered. It was very hot, and laced with whiskey. 'Whoa.'

'It's good for what ails you,' she said matter-of-factly, but with a twinkle in her eye. 'Now, Mr Private Eye, who or what brings you here?'

'I'm looking for a man called Frank Todd. I was told I'd probably find him here.'

'Irish Frank?' She sniffed loudly. 'Who told you that, then?'

'His next-door neighbour said he might be around.'

'Did he now?'

'He did.'

Smithy went past with a box of Walkers crisps. Although it couldn't have been heavy, he walked bent double with an exaggerated shuffle.

Maura rolled her eyes. 'Well, I can't help you there. He's barred.'

'Barred? For what?'

'Fighting.'

John grinned. 'I thought he was an old lad. Retired.'

'He is, daft bugger, sixty years old. But age didn't stop him making a right pig's ear of this place a few weeks back, let me tell you. Caused blue bloody murder he did. I had no choice, did I?'

She was trying to sound cross, John noticed, but he could see she was amused by what she was telling him. And a little proud.

'Is he a good friend of yours?'

'No, he's just a fella that drinks here from time to time. You ask a lot of questions, don't you?'

'That's my job.' He drank some tea. 'You've no way of knowing where I might find him?'

'Sorry, darlin', I don't have a clue.'

John could see she was lying. 'Do you mind telling me what happened?'

'When?'

'The fight.'

'It was so out of character, really. I don't know what the hell it was about. It was Friday evening and we had a dance here out the back, nothing wild, just a typical Friday-night crowd. Frank came in about seven or eight, but right away I knew he wasn't … right. He'd had a skinful, mind you, but Frank's no lightweight. He can hold his drink.' She had another swig of tea. 'He was sat at that bar there,' she nodded to the right of John, 'and he was drinking Jameson whiskey, that much I know. Then this other fella came in and sat beside him. Next thing I know, Frank's got this fella by the throat and they're knocking lumps out of each other.'

'Did you recognise the other man?'

'Never seen him before.'

'Can you describe him for me?'

'Tall, in his forties, I'd say, with very short grey hair, like the young lads wear. Oh, and he had a moustache.'

The moustached man again.

'Poor Frank, I don't know what got into him. But I can't have brawling in here – I could lose me licence.'

'How long have you known him?'

'Many years. Before he were married.'

'Did you know his wife as well?'

'Sadie? Well, she was a Brighton lass. Lovely gal, she was. She died a few years back. So sudden it was, too. She had a heart attack, poor thing, and she as fit as a fiddle her whole life. Didn't smoke, hardly drank … Frank's been a bit lost without her.'

'Katie and her brother are a great comfort to him, I'm sure.'

She gave John a funny look. 'Well, yes.'

'Can I ask you a question?'

'Ha! I thought that's what you was doing anyway.'

'Do you know if Katie and his son are Frank's natural kids?'

Maura put her cup down. 'Now, you hold on for a moment. What's all this about? How would I know if they was adopted? Come on, I'm blathering and I don't even know why. You're a cute one – you haven't even told me why you're looking for old Frank and here I am giving you his life story.'

John opened his bag. He passed Katie's photo across the table to her. She put on her glasses and peered at it. 'Oh, my Lord.'

'That's Frank's daughter, right?'

'Well, of course it is. That's Katie.'

'Okay, but it isn't.'

She looked at John as though he was nuts. 'What d'you mean "it isn't"? It *is*. I've known this girl all her life. It's Katie. What happened to her?'

'She shot herself.'

'She never!'

'She did.'

'That poor kid.' She blessed herself and laid the photo on the bar. 'She's not been quite right since her mum passed, but I never thought she'd try something like that.'

'Maura,' John sat forward, 'that girl, the girl you know as Katie Todd, well, her name is actually Katie Jones. She was kidnapped nearly twenty-six years ago in Ireland.'

Maura pulled a face. 'Go on – get away with you!'

John held her eye. 'I'm telling you the truth. And now her biological family wants to know what happened to their little girl.'

'I don't believe you. Sadie and Frank? Kidnappers? You must be barking.'

'I didn't say they carried out the kidnapping, but she'– he pointed to the photo – 'started out in one family and ended up in another.'

'If that's true, Sadie and Frank wouldn't have known. They wouldn't have had any idea.'

'Maybe not.'

'No "maybe" about it. They're good people, good Catholics, both of 'em. They wouldn't be involved in nothing dodgy. Sadie loved kids – she'd never have deprived anyone of a child.'

'And yet they raised Katie Jones as their own, and what about their son? How do we know he doesn't have blood-family, wondering what happened to their little boy?'

'You're wrong,' she said, her hand pressed to her heart. 'You have them kids mixed up.'

'You said yourself he was acting out of character in here. I think the moustached man had something to do with Katie and why she put a gun to the side of her head and pulled the trigger.'

He was sorry as soon as he'd said it. She didn't deserve his fury. 'That was harsh,' he went on, 'but I want to talk to Frank Todd and I think you can tell me where to find him.' He jabbed his thumb at the photo. 'That girl, I don't know what she went through, but I've met her mother – her real mother – and let me tell you something, *that* poor woman deserves some answers.'

He laid his hand on hers and felt it trembling. 'Please, I'm not trying to upset you, but I want you to help me find Frank. It's important.'

'I'm sorry.' She looked away for a long time, then at the photo again. 'I don't know where he is.'

John didn't push it. He knew she wouldn't tell him any more. He'd find another way. 'All right, then.' He slipped the photo into his pocket.

'I'm sorry I can't help you.'

'You helped me plenty.'

She glanced at him, her eyes fretful. 'How's that then?'

John felt a stab of guilt as he lifted his cup. He hadn't meant to upset her. 'This tea.'

'I told you it was good for what ails you.' She smiled weakly.

'Indeed you did. Well, I'd better get going. Thanks again.'

He slipped off the stool and made his way outside. He waited until Smithy appeared, then collared him at the back of the van. 'Irish Frank – where can I find him?'

Smithy scratched his scrawny neck. 'What's it worth?'

John produced a tenner.

Smithy smirked. 'Somefin's comin' to me …'

John added another tenner. Smithy pocketed the money quick-smart. 'There's a pub down on the High Road called the Queen's Arms. It's next to a Ladbrokes. He's often there of an afternoon.'

'I'll need a description too.'

'Want me to drive you down and introduce you while I'm at it?'

'Want me to stick my boot up your arse?'

Minutes later, John was walking down Quex Road with a description, the whiskey and tea warming him against the cold.

27

John stretched and felt the muscles in his back creak. He was sitting at a table in the Queen's Arms, pretending to be engrossed in the *Independent*. In fact, he had read it from cover to cover, and still there was no sign of his quarry. He ordered scampi and chips and a second pint. The barman told him his food would be along shortly.

John settled back and sipped his pint.

If Todd didn't show, he might have to order a third.

The barman had tried to engage him in conversation when he had initially arrived – asking him, for some reason, if he was from Dublin 10, but, eventually, had given up. Now he sat behind his counter, complaining to a couple of regulars about how the cost of heating the pub was breaking his heart.

Finally, just as John thought he might go mad with boredom or wring the scrawny neck of the man who played Marvin Gaye on the jukebox over and over again, a door at the side of the lounge opened and in walked Frank Todd.

John smiled.

The smile vanished when he copped a look at the two enormous men who accompanied him. And when one jerked his head at John, he reckoned this was the least smiley moment he'd had all day.

Frank Todd nodded at the barman. 'Usual, Tony.'

The man nodded and cast John a swift glance of sympathy, which John found worrying.

Frank Todd came over to him, pulled out a chair and sat down, uninvited. 'I hear you've been looking for me.'

'I am if you're Mr Todd.'

'Call me Frank.'

'Frank, then.'

Frank Todd was a small man, almost dapper, but he had an air of authority and his deeply lined face looked as if it had been hewn from granite. He wore a green tweed jacket and cords. He might have passed as a country gent, out for his yearly shop in the city, if it hadn't been for the look on his face and the two enormous men at his side, of course, who were staring at John as though his end was very near.

'Morse.'

'What?'

'You look like Inspector Morse,' John said.

'John Thaw.'

'That's the one.'

'I get that a lot.'

John looked up at the two men. 'Look, I don't mean to be funny here, but what's with the show of muscles? You want to intimidate me, you've only got to kick me in the shin, maybe call me names. I'm easily upset.'

Frank's eyes hardened. 'What do you want me for? Maura wouldn't tell me, but she sounded upset. I don't like that. It means I don't like *you* much.'

John took a sip of his pint. 'All right. I want to talk to you about your daughter.'

'Katie? What about her?'

'Have you seen her lately?'

'Sure.'

John sensed him tense up and the air around them chilled.

'But not in the last two weeks, right?'

'Get to the point.'

'Is Katie adopted?'

Frank said, 'Check him.'

Suddenly John found himself standing, his arms pinned by one goon while the other frisked him down expertly. They took his phone and wallet and handed them to Frank. Nobody in the bar paid them any attention. John wondered if they would ever remember he'd been there.

'He's clean.'

Frank opened John's wallet and flicked through it. He took one of John's business cards out, then pocketed his wallet and phone.

'I guess lunch is on you, then,' said John.

'Check his bag.'

Goon One unzipped his bag and rummaged through it. Suddenly, he stopped.

'Oh shit. You'd better see this.'

Frank sat forward. 'What?'

The goon took the photo of Katie from the bag and passed it to him.

Frank gazed at it for a long time. John waited, wishing he'd called Sarah when he'd had the chance. He also wished that the two big men would stop staring at him as if he was a plate of rashers and they were hungry pitbulls.

'This is my daughter.' Frank brandished the photo at John. 'What the fuck are you doing with it? Where did you get it?'

'You need to calm down.'

'Is she ... is Katie dead?'

'No, she's in a coma. She was shot.'

'Shot?' Frank said, as though John must be crazy. 'Who did this to her?'

'She did it to herself, not long after she blew the face off an unarmed man.'

Frank Todd moved fast for a man of his age. No sooner had John finished speaking than he was lying between the tables, wondering what hit him. He shook his head to clear his vision, only to discover that what he was seeing was less than comforting. Frank Todd stood over him, cracking his knuckles.

'Ow,' John said. He tried to move his jaw.

'You're lying.'

'Fuck, that hurts.'

'Let's try this again. Where did you get that photo?'

'I took it myself. In Beaumont Hospital two days ago.'

'Where?'

'Beaumont, Dublin.'

'What the fuck is my girl doing in hospital in Dublin?'

'I told you, then you hit me.'

'What is she doing—'

'She shot herself. She also shot a retired GP called Walter Hogan.'

'Bollix! Never heard of him.'

'Well, clearly she had.'

'It's got to be a mistake. My Katie would never shoot herself.'

'No, but Katie Jones might.'

'What the fuck are you talking about?'

'You want to do this with an audience?' John pulled out his cigarettes. He opened the packet with his teeth and pulled one out. 'Ow,' he said again.

Frank looked at him with fresh menace, but something in his eyes shifted. 'Lads, go and have a pint.'

The two men turned as one and walked to the bar without a word. John watched them go, then climbed back into his chair. 'Where do you get guys like that? Is there a special school?'

'You got something you want to say to me?' Frank said.

'You and your wife adopted Katie, right?'

'So what if we did?'

'Legitimate adoption, was it? Got all your papers?'

'Who the fuck are you to be asking all these questions? I'll ask the questions. What's my girl doing in fucking Dublin?'

John was tempted to say, 'Shooting folk', but decided against it. 'I don't know. That's why I'm here. I was hoping to find out.'

'Why are you asking questions about an adoption?'

'Because I'm working for Katie's mother.'

'Her mother's dead.'

'She wasn't two days ago.'

Frank clenched his fists. 'Are you trying to take the piss? Her mother is dead.'

'Her biological mother is very much alive.'

'So what?'

172

John lit his cigarette. 'Right.' He turned his head. 'Hit this side next time, would you?'

The muscles in Frank's jaw clenched. He looked down at the photo and back at John. He leaned in closer. 'We gave that little girl a home.'

'She already had a home. She had a mum and dad and a brother who loved her.'

'That's a fucking lie! She came from an orphanage, one of them … what do you call 'em? Them homes where they put girls who were knocked up. Her mother was only a kid herself. She didn't want her. Katie's mother gave her up.'

'No, she didn't.' John watched his face through the smoke. Frank was a hard man to read, but he'd looked as if he genuinely believed what he was saying. Was it possible Frank Todd was innocent of Katie's abduction?

'She was kidnapped in August 1980 from a beach in Wicklow, Ireland. Her parents were Charlotte and Tommy Jones, her brother is Sam Jones. They thought she was drowned. At least they did until she sent them the locket she was wearing when she was abducted. Unfortunately, they didn't get it until the day after she shot herself.'

Frank's eyes never left John's face.

'The photo of her in the locket was taken a few days before she went missing. Her mother recognised it the moment she saw it – her mother who is sitting by her bed night and day, wondering why she got her daughter back after all this time only to watch her die.'

Frank lowered his head. At the bar, the two men sipped at their drinks, but John could tell from their body language that they were watching for him to make a single wrong move.

'She had that locket the day we got her. Beautiful little thing she was, blonde, like a doll and crying her eyes out. My Sadie fell in love with her the moment she clapped eyes on her.'

Now John could see naked emotion in his face. 'Maura mentioned that Sadie died a few years back.'

'Yeah, she did.' He sighed. 'My wife, my best friend, my heart.'

'Why didn't you have kids of your own?'

'You want me social security number too?'

'Sorry.'

'You come over here with your fucking accusations.' Frank cracked his knuckles then stroked his chin. 'Sadie loved Katie more than life itself. We both did. We didn't know nothin' about no kidnap.'

'Okay. Say I believe you.' John held up his hand. 'Where did you get her?'

'I told you, from a charity. We thought we was helping unwed mothers.'

'Did you pay any money?' Frank's face turned an ugly shade of murderous. 'By way of donations … or anything like that?' John added quickly.

'Course we did, for the fucking school, for the other kids, the ones that wouldn't be given no homes. We was told they was orphans. We was *told* we were making a new life for them. I didn't know … all right, we didn't go through the usual channels, but we couldn't, could we?'

'Why not?'

Frank's upper lip curled. 'Use your noggin'.'

'You've got a record.'

'It was a different time back then, sure, but they still wouldn't let no lag adopt.'

'So you went about it through … different channels.'

Frank ran his hand through his hair and took a deep breath. He gazed up at the ceiling for a few moments before he spoke. 'Why should Sadie suffer, eh? All that woman ever wanted was to be a mum – and she was a good mum, a great mum, you hear?'

John nodded. 'I'm going to need the name of whoever supplied you with the children.'

'Why should I help you?'

'Your daughter, the girl you say you love, the girl your wife loved, is lying in a coma in Dublin. She shot a man at point-blank range. The gardaí are going to try her for murder if she ever opens her eyes. Anything you tell me might help her. She must have gone to Walter Hogan for a reason.'

'I don't know nothing about it.'

John thought of Charlotte Jones's tired, tear-stained face.

174

He grabbed Frank's arm. Suddenly, he didn't care if Frank Todd was a face. He didn't care that the two goons were up and moving fast towards him. He didn't care that this man was grieving. He didn't care what might happen next.

'Her mother, her real mother, never had a chance to watch her little girl grow up. She never took her to the zoo, to her first day at school. She never got to watch her ride her first bike, go to her debs … none of those things. Whoever gave you and your wife a daughter robbed her and her husband of theirs. Who knows how many other families he robbed? Who knows how many other lives he's destroyed? Are you going to sit there and refuse me? Are you going to fucking sit there dragging your feet and rob Katie Jones's mother again?'

'You've got some fucking nerve, talking to me like that.'

'Yeah, that's all I've got. Nerve and a pain in my jaw from sitting here watching you feel sorry for yourself.'

Frank jerked his arm free and waved the goons back to the bar. He was breathing hard. The bar grew strangely quiet. Even the song on the jukebox ended.

Suddenly Frank slapped his hand on the table. 'Right, you're coming for a drive.'

'What?'

'You want to know where I got Katie or not?'

'Of course.'

'Well, I need to check something first. Come on!'

John peered past him to the two goons. 'Can't I just follow in a taxi?'

'You're giving me indigestion,' Frank Todd snarled. He pulled a packet of Rennies from his pocket and popped one into his mouth, then stuck his cap on his head. 'How the fuck does a bloke like you stay alive?'

'Dumb luck and quick reflexes?'

'Gotta be something, cause it sure ain't your winning personality.' Frank stood up and jerked his thumb towards the door. 'Let's go.'

28

Sarah listened to the message and swore under her breath. John had called her to say he was going to stay another day, but it had gone straight to her voicemail. The phone hadn't even rung, and when she tried to call him back she kept getting his voicemail.

'Bloody mobiles.'

'What's wrong with it?' Helen said, tapping her fingers together impatiently.

'Nothing.' Sarah didn't want a John discussion so early in the day.

'What's keeping them?' Helen glanced at her watch for the fifth time in less than half an hour.

'She's in surgery, Helen. They can't rush it. He said it would probably take at least another half hour to make sure the pins were in place.'

'Poor Jackie. It's her painting arm.'

'I'm sure she'll be on the mend in no time.'

'Right.'

Sarah squinted at her sister. Helen was immaculately turned out in a black Richard Allen trouser suit with a silver shirt, and her hair looked salon fresh, but something wasn't quite right. 'Did you manage to get some rest last night? You look exhausted.'

'Not really. You?'

'By the time I got Mum home and into bed, there didn't seem much point in trying and I wanted to check out the car this morning.'

'I can't believe someone hit her and just drove off,' Helen said.

'Me neither.'

'I can't believe the bloody gardaí were so sceptical when you told them.'

'I'm used to it. At least they said they'd investigate, check CCTV cameras.'

'Still – how bloody dismissive.'

'She'll be all right, you know. The doctor said—'

'Oh, doctors.' Helen snorted. 'Like they know everything.' She picked up a copy of *Marie Claire* and started to flick through it.

Suddenly, Sarah realised what was wrong. 'Helen, where are your wedding and engagement rings?'

'What?'

'Your rings.' Sarah pointed. 'You're not wearing them.'

'Oh.' Helen inspected her hand as if she were seeing it for the first time. 'I'm getting them cleaned.'

'Cleaned?'

'Yes.'

'I didn't know they got dirty.'

'Of course they do.'

'Even the band?'

'Especially that.'

Helen picked up the magazine again and it was clear the conversation was over. But Sarah knew something was troubling her sister.

'Helen, I—'

'By the way, I spoke to Gloria about your apartment.'

'You did?'

'Yes.' Helen gave her the same look she might give bacteria on a Petri dish. 'Why did you send John round to check up on her?'

'What?'

'The reason she didn't want to handle it any longer is because he scared the crap out of her the other evening.'

'John?'

'Yes, *John*. He was in looking around and she said he was very intimidating.'

Sarah frowned. 'You're telling me that John Quigley intimidated my estate agent?'

'Oh, please, are you going to say you didn't know?'

'I didn't. John was at my apartment?'

Helen sighed dramatically. It annoyed her to have to repeat herself, as her younger sister knew. 'That's what Gloria *said*. And let me tell you something, Sarah, she wasn't one bit impressed.'

'But that doesn't make sense. She must be mistaken.'

'Oh, really? John Quigley – private detective, there aren't too many of those around, thank God.'

'I can't believe John—'

'There you are!'

Sarah's mouth snapped shut as Barry Swan, Jackie's fiancé, came huffing down the corridor towards them. Sarah watched him with mild revulsion. She thought him an effeminate creepy little toad. No matter how hard she tried, she couldn't warm to him. His soft womanly body and tight-fisted ways stopped her trying too hard. But Jackie adored him, so she kept her feelings to herself.

'I've been looking all *over* for you.'

Helen put down her magazine. 'We've been right here, Barry.'

'Well, I couldn't *find* you.' He stopped in front of them and bestowed a disapproving glance on Sarah. 'Sarah.'

'Barry.'

He turned back to Helen. 'Any word yet?'

'She's still in surgery.'

'God. Think they'll be much longer?'

'We'll have to wait and see.'

'I need to get into town, talk to Fiona. Jackie has an exhibition in two weeks, you know.'

'They can still exhibit her paintings, Barry,' Helen said in a tense voice. 'She doesn't have to be there.'

'But she *loves* talking to her clientele and they *adore* her.' He folded his arms over his chest and, for a moment, Sarah could have sworn he was actually pouting. 'She probably won't sell half as many if she's not there in person.'

'Then ask Fiona to postpone.'

'Do you think I should?'

'Well, don't you?'

'Probably. After all her hard work, it seems such a shame to present it without her. I can't imagine Fiona would mind, though, especially when I explain about the accident.'

'Don't you think,' Sarah said, 'you should wait until you've talked to Jackie about this?'

Barry glanced at her and Sarah was unnerved to see such hostility in his eyes. He looked as if he wanted to slap her.

'Well, of course. I'm just trying to do what's right for her. It's such a shame she was in a crash so close to her biggest ever show.'

'Yes, it is.' Now she got it. Barry held her responsible and Sarah didn't like it. It was bad enough that she blamed herself.

'Sarah was at the pound this morning,.' Helen said. 'It looks like someone really tried to run Jackie off the road.'

'What?'

'There's evidence that someone struck her car,' Sarah said, 'which probably forced her across the road.'

'I don't believe it. Do the gardaí know?'

'Yes,' Helen said, 'but she was probably over the limit.'

'She shouldn't have been driving last night.'

'You throwing that bone at me, Barry?' Sarah said angrily, the colour rising in her cheeks.

'It kills me that after all her hard work, she's going to miss her big night. Poor Jackie. She's so good – so *available* to everyone. She really needs to learn how to say no once in a while.'

'Barry, did you see a coffee machine near here?' Helen said.

'There's one in Reception.'

'Right.' Helen stood up. 'Sarah? You want one? Barry?'

'Helen, you sit down. I'll go.'

'No, thank you, Barry, I need to stretch my legs. Sarah?'

'I'm fine, thank you.'

Sarah listened to Helen's heels click away across the tiles. Her head was a mess – Jackie, the van, Barry's accusatory tone, and there was what her sister had told her about John. Why would he try to sabotage her attempt to sell her apartment?

'Will you excuse me? I've got to make a call,' she said.

Barry shrugged. With Helen gone, he dropped any attempt at civility.

Sarah dialled John's number again and walked a little way down the hall. It went straight to voicemail.

'Damn it, John, where are you? Call me as soon as you get this.'

She dialled Gloria Bradshaw.

'Hello?'

'Gloria?'

'Yes?'

'Gloria, hi, it's Sarah Kenny.'

'I'm just about to head into a meeting.'

'I won't take up much of your time.'

'Okay, then. What can I do for you?'

'Gloria, I'm with Helen and she tells me John Quigley was in my apartment. She says he tried to intimidate you.'

'Well, I never actually said "intimidate", but he *was* acting strangely.'

'John Quigley?'

'Yes, Helen says he's your partner.'

'In the agency, yes.'

'Well, I must say, he's a very unpleasant person.'

Sarah tried to think. This was so weird. Why had John not mentioned it? What would he have been doing there in the first place? 'What did he say to you exactly?'

'He just arrived and asked to look around and … well, there was something off about him … then he kissed me.'

'He *kissed* you?'

'Yes, on the forehead. I'm telling you, Sarah, in all my years as an agent I never – anyway, he kissed me and told me … oh, what was it now? He told me to stay pretty. Can you imagine? And let me assure you, it wasn't a compliment, the way he said it.'

Suddenly Sarah couldn't breathe. She put her hand on the wall and bent over to steady herself.

'I mean, at one point I thought about calling the gardaí. And when Helen said he was your partner, I was stunned. If you wanted to check up on me, I—'

'Gloria, what did this man look like?'

'What?'

'What did he *look* like?'

'Sarah, I don't have time for games. Whatever you and that partner of yours have going on, I don't want to be involved. Helen was telling me some very unsavoury things about him. Frankly, I didn't want your apartment and I was selling it as a favour for your sister.'

'Gloria, please, can you just tell me what this man looked like?'

Gloria tutted. 'All right, Sarah. He was big, late thirties, English accent. He had one very blue eye and the other was all white, like he had a cataract. He had very pronounced cheekbones too.'

'Okay. I don't need to hear any more.'

'Right.' Gloria sounded annoyed. 'Look, Sarah, I'm a busy woman. I don't have time for this sort of thing.' She rang off.

Sarah tried to get a grip on herself. She clicked off the phone and returned to her seat.

'Everything all right?' Barry said, sounding as though he couldn't care less.

'Sure, work.'

'Right.'

Sarah stared at her feet. Barry examined a bad print on the wall as though it was an original Monet. After a few moments, Sarah tried to call John again, but her hands shook so badly she could barely hold her mobile, let alone dial a number. She slipped it into her pocket and folded her arms. But a burning pain was working its way through her body and it was all she could do not to vomit.

'Sarah? Are you all right?'

'What?'

'Are you all right?' Helen stood over her, a steaming Styrofoam cup in her hand. 'You're as pale as a ghost.'

Sarah nodded. 'I'm … Helen, I'll be back shortly. I've got to go.'

'But what about Jackie?'

'I'll be back.' Sarah got up and put on her jacket.

'Sarah, what's wrong?'

'Nothing. I'll be back shortly.' She kissed her sister on the cheek and hurried away.

Barry watched her go. 'She's off,' he said querulously. 'Always running away.'

29

John couldn't have been less comfortable. He was squatting between a filthy toolbox and the metal that ran across the back of the cab. At the start of the journey, he had been sitting on a pile of pallets. It was secure, lashed together and tied to a metal bar that ran along the side of the truck, but the goons seemed to take a perverse pleasure in going round corners on two wheels.

The first time they had done this, John had gone flying and ended up in a winded heap at the back doors. After another spill, he decided the floor would be safer.

After about ten minutes the van had stopped and he heard the goons get out. Frank said he'd see them after, and then it was Frank driving. Frank – if anything – drove harder than the goons.

After the best part of an hour – by which time John had developed some considerable skill at judging when a corner was coming up – the van slowed, then stopped.

Frank climbed out and opened the back door. 'Are you telling me the truth?'

John was delighted to find himself in one piece, although less than thrilled to see that the knees of his last remaining clean jeans were covered with oil.

'Ah, shit,' he muttered.

'What?'

'I'm officially out of clean jeans.'

'That's the least of your problems if I find out you've been lying to me,' Frank said, so viciously that John wished he had been allowed to stay at the Queen's Arms.

Outside, he saw that they were in a leafy street. Large Georgian houses stood elegant and proud in the late-morning sun. 'Where are we?'

'Never mind, I'll be back in a second. You stay here.' Frank slammed the door on him.

John tried the handle, but it didn't open from the inside, and there was no way into the cab.

He lit a cigarette and settled back to wait. He wondered idly if he'd ever see Sarah again, then decided that was too morose a thought even for a man trapped in the back of a van in the middle of God knew where.

Frank walked up the drive of the nearest house, then went round to the side and rang a discreet brass bell at the garden door.

After a moment, a woman opened it. She was small, barely more than five feet, slender and immaculately turned out. She had blue eyes and a kind face, with a few laughter lines. She wore her highlighted hair in a soft bob. She had clearly been baking: there were traces of flour on her sleeves and she wore a spotless lemon-striped apron over a dark shirt.

'Frank!' she cried, her lilting Northern Irish accent as strong now as the day he had met her. She wiped her hands on the apron and opened her arms. 'What a surprise.'

'Hello, Lizzie,' Frank said, stooping down to kiss her cheek. 'How's it going? Lookin' as beautiful as ever.'

'Oh, now, sure, it's a struggle.' She looked past him, saw he was alone and smiled. 'What brings you here?'

'I need to talk to you. It's about Katie.'

The smile stayed in place, but Frank wasn't fooled. Despite her manner, there was a cold shrewdness to Lizzie. 'Can I come in?'

Her face fell. 'Oh, Frank, why didn't you call and say you were coming? This is such a bad time. You know how it is, I've a terrible load on … if you'd rung earlier, I might have had time for a visit. Why don't you come back tomorrow?'

'I won't take up too much of your time. I promise.' He wasn't asking, and apparently Lizzie picked up on this.

'Well, of course,' she said. 'Come in and I'll put the kettle on.'

He followed her down a long dark hall. The smell of baking wafted through the house and Frank's belly rumbled.

She led him into a bright, spotlessly clean kitchen and went to the stove. There was pastry rolled out on the worktop and a basin of peeled apples beside it.

'Doin' a spot of cooking, Lizzie?'

'Oh, now, it's just a few pies for the church's monthly sale of work. Father Vincent says they fly, so they do.'

'I'll bet.' Frank leaned against the fridge and watched her move about.

'Sit down there now, Frank.' She indicated a table covered with shiny blue oilcloth. 'Will you have tea?'

'Sure, I'd love a cuppa.'

He sat down and Lizzie bustled about her task. She set out a plate of biscuits and some milk, then poured the tea. It was all very civilised, a proper little party, right up to the point when Frank said,. 'Someone was telling me earlier that Katie didn't come from no unwed mothers' home. They told me she was kidnapped.'

A deathly silence fell over the room.

'What's that now?' Lizzie said.

'You heard me.'

'Your Katie?'

'That's right.'

'Ridiculous.' She poured tea into the cups. 'Whatever next?'

'So she's an orphan? And Robbie?'

'Of course she is, and Robbie too.'

'That's what I said.' Frank took up a biscuit. 'I knew this would be easy to sort out. Tell you what, you get the paperwork I need and I can give it to that weirdo family claiming my kid is theirs, will you, Lizzie?'

'What family?'

'Some crowd in Ireland, strangest thing – Jones, they're called – they're claiming my Katie's theirs.'

'Oh.'

'So, about that paperwork …'

'Well, it was so long ago, I don't know if I can even find—'

'Before you get talking, Lizzie, this fella who spoke to me hasn't informed the cops about his investigation. Nobody knows about you – or your connection to me, for that matter. If there were any … oddities, it would be easy enough to clean up any mess, wouldn't it? Course, I'd have to know the score, now, wouldn't I? Last thing I need is to be kept in the dark.'

Lizzie shot him a look, and suddenly Frank felt cold. Now he knew for certain that Quigley had been telling him the truth, but he'd hoped Lizzie would laugh and prove him wrong. She hadn't. She looked worried for the first time since he'd known her.

'Who is this person filling your head with these terrible thoughts, Frank?'

'Doesn't matter. So what's it to be. Them kids – they was orphans or they wasn't?'

The seconds ticked by. Frank dunked his biscuit into his tea and ate it.

Lizzie put down her cup and rested her hand on his. 'Frank, those poor children needed homes. They were barely existing where they were.'

Frank's expression never changed.

'And you and Sadie … don't you remember how happy you were? Don't you remember how desperately Sadie wanted kids? She cried, Frank, cried in this very kitchen!' Her hand fluttered to her face, then back to Frank's hand. 'I helped you, Frank, and I helped Sadie. I helped make your lives complete.'

'I seem to remember it weren't exactly out of the goodness of your heart,' Frank said softly, and rubbed the fingers of his free hand together.

Lizzie reeled back. 'Well, we had expenses … donations and—'

'*Donations*? Was this to the orphanage, then?' Frank asked maliciously.

'No, to the charity that ran it. It was a very difficult time, Frank.'

'What orphanage did they come from?'

'It was a religious order.'

'Yeah? What was its name?'

'I don't remember.'

'You don't remember where you got a two-year-old girl and a four-year-old boy?'

'What does it matter now? You have your children.'

Frank's face closed. 'What orphanage did Katie come from?'

'It … was in some place over in Dublin.'

'Whereabouts in Dublin?'

'I—' Her hands trembled. 'It was so long ago. I—'

Frank took out the photo John had given him and slapped it onto the table in front of her. Lizzie gave an involuntary moan.

'Look at my little girl, Lizzie.' Frank leaned close to her. 'Look what she done to herself. Why would she do that? Who the fuck is this guy she shot? Walter Hogan.'

'I don't know.'

Frank stared at her coldly. 'The right answer would have been, "What guy she shot." You're slipping, Lizzie.'

'What?' Her features had blanched. 'Frank, please, you have me so confused. I don't know what's going on … Frank, I swear to you, I don't know what this man has been saying to you, but he's wrong. *He's wrong.*'

'So tell me where you got them, then. We can sort this out in no time.'

Suddenly, she seemed to be having trouble breathing.

Frank was unmoved. He had known Lizzie a long time and had seen her pull many a stunt. 'Come on, out with it.'

'Please, I'm a sick lady.'

'Sick you may be, a lady you ain't.'

She began to cry. 'You don't understand! They would have died.'

'With their fuckin' parents?'

'I didn't get them from their parents.'

'No, you fuckin' kidnapped 'em.'

'How can you say such a thing? I didn't.' She clutched at Frank's hand and sobbed when he pulled it away from her. 'I swear to you, I didn't.'

'No? Then where did you get 'em?'

'I can't! He'll kill me.'

'Who? What fucking guy is this?'

'Frank, please.'

Frank punched the table with such force that Lizzie yelped.

'Don't you fucking "please" me. Now, you listen to me, Lizzie. You and me, we go back a long way, and I don't wanna fuck you over, but I'll bring a whole world of hurt down on your fucking head if you don't talk to me. I gotta kid in a coma cause she shot herself. I gotta son inside who's a fucking basket-case and Milo's boy's dead too. Now, if there's something you know, you'd better fuckin' talk, you miserable bitch. Where did you get them kids?'

'I *can't.*'

'You better, or I swear to God …' Frank clamped his hand round her wrist.

Lizzie cried out. 'Frank, please!'

'Please?' Frank sneered. 'Please what? It's not like I'm asking you for anything you can't provide, is it? Right, Lizzie, your last chance.'

She whispered something.

'What was that?'

'It was Nico. He took her, I had no choice … he said if I didn't help him he'd kill me.'

It was as if someone had flung a bucket of icy water into Frank's red face. The colour drained from it and his mouth flapped open. He was appalled. When he'd collected himself, he snapped, 'Took her from where?'

'I don't know. Somewhere in Ireland.'

'And Robbie?'

She shook her head.

'Did Robbie come from Ireland too? What about Milo's boy?'

She was sobbing.

Frank said nothing for a few moments. Then he upturned the table, sending tea and biscuits everywhere. He roared, a sound so anguished that Lizzie cringed. Then he lunged at her.

'Frank!' She shrank away from him and, at the last second, Frank pulled his punch.

'You're a fuckin' bitch. I'll see you rot for this.'

'I'm sorry, Frank – I'm so sorry.'

Frank kicked over his chair and stormed out of the house.

30

Sarah drove fast, blasting her horn at a taxi that pulled out in front of her at Jury's Inn, getting the finger for her trouble. Enraged, she swung the Manta into the next lane and accelerated past him, then swung back in front of him, causing him to jam on his brakes.

Sumo was thrown against the passenger window. He yelped.

'Oh, Sumo, I'm sorry.' Sarah looked at him in the rear-view mirror as he righted himself.

Jesus, she was going to get them killed.

She slowed down and by the time she had parked up on the footpath outside her house, she was almost less than hysterical. 'Wait here, okay? I'll be right back.'

She got out and, with John's tyre iron in her left hand, ran up the steps to her apartment, taking them two at a time. She let herself in and slammed the door behind her. 'Okay,' she yelled into the silence. 'If anyone's here, you better come out! I've already called the gardaí! They'll be here in a minute.'

She waited. The apartment remained silent. She advanced slowly, checking each room. Once she was sure nobody would leap out at her, she collapsed into her leather armchair.

Stay pretty.

How often had he said that to her? How often had he leaned

across her and uttered those very words? *Stay pretty*. How could two words be so loaded? They meant don't cause me any trouble and I won't have to rearrange your face.

Stay pretty.

He didn't wear a beard.

It couldn't be him. Could it?

Stay pretty.

She needed confirmation.

She went into the hall and noticed straight away that her address book was gone. She did a quick search for it, but it wasn't in the apartment.

It had to be him. He knew where she lived. He knew where her sisters lived.

'Fuck.'

She went back into the sitting room and picked up the phone. After a moment, she dialled a number she knew by heart and waited, praying she was wrong.

'Yeah?' a gruff voice answered.

Sarah heard music in the background and laughter. She closed her eyes tighter.

'Who's there? Speak – I ain't got all day.'

'Sid?'

'Yeah.'

'It's me.'

'Speak up, kid, it's a bad connection.'

Sarah felt a tear slide down her cheek even as she smiled. Sid and his bad connections! He was half deaf, but he hated to admit it. If he did, he might have to admit, too, that he was getting old.

'Sid, it's me. It's Sarah.'

There was a long pause. A very long pause.

'Sid?'

'Hold on.'

In the background, she heard him barking orders to someone, then a door opening. After a moment, the background noise was gone.

'Hey there, kid. How you been, my darling?'

'Oh, Sid.' Sarah knew then, from the sadness in Sid's voice, that she was right, and she began to cry.

'Come on, now.'

'He's out, isn't he?'

'Yeah.' Sid sighed heavily, and Sarah could picture his face as clearly as though he was standing in front of her. He was a small, muscular man in his early sixties, hard as nails with stubbly grey whiskers and deep-crinkled skin round his pale Nordic eyes. He had come up the hard way in life, the product of a Swedish mother and an East End father. His mother had abandoned him as a baby, almost as soon as she realised London wasn't all Biba and Mary Quant, as she had been led to believe. Sid's father had been a dock-worker: a hard-drinking man, a grafter and a bruiser. Between a succession of girlfriends and sisters, he had raised his son on tough love, teaching him to keep a shield up and to fight his corner. To fuck up a rival before a rival fucked him up. To be a man's man.

And the Sid she knew was a man's man, albeit with a heart as big and soft as a marshmallow mountain. It had been Sid who had patched her up when Vic had beaten her to a pulp. Sid who'd 'put a word in his shell-like' that he didn't appreciate his lounge girls looking like they'd gone ten rounds with Muhammad Ali.

Sid who had helped her get away when no one else would.

She clutched the phone tighter. 'How long?'

'About two months now. He was round 'ere askin' 'bout you. He found the twins, too, but they told him they didn't know where you was. Not sure he believed them, but I warned him not to start any shit. Told him last I heard you was in Spain somewhere. If I'd 'ad a number for you I'da called.'

She felt a stab of guilt. The twins were two gorgeous girls from São Paulo. They were hard-working, funny and sent money home to their family every week without fail. 'I'm sorry about that. Tell them I'm sorry, won't you?'

'It's all right. The girls are cool. You made a clean break, and I respect that. Anyway I got that beautiful card, didn't I?'

'He was here, Sid.'

'You seen him?'

'No, but he was here and – oh my God.'

'What?'

'My sister was in an accident last night ...' Sarah slammed her fist against her thigh.

'You think it was him?'

'I don't know ... maybe.'

Sid didn't say anything.

'Sid?'

'I don't know what to tell you, darlin'. He didn't hear nothin' 'bout you from me, and that's a fact.'

'But how the hell did he get out? I don't understand.'

'He said new evidence came to light. He said the case against him was ... how did he put it now? Oh, yeah. As bogus as my fucking teeth.'

'Oh Jesus, Sid, did he try to hurt you?'

'Nah, sweetheart.' Sid gave a throaty chuckle. 'Come on! He knows better than to fuck with the likes of old Sid. But if his case sprang a leak, then it's gotta be Betty, ain't it?'

Sarah closed her eyes. Sweaty Betty, the coat-check girl, she'd seen Sarah leave the day Vic had been arrested. She was the only one who could have pointed the finger at her.

'She never liked me.'

'She never liked anyone, that one. That's her problem. But she had a soft spot for patter, and you and me both know, Vic can fucking charm the birds down from the trees when he feels like it. I should have got rid of her a long time ago.'

Sarah closed her eyes and leaned her head against the wall. 'I don't know what to do, Sid.'

'Get gone. That's what I'd do in your shoes. Lay low for a while.'

'I can't just up and go. I've got responsibilities.'

'You got a responsibility to yourself to stay safe.'

'I've got a new life here.' Suddenly, the strength left Sarah's legs and she sank to the floor. 'I can't do this any more, Sid. I can't keep running.'

Sid sighed. 'He ain't gonna come at you directly, girl, you know that. If he's gonna do something he'll do it Vic's way.'

'I know,' Sarah whispered.

'Maybe it'd be best if you moved. Head down south or something.

I got a mate down the Costa – he owns a fancy bar. I could give him a call and—'

'I'm not running any more, Sid,' Sarah said softly.

'Look, darlin', that's all very noble and shit, but this guy … you know what he's capable of.'

'I've changed too, Sid.'

'Put on eighty pounds of muscle, have ya? Can you wring a man's neck with your bare hands?'

'No, but—'

'Then it don't matter, and even if you had, it still don't matter.' He cleared his throat. 'Now, listen to me, if he's there, he's there for a reason, and that reason is to harm you and yours. You wanna protect you and yours, then the best thing you can do is get your skinny little arse as far away from wherever Vic is.'

'I've got to go, Sid.'

'Listen to me. Don't try nothing stupid with that man. I know you ain't forgotten. You know him. You know what he's capable of. Please, darlin'.' Sid sounded very upset. 'Let me call this friend.'

'No, you've done plenty for me, Sid, and I appreciate it, all of it. You've got my heart, Champ.' It was his pet name. *Rocky* was Sid's favourite movie and he knew every line from the film and grew misty-eyed when Rocky Balboa ran the steps.

She hung up and scrambled to her feet.

Stay calm. So what if it was him? He was flesh and bone. So what if he was here? She wasn't a kid any more – she'd changed. She'd shot a man, for Christ's sake.

She had barely made it to the bathroom before she vomited all over the tiled floor.

31

John was jolted out of his reverie by the sound of the van door slamming. Seconds later, the engine roared into life and they were off. Frank drove like a lunatic and, after twenty minutes of hanging onto the pallets, John was relieved when the van skidded to a halt.

The door opened and Frank said, 'Out.'

John blinked in the winter sunlight. 'Where—'

'There's a Tube station over there. Take the green line – the District – and it'll bring you back into town. Here's your bag. Your phone and shit's inside.' Frank shoved his gear into his arms and began to walk away.

'Wait!'

John ran after him and caught him before he got back into the van. He grabbed the older man by the shoulder and swung him round. 'Hold on a minute.'

'Get yer fuckin' hands off me.' Frank took a swing at him.

'Whoa!' John danced back just in time and held up his hands in front of him. 'Hold on now. What's going on? Where are you going?'

Frank's eyes were blazing. 'You was right. My Katie was taken from her family.'

'Okay, so now you've got confirmation.'

'I can't fuckin' believe it. And Robbie, my boy. Milo, too. It's a fuckin' nightmare.'

'Oh.'

'That fuckin' bitch.' Frank was pacing in a circle. 'She lied to me – she lied to my wife.'

'Who?'

'Fuckin' Lizzie, that's who! I shoulda known, I shoulda fuckin' known.'

'You must have known something was up. You chose to use this Lizzie and you knew kids didn't just pop up out of the ground.'

Frank looked ready to take another swing at him, but instead he turned on his heel and walked to the van.

'Where are you going?'

'To talk to the Greek.'

'Who?'

But Frank wasn't stopping, so John made a decision. 'I'm coming with you.'

'The fuck you are.'

John ran past him and stood in front of the van's door. 'You take me or I'm turning everything over to the cops right now.'

'Get out of my way!' Frank grabbed the front of his shirt.

'If you really love Katie, you'll take me with you.'

Frank's hand dropped to his side. 'What?'

'I need to make a call, but if there's a connection between your daughter and the man she shot, it might have some bearing on her case.'

'What are you saying?'

'I don't know yet, but I've been thinking. The man Katie shot was a retired GP. Maybe he had something to do with getting kids for adoption. How much money did you pay for her?'

'That's none of your fuckin' business.'

'I'm trying to help you.'

'Eighty thousand for her, a hundred thousand for my boy.'

'Jesus!' John said. Back in 1980, that was serious money.

'How the fuck do you think the miserable bitch can afford to live in that neck of the woods?'

John wasn't sure which neck of the woods Frank was talking about, or even if Frank was still talking to him. 'How many kids did she supply?'

'The fuck should I know?'

'Who's Milo?'

'What?'

'You mentioned someone called Milo.'

'Yeah? Well, I shouldn't have.'

'Frank, listen—'

'No, you listen. Milo's fuckin' business stays just that. Milo's business. You say you want to help my girl, then start talkin', cause I'm about to start walkin'. Got it?'

'Look, I'm not trying to rile you, but you need to calm down for a moment.'

'Hey, fuck you. This is my kid we're talkin' about.'

'You know what? She isn't,' John said angrily. 'She's Charlotte Jones's kid, and right now that poor woman wants to know what the hell happened to her daughter. She needs to know why her little girl grew up without her, why she shot a man in cold blood and why she shot herself.'

'You think I don't want to know that too?' Frank's voice cracked. 'I love that little girl, love her with all me heart.'

'I know you do. I can see that.'

'I didn't mean for none of this to happen. Sadie'd turn in her grave if she knew. I don't know what the fuck's happened. First me boy goes off the deep end, then Katie. She wouldn't even talk to me these last few weeks, broke my fuckin' heart. Then she goes and gets shacked up with some weirdo—'

'Drake?'

'That's him. Tall skinny freak, loony toons.' Frank twirled his finger by his temple. 'I tried to talk to him this one time and he wigged out. I tell you, he's barkin'.'

John patted his shoulder awkwardly. 'But if we're going to help Katie, we need to find out what's going on, and we can't do that if we're barging around like bulls in a china shop.' He pointed to his swollen jaw. Suddenly the fight went out of Frank. In the late-morning sun, he looked like a frightened, angry old man.

'Look, we'll talk to this guy together. I've got a friend back in Ireland and she'll do a bit more digging on our GP, see if she can't come up with something. How about that?'

'All right.'

John held out his hand. They shook, then Frank took out his keys. 'I'll do the talkin' to the Greek.'

'Okay.'

'You get in my way, I'll break you.'

'Right.'

'And don't start any of your fuckin' smart mouth.'

'Scout's honour.'

Frank looked at him for a long time. 'I must be fuckin' nuts.'

John agreed, but wisely kept his opinion to himself.

Lizzie sat on the bed and poured herself a large scotch. She carried it to the window and looked out across the street.

'He was heading to find Nico,' she said into a small mobile. 'I don't know, do I? But he said there were no cops involved and as far as I can see he's on the level. Frank won't want the police sniffing about.' She let the curtain slip back into place. 'I don't care what you do, Mark, but you've got to see to it that he never makes it to the cops. You've got to get there first. I don't want to hear excuses. The girl must be taken care of, too … Don't give me that. You messed up. You should have checked. I'm very disappointed in you. You've let me down.' She paused to sip her drink. 'Don't make the same mistake again.'

She hung up. Although Frank's anger had shaken her, she had almost fully recovered. Lizzie was not a woman to be overawed in any situation and she could turn on the waterworks like a tap. That particular talent had served her well.

'There, now, my little ones,' she said to the two babies that gazed up at her from the crib. 'Did the noise frighten you? Nasty men, don't you worry about a thing.' She offered a rattle to the blond one and smiled as he took it from her. Oh, he was a cutie all right. He'd fetch a pretty penny.

It was so much easier these days. You didn't have to search far and wide for the right type of kids. It was all so clean and hassle-free. You could just buy them. No real chance of being caught by the authorities. And half the silly bitches who dropped the brats out could hardly feed themselves, let alone anyone else. Sluts and tramps, the lot of them. And there was always a market for the babies if they looked right and were disease free. Every year, the waiting list grew longer and the money kept going up. The adoption board was a joke, with their questions and tests. Kow-towing to the birth mothers, making folk feel like shit. Good people being pushed through the wringer – and for what? They didn't want the hassle of red tape, constant interviews and questions about their private lives. Why should decent people anywhere have to put up with that nonsense when every brain-dead sink-head popped out kids with no one to look down on them. It wasn't right and everyone knew it. She was doing the world a service.

Lizzie straightened her shoulders, feeling a surge of sanctimonious self-justification. She gave poor kids a chance to live in luxury and wealth. She made a bit of money and the birth parent got a few quid. Everyone should be happy. It was a crying shame people couldn't get their stupid heads round it. It wasn't her fault that a few of the kids turned out to be wack-jobs.

Nico had been a mistake. He was weak – she'd known it all along. There had always been the possibility that he'd bring trouble on her. She should never have got involved with him back then, but it had been the early days and she had needed the contacts. Not like now. Now, *she* was running the show. She didn't make mistakes.

She smoothed one baby's hair and rested her arms on the crib. It was a shame old Frank had found his conscience in his old age. Stupid, sentimental old fool.

She thought about what kind of wreath she would send as she played peek-a-boo with the second baby, a little Romanian with huge brown eyes. Nothing too showy, something classic, she decided.

She smiled as the baby grinned at her toothlessly.

32

Sarah drove back to Clontarf. She led Sumo through the side gate and released him into the garden, then let herself in through the back door. Her mother and Belinda were sitting at the kitchen table with the newspapers spread out in front of them.

The kitchen was warm and sunny. It all looked so normal. Sarah paused in the door for a second, uncertainty washing over her. How could the world go on as though nothing was wrong? Why didn't everyone sense the imminent danger?

'You're back early,' her mother said.

'Everything all right?' Belinda asked. 'We've been trying to reach you.'

'Sure, I just need to do something.'

'Your sister called, looking for you.'

'My phone's been off for a few hours.'

Belinda stood up to fill the kettle. 'She said to tell you Jackie's out of surgery.'

Damn! She'd even forgotten to call Helen. 'That's great,' she said. 'Did she say anything else?'

'They got the blood test result back and Jackie was just under the limit.'

'Oh, thank God!' Sarah pulled off her hat and rubbed her eyes to hide that she was close to weeping. 'That's brilliant news.'

'They're probably going to keep her in for a few more days.'

'Right.'

'Are you okay, Sarah? You're very pale.'

'I'm fine.'

'You need a steak,' her mother said. 'Get some iron into you.'

'I'm fine, Mum.'

'Pudding and toast then.'

'I'm *fine*, Mum, honestly.' Sarah kissed the top of her mother's head. 'I need to make a few calls – I'll be down in a minute.'

'I'll make you some coffee,' Belinda said.

Sarah glanced at her. She was being unusually kind. 'Thanks.'

Sarah ran upstairs and into her room. If he had been in her apartment, then it was probably safe to assume he knew she hadn't been staying there and that she was here. She had to get her mother out of the house. She had to make sure that if Vic struck, Deirdre wasn't caught in the crossfire.

She glanced at her watch. It was now after two. Time was getting away from her. What was Vic planning? He had used John's name as a warning to her, she knew. And Jackie – he'd been behind the accident too. She had to tell Helen, warn her to take extra care. She had no choice.

She must tell John too – and watch his eyes cloud. Watch confusion and mistrust replace what had been growing there.

Victor. Even his name made her tremble. Made her want to run and hide.

No.

She had run before and she wasn't going to run again. She could take care of this before it destroyed her life. She could do it. She could stop him.

But, first things first, she needed help. Her hands shook as she dialled the number. She took a deep breath.

'Hello.'

'Helen, it's me.'

'Sarah? Where the hell have you been? I thought you were coming back.'

'I'm sorry. Something came up.'

'Oh *really*.'

'I have to ask you a favour.'

'What sort of favour?'

'I need you to take Mum for a few days.'

'What? Why?'

Sarah gritted her teeth. Helen had every right to tell her to get stuffed. 'I have to work on this case, and John's in London—'

'Why?'

'Helen, the case involves a gun dealer, and I can't be sure ... but I've got a lead and I have to follow it up. It would only be for a couple of days.'

'Jesus Christ!' Helen exploded. 'Our sister's lying in a hospital bed and you want to fuck off on some case?'

'It's my *job*, Helen, it's not like I can turn work down.' Sarah hoped she was doing the right thing because Helen would never let her forget this – she'd probably never forgive her for it either. 'I'm asking for your help, Helen.'

'You are out of control. This kind of ... Jackie could have been killed last night and you hadn't even the decency to wait at the hospital this morning to see that she was all right. Now you want to uproot our mother from her home and dump her in mine while you go off playing cops and robbers.'

Sarah bit her tongue and said nothing. She had heard the fury and hurt in Helen's voice and, worse, the disappointment. There was nothing for it but to let her get it all out of her system. 'Helen, please, I wouldn't ask if I wasn't desperate.'

'All right, then. Just for a couple of days – but this is one liberty too many.'

'I really appreciate it.'

'Make sure Belinda's okay with it first.'

'Of course.'

Helen sighed heavily. 'You'd better come in and see Jackie. She was pretty out of it earlier and doesn't know who was here – but she'd better see your face today, do you hear me?'

'I'll pop in later, I promise.'

'You can drop Mum over, I take it? I've got to go to work now.'

'Absolutely.'

'And you'll make up her room. That's not Belinda's job.'

Sarah had never heard Helen sound so disgusted, and she didn't blame her. She felt like the world's worst sister, its biggest loser and fraud. 'I'll talk to you in a while.'

Sarah tried John, and it went straight to voicemail. 'Dammit, John, what's going on over there? I'm starting to worry. Ring me, will you?'

She hurried downstairs and drank the coffee Belinda handed her standing by the sink. She hoped there would be no hassle with the prickly carer.

'Belinda, can I talk to you in the other room for a second?'

She need not have worried. Belinda seemed almost eager to look after her mother at Helen's home, and Sarah felt a small stab of resentment, but quashed it quickly. She needed Belinda to help get Deirdre ready and explain what was going on. Deirdre was not happy. 'I don't want to go to Helen's house, I want to stay here,' she said, glaring at Belinda, who was taking clothes out of her drawers.

'It's only for a couple of days, Mum. Think of it as a mini-holiday.'

'A holiday?' Her mother looked confused. 'I'm going on holiday?'

'Sort of.' Sarah could feel a headache building behind her eyes. She helped her mother into a green cardigan and began to brush her hair.

'I don't know,' Deirdre said. 'I want to stay here. Is *she* going?'

'Belinda? Yes.'

'I told you before,' her mother huffed, 'I don't like her.'

'Mum, that's not nice.'

'I want to stay here.'

'It's just to Helen's.'

'I don't want to go. I want to stay here.'

'Well, you can't,' Sarah snapped. Belinda straightened and gave her a look. 'Sorry, Mum, but it's for the best.'

Deirdre said nothing, but Sarah could see her hands twisting the fabric of her blouse in distress. She put down the brush and bent down until her face was inches from her mother's. 'Mum, I'm sorry,' she whispered. She leaned in and kissed her mother on the forehead. 'I'm sorry for being short with you. I love you.'

Her mother nodded, but her hands didn't cease fiddling.

'Belinda, I'm just going to feed Sumo and give him some water. Will you finish here?'

'Sure,' Belinda said, disapproving.

Sarah went downstairs, heaviness descending on her with every step.

Belinda followed her. 'Sarah?' Her dark brown eyes were thoughtful and alert. 'What's going on?'

'What?'

'What's going on?'

'Nothing. I have to … there's this case and—'

'Why are you bustling us out of here like the hounds of hell are behind you?'

It was all Sarah could do not to cry. Behind her, the clock read ten past three. 'I don't know what you're talking about.'

'Is it about that man who came to the door today?'

Sarah thought her heart might burst out of her chest. 'What man?'

'He was calling about a car, or so he said. He wasn't fooling me, mind. I could see him checking the place out.'

'What did he look like?'

'Nondescript, blue eyes, sort of fat, in his thirties.'

'Did he have a beard, a funny-looking eye?'

'No.'

'Good.' Maybe there was more than one. Vic usually worked alone, but perhaps he'd changed his *modus operandi*.

'Are you sure you're okay?' Belinda said.

'I'm fine, but I've got to get ready. You go back to Mum. I'll lock up here.'

She gave Belinda a tense smile and slid away from her before she had to deal with any more questions. She ran around the house checking all the doors and windows, then stood in the middle of her mother's living room and clutched her head.

She needed protection, she needed help. She needed to talk to John, she needed—

She caught a glimpse of her face as she walked past the mirror over the fireplace and stood stock still.

The fear. This was how he wanted her.

No. She didn't need anything. She had to take care of something. Victor was a malignancy. She had cut him out before, but this time she would cauterise the wound. This time he would not return, she would make sure of it.

33

The unfamiliar streets blended into one as they drove across the city. Frank raged to John about Lizzie, how she had sworn that the kids were from a home.

John let him talk, but he was thinking of something Drake had said. Obviously Frank had tried to talk to him about Katie's whereabouts, but what about the second man who had gone to the nursing home – where did he fit into it all? If he wasn't the moustached man, how many men were after Katie?

He took out his phone and switched it on. It beeped. Messages.

John listened. Sarah.

He called her immediately.

'Where the hell have you been? Are you all right?'

John glanced at Frank's set jaw. 'Let's just say I had a few communication problems. You sound upset.'

'Jackie had an accident last night. She's in hospital.'

'She okay?'

'Broken arm and concussion.'

'What the hell happened?'

'She had a car crash.'

'I'm so sorry, Sarah.'

'Thanks. What's going on with you?'

'I found Frank Todd. I'm with him right now, in fact.'

'Isn't he the kidnapper?'

'No.'

'Maybe it's because I've had a long night, but I'm confused.'

'He says he didn't know Katie had a family. He and his wife adopted her in good faith.'

'So where—'

'But it wasn't a legit adoption …' John explained as much as he could, noticing Frank's knuckles growing white on the steering wheel, '… so we're on our way to see this Greek guy right now.'

'When will you be back?'

'Tomorrow, probably.'

'I need you to talk to the sister of the GP – what was her name again?'

'I don't remember, I'll have to look it up.'

John was surprised, she never forgot names.

'Okay, find out if her brother was involved in any kind of adoptions or with foster families. There has to be some reason why Katie went to his house that day.'

'Other than to shoot him, you mean?'

'Don't be like that.'

'Sorry, I'm just tired. Should I call Sam and let him know you've located Todd?'

'Don't mention anything to him or Charlotte just yet. Wait until I've talked to this Greek guy. Then we should consider what they want to do. They might not want the gardaí involved.'

'Of course they will.'

'Wait until I've talked to this guy.'

'You might be just tipping him off by talking to him.'

'Sarah, let me handle things my way. I'm the one who's here. I'll call you later.'

'Right.'

She was gone. John glanced at his phone in surprise.

'She thinks my girl did it?' Frank said.

'Well, in fairness, there's no reason for her to think anything else.'

'She wouldn't do it.'

'You're her father, so you're bound to say that.'

'You don't understand. Let me tell you a story about Katie. When she was eight she was coming home from school and she found a magpie by the side of the road. It must have been attacked by a cat because it was bleeding and manky-lookin' and it was squawkin' and tryin' to hop away. But Katie went right up to it, lifted it and brought it home with her. Nearly as big as her, it was. So she arrived home, this little blonde angel, with this great big squawkin' thing in her hands, covered in blood and shit. Now, course, Sadie took one look at it and freaked out and said she couldn't have it in the house.' He laughed softly. 'Anyway, when I got home Katie was up in her room. She'd got a box down from the wardrobe and she had that fuckin' bird all wrapped up and in it. It was still squawkin', but it'd given up fightin'. And I said, "Baby, it's goin' to die. Better let me bring it to a vet."' Frank chuckled. 'Course I wasn't gonna bring it to no vet and I think, young and all as she was, she knew that. So she said, "No, Daddy, I'll help him." So I thought, Fuck it, it's on its way out and the kid's gotta learn that shit dies. So I said, "All right."' He shook his head.

John had heard the love in his voice, the pride. It was as clear as the nose on his face.

'You know what? That fuckin' bird was still hangin' about the place two years later.' Couldn't fly and never looked right, but it lived.'

'That's remarkable.'

'No, that's Katie,' Frank said. 'Why d'you think she wanted to be a nurse? She's a healer, always has been. She doesn't take life, she gives it. That's why she works with them oldies. She thinks she can help them live out their lives with dignity. And I don't care what no fuck says, I don't believe Katie shot no one.'

John didn't say anything. There was no point. Blood aside, Frank Todd was Katie Jones's father and she was his little girl. He wouldn't believe anything bad about her.

'Frank?'

'What?'

'The day you had the fight in the social club? With the moustached guy?'

'What about it?

'Who was he?'

Frank took a packet of cigarettes from the dashboard. He offered them to John and put one between his lips. 'He said he was a detective, like you.'

'A private detective?'

Frank nodded. 'Cheeky fuck he was too. Start giving me gyp about my son, asked all sorts of questions about Katie, about whether she ever suffered from depression and some other shit like that, so I popped him one.'

'He was asking about her mental health?'

'Yeah, and was there any family diseases and some weird shit like that. I never heard the fuckin' like of it. I said to him, "Here, even me priest don't ask them questions."'

John frowned. 'He say why he wanted to know?'

'Some job Katie'd applied for, but I knew that was a load of shit. Katie had a job she liked. She wasn't thinkin' of changin' nothin'. And after that he had a few problems talkin' around my fist.'

34

Sarah pulled up outside Helen's home. It was an old house, early Victorian, with bay windows and set in mature gardens. Paul had bought it twelve years previously and gutted it. Now it was Victorian on the outside, high tech within. Despite the grandeur, it was the most soulless house Sarah had ever seen. It suited Paul down to the ground.

'Okay, Mum, we're here.'

Deirdre was staring fearfully at the imposing front door. 'Sarah, I—'

'I'll get your bag.' Sarah climbed out and closed the door. She could feel Belinda's eyes on her as she moved to the boot. Her head pounded.

They rang the doorbell and Mrs Higgins, Helen's housekeeper, came out to greet them. She was about two hundred years old and a terrible housekeeper. Sarah had never understood why Helen kept her on. Jackie had said that the one time Paul had brought up the subject of letting Mrs Higgins go, Helen had pitched a blue fit and the matter had been dropped.

It was odd because Helen – as Jackie had said over a glass of wine – was not one for sentimentality.

'Hello,' Sarah said. 'Did Helen tell you we were coming?'

'She did, she did. Come on in now.' She leaned in closer – Sarah could smell Oil of Olay and face powder. 'How's your mammy doing?'

'Oh, she's fine.'

'It'll be nice having her for a few days. She was always such good company.'

'Yes.'

'I took the sheets out.'

'Don't worry, Mrs Higgins. I'll make up a bed.'

'Will she have a spot of lunch, do you think?'

Sarah smiled tightly. These days, many people expected her to talk for her mother as though Deirdre no longer had a voice of her own.

'Why don't you ask her, Mrs Higgins?' she said, with more force than she had intended, 'and I'll go make up her room.'

Sarah hurried up the stairs to the second floor. There were three bedrooms here and two bathrooms. Helen and Paul's bedroom occupied almost all of the upper floor. It was a waste of space, Sarah thought, and wondered, not for the first time, why Helen and Paul had no children yet.

She opened the door to a guest bedroom and began to make her mother's bed. She was putting on the sheets when her mobile rang.

'You can move her all you like. It don't matter.'

All the strength left Sarah's body. She sat down heavily on the bed. 'I knew it was you.'

'Well, you're a clever girl, ain't you? I always said that.'

'What do you want?'

'Me? I want what all men want. A job, a life, a nice-looking woman, family, kids, white fences—'

'What do you want, Vic?'

'I wouldn't mind the last three years of my life back.'

'Well, that's not likely to happen, is it?'

'Guess not. So, failing that, I'll have my woman back.'

'I'm not your woman.'

'I beg to differ.'

'It's over.'

'You don't get to decide that.'

'Leave me alone, Vic.'

'You shouldn't have fucked with me, Sarah. You shouldn't have done what you did. I know it was you, you fucking cunt. You set me up.'

'You left me no choice.'

'*Choice*? What's fucking choice got to do with anything?'

Sarah said nothing.

'We need to talk.'

'I don't want to see you.'

'Meet me tonight.'

'No.'

'I ain't asking,' Vic said softly. 'Make sure that fucking dog's locked away too. I see it I'll kill it, and what would your boyfriend say then?'

'I don't have a boyfriend.'

'Shame he's away. I was really looking forward to meeting him.'

'I told you, I don't have a boyfriend. And I'm not going to see you.'

'Do you know how easy it was to edge your sister off the road?' Vic said, and now there was no trace of humanity in his voice. It was cold, unemotional, the way it used to get back in the days when they dated. Despite her best efforts, Sarah was shaking. She closed her eyes and fought it.

'Bump and she was gone. It was easy. Now I want you to imagine what I could do to your mother. Be doin' her a favour – old bag's already half gone, ain't she?'

The hair rose on Sarah's arms, but she forced herself to remain calm. He was trying to upset her. He wanted to hear her cry. That was how he operated. He liked to play with his victims first, break them.

'Vic, if you come near me or my family, I will kill you, do you hear me? I will kill you.'

'Bitch, you couldn't—'

Sarah hung up. When the phone rang again, she flung it across the room. It hit the wall opposite and smashed into little pieces.

She stood up and finished making the bed on auto-pilot. She was thinking. Vic was just crazy enough to turn up at the house, he really was.

But as she straightened the pillows, she was thinking maybe she should let him.

She ran downstairs and made sure her mother was comfortable in front of the television, then went to say goodbye to Mrs Higgins, who was making tea and sandwiches in the kitchen.

She met Belinda in the hall.

'Are you off, then?' Belinda asked.

'Yes.'

'When will you be back?'

'I don't know yet.'

Belinda nodded, but her eyes didn't leave Sarah's face.

'Belinda, be careful,' Sarah said. 'Please make sure Mum doesn't go anywhere alone.'

'Of course.'

'And make sure you know who's at the door and stuff. The city's full of weirdos.'

Belinda patted Sarah's hand. 'I'll take good care of her. You mind yourself, girl.'

'Will do.' Sarah zipped up her jacket, went out and got into her car. She took off, scattering pale gravel across the lawn.

35

Willie Staunton parked the Toyota in the garage and climbed out. He stretched his back and cracked his neck. He was tired after the drive. He had spent most of the early afternoon in Dundalk. Now, he was glad to be back. He wanted to go home and take a nap, then get ready for the night's action. But first, a little preparation.

He opened the boot and took out a plastic container. He walked with it to the pump and filled it with four litres of petrol. Satisfied, he closed the lid and put it back into the car.

He bought coffee, two doughnuts and a newspaper, and paid for the lot with cash. On his way home, he made a phone call, establishing his alibi for the night. Just to be on the safe side he made a second call, confirming the first. When 'Gay Bar' came on the radio, he banged his hand on the steering wheel in time to the music, his spirits lifting.

Oh, yes, he was ready.

Sarah drove across town, her head spinning. She dropped in at the house and picked up her replacement mobile. She had been stupid to break her phone – she should have just turned it off. She slipped her SIM card into it and left the shattered remains of the other on the kitchen table.

Sumo barked at her from the garden. Sarah took a packet of rashers from the fridge, opened it and tossed them to him. 'Hey, Sumo. You're going to have to stay here for a while.'

She walked past him and opened the shed. Inside she saw the collection of junk accumulated over the years: a decent petrol lawnmower and the collection of tools, some rusted, some perfect. She lifted the hammer, slipped it into the crook of her arm, then tried the hoe – too awkward. Instead, she took the rusty sickle from its hook and kicked the door shut.

'Sumo, I'm relying on you to keep an eye on the place until I get back. Anyone comes near, you have my permission to eat them.' She patted him, went back inside and put all the tools into the cupboard by the back door. She ran upstairs and grabbed a can of hairspray and a lighter too, just to be on the safe side. If he came for her, he'd be sorry. She wasn't the person she had once been.

God! she laughed. Who was she trying to kid? She was so frightened she could scarcely see straight. Did she really think she was going to take on Vic with a can of hairspray and some old gardening tools? She should have taken Sid's advice and run. But to where? And for how long? She might as well be dead.

And then there was Jackie. She had unleashed this man on her family. Helen was right, she was a walking fucking disaster.

'*Get a grip*!' she admonished herself. She dashed away the tears that had started to flow, furious with herself. There was no time for that. She had to get moving. If she was moving, she was safe.

She was sure she hadn't been followed, but he didn't need to follow her. He already knew where she lived, and her phone number and God knew what else.

First, she had to see Jackie. And what was it John had asked her to do? See the dead doctor's sister. She'd have to go to the office for the address. Sarah took a deep breath, picked up her car keys and set off.

As she stood over her sister's hospital bed, Sarah felt her heart might break. Jackie looked ghastly. Her normally rosy skin was yellowish.

Her right arm was plastered from fingers to shoulder and a drip was connected to her left hand. The nurses or Helen had done a bit of a clean-up job, but dried blood was still encrusted in her hair and round her nostril. The right side of her face was battered and she had eight stitches over her right eyebrow.

'Hey, darling.' Sarah sank into the chair at the head of the bed and brushed a lock of hair from her sister's forehead. 'Jackie? Can you hear me?'

Jackie opened her eyes, licked her chapped lips and moaned.

'I know you're thirsty, love, but the nurse says you can't have any water yet.' Sarah held up a plastic cup. 'But I've got some ice here. Do you want a piece?'

Jackie rolled her head and closed her eyes again.

'She's pretty out of it.'

Sarah turned. Barry stood behind her.

'The anaesthetic's knocked her for six,' he said. 'She's probably going to sleep right through.'

'They put the plate in?'

'They had to. The break's not clean. The surgeon said it was sort of spiralled.'

'Jesus.'

Barry picked up the bag at his feet, and Sarah noticed he was carrying water and yellow tulips. 'Where did you get those this time of year?'

'Let's just say it wasn't easy.' He took a vase from the bag and filled it with the water, put the flowers into it and fluffed them out. 'I wanted her to see them when she woke up. They're her favourite, you know.' He leaned across and kissed Jackie's stitches. 'I'm here, Jackie.'

Sarah watched him take her sister's left hand and caress it between his own. Suddenly, she knew what Jackie saw in this odd, effeminate little man.

He loved her. Now, she felt as if she was intruding. 'Will you tell her I was here?'

'You're leaving?'

'I really have to go.'

'Of course I will.'

'Thank you, Barry.'

Sarah slipped away, feeling more depressed than ever. She missed John. She took out her phone and began to dial his number.

No. She slipped the phone back into her pocket. If she called him, he'd come. And she wasn't about to place another person she loved in danger.

She parked on double yellow lines and galloped up the stairs to the office. She found the name she needed in the file and made the call.

Initially, Yvonne Hogan sounded hostile, but eventually she agreed to see Sarah that evening.

She was about to jump into the car when she felt a tap on her shoulder. 'Sarah Kenny!' She turned around and got a smack in the face. 'You're a fucking bitch!' said a chubby, red-faced woman.

Sarah fell back against the car. She raised a hand to protect her face and her attacker advanced on her. 'Bitch! You've ruined me!'

Sarah ducked another shot, but had no room to move. Caught off balance, she had no choice but to brace herself against the car, cover her head with her arms and kick out at her assailant, with her bad leg.

She connected with the woman's belly, knocking her backwards onto the pavement. She stared down at her assailant, who was clutching her stomach as though she'd been shot. She glared at Sarah. 'You kicked me.'

'Who the hell are you?'

'As if you don't know!'

Another set of hands reached for her. This time, Sarah didn't wait to be struck. She lashed out with her elbow, connecting solidly with something behind her.

'Ow!' Rodney Mitchell coughed and clutched at his chest. 'Sarah? Jesus, are you all right?'

'Oh, Rodney, I'm so sorry.'

'I shouldn't have sneaked up on you like that.'

If John had been there, he would have indulged in a fit of eye-rolling. Rodney Mitchell was so desperately in love with Sarah he would have found good reason for her to dance on his head in a pair of six-inch heels.

'Everything all right?' he asked.

Sarah pointed at the woman on the ground. 'She attacked me – hit me in the face.'

'I saw her from across the street.'

'You deserve it, you snotty cow. Where do you get off destroying marriages? You're heartless – heartless!'

She tried to scramble to her feet, but Sarah kicked her leg out from under her. A bemused crowd was gathering around them. 'If you hit me again, I'll have you arrested.' Sarah warned.

'You fucking *homewrecker*!'

'Homewrecker?

'Don't come the innocent with me!'

'I don't even know who you are.' But something about her did look a little familiar.

'You do! You know my husband, Geoff.'

Sarah was bewildered. 'Who?'

'Pervert!' the woman screeched.

'Er, maybe we should go inside,' Rodney said softly.

'Twenty years we've been married! Twenty years – until you came along. Now it's over!'

A few of the crowd glanced Sarah's way. A woman Sarah recognised from the bookie's screwed up her nose in moral condemnation.

'And I love him.' The woman burst into ugly sobs. 'I love my Geoff so much.'

Suddenly, Sarah remembered. 'Oh my God, you must be Carmel Granger!' She began to laugh and couldn't stop.

Some of the crowd were muttering, but that made her laugh all the more.

'It's not funny!' wailed Carmel.

'You hussy,' an old lady with a trolley said to Sarah angrily. 'Carrying on with another woman's husband. Have you no shame?'

'Sarah, are you all right?' Rodney was looking a little alarmed now.

'Ooh-hoo,' Sarah said, trying to catch her breath.

'Disgusting,' said another.

'Hoo.' Sarah wiped her eyes. She glanced at Rodney, who evidently thought she'd lost her mind. 'Oh, Jesus, I'm all right – honestly.' She held out her hand to the woman on the ground.

Carmel Granger looked at it suspiciously.

'Do you want a hand up or not?' Sarah said.

'Not from you I don't.' Carmel smacked her hand away and scrambled to her feet in such an ungainly fashion that Sarah began to laugh again.

'It's no laughing matter,' Carmel said. 'You've destroyed my life.'

'No, I didn't. *You* did,' Sarah said, serious now. 'You were cheating on your husband and he's kicked you out, right?'

The crowd turned confusedly to Carmel. Was *she* the bad one?

'It was no one's *business*.'

'Wrong. It was his business, and then it became our business when he hired us.'

'What am I going to do? I love him!'

'So tell him.' Sarah tested her cheek with her fingertips. No blood, but it stung. And no wonder! Carmel had arms like two sides of beef.

'I'm going to sue you!'

'For what?'

'Defamation of character and … slander.'

'For *slander*?' That made Sarah laugh again.

Suddenly – inexplicably – she felt a load lift off her shoulders. She didn't know why, but it did. 'Spare me the theatrics. You think this is some kind of soap opera? You can't go around bashing people about the place. Get the hell out of here before I have you arrested for assault.'

'You kicked me!'

'In self-defence and don't bother denying it, I've got witnesses.' Sarah waved at the crowd. 'Rodney, I'm sorry I whacked you. I'll catch you later.'

'Are you sure you're okay? Your cheek's bright red.'

'Rodney,' Sarah said, 'I've been having a rough day, but sometimes you need a sense of perspective slapped into you.' She kissed Rodney Mitchell's cheek, got into John's car and drove away, leaving the bemused crowd, the wailing woman and the love-struck solicitor in her wake.

36

The sun was low in the sky when John and Frank reached their final destination – a run-down-looking cul-de-sac deep in London's East End.

Frank pulled into a litter-strewn alley and killed the engine. He jerked his head at a set of filthy windows set high in a brick wall. There was a dull glow behind the grimy glass. 'Door over in the alcove leads into his storeroom, and his office is upstairs.'

'What if he's not there?'

'He's always there.'

'Don't you think Lizzie will have called him to warn him we're coming?'

'Not if she knows what's good for her,' Frank said. 'Don't make any difference if she did or not. He's not going anywhere. This is his lair.'

'Who is this guy?'

'He's a fucking slimeball, that's what he is, a nonce.'

'Really?'

'Rumoured to be.'

'Can't always buy into rumours, Frank. Least, that's what my partner would say.'

'You partner sounds about as smart as you.'

'Smarter, I'd say, but I could be wrong. She's definitely not as pretty.'

'I warned you not to come the smart arse with me, kid. I'm pretty fuckin' sick of people today.'

John stroked his jaw. 'Yeah, I kind of got that.'

'I said I was sorry.'

'That's sweet, but it doesn't make it hurt less.'

Frank sighed and lit another cigarette. Now that he was there, he seemed reluctant to get out of the van. Despite his quick fists and general crankiness, John got the feeling there was a lot to like in Frank Todd.

'Sadie always wanted kids, you know,' Frank said. 'It was like a passion with her. It was all she talked about, the day we'd have kids, what they'd look like, what she was gonna do with 'em. She had it all planned out. The first miscarriage almost broke her. She cried for weeks afterwards. But not after the second. Ain't that strange?'

John said nothing. He thought Frank wasn't really expecting an answer to that one.

'After the third, she just stopped talking about them – kids, I mean. It was like she threw a switch. Stopped going over to 'er sister's house and stopped draggin' me to christenings and birthday parties.' Frank took a drag of his cigarette and blew twin jets of smoke out of his nostrils. 'First I thought she'd come round and we'd keep tryin', but no. She said she didn't want to go through it again, lose another.'

'Sure, I understand.'

'But it was like watching her wither up and die. I mean, she was still my Sadie and I loved her, but she was only partly the woman I'd married, the woman I loved. I know this is going to sound weird, but I swear she was wasting away.' He ran a hand over his brow. 'I'm not explaining this very well.'

'I get it.'

'I was scared she might do something. I couldn't watch her every minute. I'd see her looking at kids when we was out shopping, the pain in her eyes – she never spoke about it, mind. But ... I couldn't let it happen. Not to her. She didn't deserve it.'

'I know you loved your wife, Frank.' John looked away. 'But Charlotte Jones didn't deserve what happened to her either.'

'You're right. Sadie would never have forgiven herself if she'd known. She'd never have forgiven *me*.'

'You saying you knew something was wrong?'

'No, but I didn't want to know either.' Frank smoked for a moment. 'This woman, Katie's birth mother, what's she like? She nice?'

'From what I know of her. Her daughter looks just like her.'

Frank ignored the jibe. 'Will you tell her I'm sorry?'

'Not sure she'd be interested in your apology.'

Frank took that in and digested it. 'No, I don't suppose she would be.'

'Why do you think Katie was avoiding you recently?'

'I don't know.'

'You must have some idea. Do you think she discovered you weren't her biological father?'

'I don't see how she could have.'

'But you said yourself, a man was asking questions about her.'

'The guy with the 'tache?'

'Yeah, him. I was at the nursing home and they told me a man fitting that description had been there, and that Katie had spoken to him.'

'Huh,' Frank said.

'He give you a name or anything?'

Frank sat back and dug out his wallet. He opened it and pulled out a dog-eared card. 'Here.'

John took it. It was a cheap card, the kind people printed in a booth in a shopping centre. Exactly the sort John carried, in fact. There was a name on it, Harry D'Angelo, and a phone number.

'Harry D'Angelo?' John raised an eyebrow.

'Yeah, that's what I thought,' Frank said.

'You try calling him?'

'A few times. It goes straight to a machine.'

'Can I keep it?'

'Sure.'

John put the card into his wallet. He jerked his thumb towards the light. 'This guy, he dangerous?'

'He's not a puppy – he's got teeth.'

'We've got to be careful then.'

'You worried about your skin?'

'Sure. It covers my body.'

Frank ground out his cigarette in the ashtray. 'Come on, smart arse, let's go.'

They climbed out of the cab and John wrapped his scarf around his neck. The temperature had dropped and now it was near freezing.

They walked across the cobbled street and towards a set of wooden double doors set in an alcove. They stood ajar. Frank grabbed the left one, which shuddered back on greasy tracks.

'What is this place?' John asked as they stepped into a dark space.

'It's a textile warehouse. The Greek imports cheap fabric and sells it to them stuck-up interior designers at a two hundred per cent mark-up.'

'Nice.'

'He could sell fleas to a dog.'

'You don't say.' John waited for his eyes to grow accustomed to the gloom. 'He always leave his doors unlocked?'

'No. There's usually a guy here, Carl.'

They stood still and listened.

'I don't hear anything,' John said after a minute.

'Me neither.' Now Frank's voice had a trace of something else in it. 'Come on.'

'No punching. We're here to talk to him, right?'

'Sure.' Frank picked up a long wooden spool and tilted his head towards a set of wooden steps behind John.

'Frank—'

'Come on.'

Something was off, John could sense it, but he followed Frank all the same.

They climbed the stairs, Frank leading the way, and reached a landing, then saw light under the Greek's door. A shadow moved across it.

'Bastard's here all right,' Frank said, speeding up.

John's spine tingled. There was a funny smell in the air, something foul and sweet. He climbed the last step and made his way down the corridor.

Frank grasped the office door handle at the same moment as John noticed a pair of legs sticking out from under a trestle table on the factory floor. 'Frank, wait—'

'Knock fucking knock, Kastrinakis.' Frank pushed open the door.

That was as far as he had got when someone charged him, flicked out a hand and struck him a blow to the chest. Frank was caught unawares. He grunted and tumbled backwards, landing awkwardly.

The man, wearing a black balaclava and black clothing, jumped over him and skidded to a halt when he saw John.

John found himself looking into the deadest pair of eyes he had ever seen. They were amber, like a cat. He held out his hands in front of him, wishing to God he had one of the spools Frank had been smart enough to take, even if it hadn't done him a lick of good. 'Whoa there, fella. No need to—'

The man tightened a strap round his waist and, without a word, leaped up and kicked John in the chest.

John fell backwards as the man put two hands on the railing and vaulted over it, landing almost soundlessly on the factory floor. By the time John had recovered from the shock and looked over, he was running out the door.

'Fuck it,' John wheezed – the blow had knocked the breath out of him. He considered giving chase, then thought better of it. His gammy leg wasn't up to it. 'Man, what the fuck was that?' He walked back to Frank, wondering why he was still down. 'You okay?'

'I don't think so,' Frank said.

Something in his voice made John's heart quicken. 'Frank?' That was when he saw the hilt of the blade jutting from Frank's armpit and the stain spreading rapidly down from it.

'What the …?' John dropped to his knees.

'He got me.'

'Ah, Jesus. Don't move, I'm going to call for an ambulance and—'

Frank shook his head. A bubble of blood stood at the corner of his mouth. 'Tell … Katie … I'm sorry.'

'You can tell her yourself.'

'Lizzie …'

'Frank, man, hold on now,' John said, fumbling for his mobile. He got it out and dialled 999. 'Where are we?'

'Spitalfields,' Frank whispered, as more blood covered his lips and chin. He closed his eyes.

John realised he must have been hit in the lungs for the blood to be foaming like that.

An operator was on the line.

'Hello? I need an ambulance … What? … No, an ambulance. I'm in Spitalfields … What? … I don't know – I don't fucking know where I am. Hold on.' John stood up and turned in a circle. Where were they? 'Hold on.'

He ran into the office to look for headed paper – anything. There was a desk, all right, and a chair, and in that chair sat an obese man. John stared into his huge black eyes. The man's head had been pulled back and his throat cut from ear to ear.

'Oh Jesus …' John said. There was blood all over the man's chest, on the desk and splattered over the lamp that stood on it.

John could hear the operator calling from a distance.

An address.

He edged closer to the desk and saw a selection of opened, blood-splattered mail. He eased an envelope towards him, grimacing, and glanced at the address on the front. The mill. This was the mill. Perfect.

John read it out to the operator and hung up without leaving his name.

He raced back to Frank. The older man was in a crumpled heap. He was very pale and when John pressed his fingers to his throat the pulse was weak and thready. 'Ah, shit, Frank, try to hold on – please.'

'Lizzie, she's …' Frank whispered, so softly that John could hardly hear him.

'She's what?'

Frank nodded and, with a supreme effort, spat, 'She …' He coughed and more blood bubbled over his lips.

'Never mind, don't worry and don't talk any more. Try to relax. There's an ambulance on its way and—'

Frank smiled. Then his eyelids fluttered once, twice. He sighed, and was gone.

'Frank?' John placed his hand against Frank's chest. Nothing.

He bowed his head. 'Dammit!' He punched the wall over Frank's head so hard that pieces of chipboard flew everywhere, then looked at his hands. His knuckles were shredded and bleeding. The pain was a welcome relief from the impotent rage he felt.

37

Sarah sat on a hard-backed chair and took another sip of tea. She tried hard not to pull a face. It was disgusting, weak and watery, but she drank it anyway.

Yvonne Hogan lived in a small cottage in Blackrock, a stone's throw from the coast. It was the sort of house Sarah normally adored, small and charming on the outside. As soon as she set foot inside, she changed her mind. The rooms were dark and stuffed full of furniture and it was cloyingly hot. Even though Sarah had already stripped off her coat, scarf and jumper, she was sweating.

In contrast, Yvonne Hogan was rubbing her hands as though she was frozen. She was a tall, hard-faced woman of fifty, prematurely grey and so thin Sarah wondered how she found the strength to stand, let alone pace and gesticulate as she was doing right now.

'It's hard, you know, so hard without him,' she said, sniffing loudly. She spun on her heel and reached up to the bookshelves on the right of the chimney breast. She pulled out a blue leather-bound photo album and sat on the chair next to Sarah. She opened it and turned the pages. Her hands rested on a recent photo of her and her brother taken outside a bar somewhere. 'We were so close. He was all I had.'

'I'm very sorry for your loss, Miss Hogan.' Sarah put down her cup and saucer on a doily-covered table. 'Dr Hogan was retired?'

'Yes.'

'If you don't mind my saying so, he was very young to have retired.'

'He was not well.' Irritation showed in Yvonne's face. 'He had been very sick lately.'

'Oh, I didn't know.'

'Well, why should you?' She looked back at the photo. 'He took early retirement last year. He wanted to travel, see a bit of the world. That's what makes this so tragic. He had such plans. We were going to take a trip to Venice later this year, then go on to Rome.'

'Rome?'

'Oh, yes. My brother was a spiritual man, especially in his last few years. He very much wanted to see the Vatican and the Holy Father.'

'Sounds lovely.'

'It would have been. It was very important to him. Then that *woman* robbed him of it. I don't know why you're working for her.'

'Not her, her brother.'

'Huh! Well I had a brother, and look what she did to him. Walter was a saint, an absolute gentleman – you can ask anyone. He never harmed a fly, dedicated his whole life to looking after others. Shot down in his own home. It's not right.'

'No, it's not.'

'He had a calling.' She pursed her lips, turned another page and pointed to a black and white shot of the Hogan family standing outside the cottage. 'My parents paid for him to go to medical school. My father was a bookmaker. Walter was the first medical man in the family.'

She said this with pride, but Sarah saw her eyes flicker. College fees would have been a struggle, even for a bookmaker. She wondered how far Yvonne Hogan's parents had sacrificed their daughter's dreams to bolster their son's. 'Was your brother always a GP?'

'Oh, yes. He had the practice in Howth for many years. He joined old Dr Pierce straight out of college and when Pierce retired back in 1978, Walter took over.'

Jesus, Sarah thought. Katie Jones had really picked a squeaky clean victim. 'Did your brother ever work for any charities or foundations?'

'Why do you ask that?'

'I'm trying to get some idea *why* Katie Jones shot your brother. There's no evidence to show she knew him.'

'She's mad, that's why.'

'You know,' Sarah leaned in a little closer, 'I think it was a case of mistaken identity.'

This was clearly the line Yvonne had been waiting to hear. She beamed at Sarah. 'I was saying that to Ellen Spencer – she owns the local shop – the other day. Honestly, you should hear the way they've been talking round here. You'd swear it was Walter who'd shot that girl. People have minds like gutters.'

'Indeed they do.' Sarah thought that Yvonne herself wouldn't be too shy about a bit of gossip if the occasion arose. 'So I'm really trying to backtrack over your brother's life, find something that might have caused Katie Jones to seek him out and attack him.'

'There was something.' Yvonne rolled a bony shoulder and closed the album. She tapped her index finger on the spine. 'Years ago, maybe. I seem to remember him talking about being involved in something or other.'

A dribble of sweat ran down the back of Sarah's neck. 'Do you remember what it was?'

'Some private organisation, a charity.'

Sarah waited. The seconds ticked by.

'I believe they paid for vaccines and other things. For the *poor*.'

Sarah noticed she said 'poor' in the same way that John said 'non-alcoholic beer'.

'That was very charitable of him. Do you remember what the organisation was called?'

'Oh,' Yvonne raised a hand to her mouth, 'it was so long ago now …'

Sarah smiled patiently. She considered taking another sip of tea but couldn't face it, politeness or not. 'I'm sure it's probably got nothing to do with anything, but at this point in my investigation I need to check everything.'

'Well, I don't see what Walter's charity work would have to do with this girl.'

'Me neither, but it's better to be sure.'

'The Cradle Foundation – that's what it was called. I don't know if it even exists any more. My brother volunteered his time for them, immunising babies and providing care for unmarried mothers, and so on.'

Sarah took out her notebook and wrote this down.

'Poor Walter. He was a saint,' Yvonne continued.

Sarah put on another patient smile. Inside she felt like screaming.

'I'll see if I can find a particular notebook. One moment, please.' She stood up and left the room.

Sarah undid an extra button on her shirt and fanned her neck. The heat had almost wiped her out. How could anyone live like this? And it must cost a fortune. She tipped the rest of her tea into the plant wilting on the table beside her and put the cup back on the saucer. She checked her watch. Twenty to five.

She wondered where Vic was.

Bothered and impatient, she picked up the album and began to flick through it. Her eyes skipped over the photos, black and white, sepia-tinted … She smiled at some of the hairstyles and fashions. God, the sixties and seventies were something else altogether. Flares, synthetic polo necks, wide lapels, cord jackets, big hair, bigger moustaches, crazy patterned jumpers. Crazy everything.

She flipped along.

Yvonne and Walter outside the house, Yvonne and Walter eating ice cream on Bray Front. Walter and a friend sitting on scooters, Yvonne smiling shyly at a young man with slicked-back hair wearing a Crombie jacket.

It was funny to see people age year by year, Sarah thought, remembering the photo albums in her own home. She flicked the page – and frowned.

The photo was tattered and faded. In it, Yvonne and Walter sat on a low wall outside a shop. Another couple were sitting on the ground below them. The boy was dark-haired and could only have been in his twenties; the moustache he had grown did little to age him. The woman seemed older. She was small, red-haired and sly-looking. She was eating ice cream that was dripping onto her hand. But it was not the people Sarah was interested in, it was the car to the forefront of the picture.

It was blue. It looked sporty. It had go-fast stripes on the wing. She breathed out slowly.

'Now, I can't find the little box I used to have,' Yvonne said coming back into the room. 'But I did find this old diary and I'm nearly certain I wrote something about it at the time...'

'Miss Hogan,' Sarah proffered the album, 'where was this taken?'

Yvonne peered at the photo. 'I'm nearly sure that's Greystones. We used to holiday there with our parents when we were children. My mother was from there, you see, and she took over the house when her father died. That picture was taken ... let me see ... 1980. I know because I had that awful perm and it was hot and the heat made my hair frizzy.'

'Are these your friends?'

'Yes – well, no. She was a friend of Walter's. They'd been at college together. She was a student doctor.'

'And the man?'

'I don't remember his name. I think he was her boyfriend – oh, what was he called? Something unusual. Foreign ... my memory, these days. He was a lovely man too, the complete opposite of her, very shy. Hardly spoke a word, poor thing. I think he was half afraid to open his mouth around Elizabeth – very bossy, she was. You should have heard the way she spoke to him.'

'That's a lovely car.'

'Oh yes, Nico's rocket! After Niki Lauda! How funny, I'd forgotten all about that.'

'Niki who?'

'Lauda, he was a racing driver. Oh, Walter loved cars, and that was his name for Nico's car.'

'What kind of car is that?'

'An Alpine. Nico let Walter drive it once and it was all he could talk about for weeks after.'

'Nico.' Sarah said the word carefully. 'And where are they now?'

'I have no idea,' Yvonne said, a note of suspicion in her voice. 'Why are you asking about them anyway? What have they got to do with that murderer?'

'Nothing,' Sarah said. 'I was just curious.'

Yvonne took the album from her and closed it. She put it back up on the shelf. 'Well, if you don't mind, I've really got to get ready for evening mass, so—'

A phone rang in the hall. Yvonne jumped slightly. She was clearly not used to getting calls. 'Will you excuse me for a second?' She hurried out of the room. As soon as she was gone, Sarah was up in a flash. She grabbed the album, opened it and removed the photo from under the plastic sheeting. She slipped the album back and flung herself into her chair barely seconds before Yvonne Hogan returned.

'Those marketing companies! So annoying and rude. Imagine calling at this hour of the evening.'

'We get them all the time too. Very irritating.'

Yvonne tightened her cardigan and looked at Sarah expectantly.

Sarah took the hint. 'Thank you very much for your time.'

38

John sat in the interview room, head bowed, hands hanging between his legs. There was blood on his jeans as well as oil now, and whatever else he had picked up during the day. He didn't mind that, but his hands bothered him. He had washed and dried them five times, yet he thought he could still detect traces of Frank's blood under his nails.

He tried not to think of Frank. Despite his past actions and even the wallop to the jaw, John had liked the man. He hadn't deserved to die like that.

He was exhausted. He was thirsty, he was filthy – God, he stank – he wanted to book into a hotel somewhere, take a long hot shower and maybe even a nap. He took out his mobile and tried Sarah's number, but there was no signal in the police station.

He glanced at his watch. It was ten past six. He wasn't under arrest, but he wasn't free to go either. He had been there for more than two hours already: he had given and revised his statement twice. He had handed over his card, his driving licence and his passport as proof of identity and yet they still weren't satisfied. Finally, he had had no choice but to give Sergeant Steve Magher as a referee. He watched one cop go through his sports bag, then waited patiently while another contacted Steve. In desperation, he had even offered to take a lie-detector test, but that hadn't been necessary, although it did make the sergeant, one Marcus Dell, call him a smart arse.

He had answered as many of their questions as he had felt comfortable with while still protecting his client's privacy. All the cops could get out of him was that Frank had called him in to investigate his daughter's disappearance and that he had wanted to talk to the Greek. He thought Frank wouldn't mind – might even have appreciated the bend in the truth.

The cops knew he wasn't giving them everything – they had told him so more than once. It had maddened the two officers who had interviewed him and John guessed that was why he was still there.

He hadn't mentioned Lizzie. He wanted to make sure he got to talk to her before anyone else did. Of course, he still had to find her.

No first he wanted to talk to Harry D'Angelo, and he needed to talk to Drake again.

John sighed and closed his eyes. Something was going on and his weary mind was not making much sense of it. If the Greek had been involved with Lizzie in Katie's kidnapping, why was he dead? Who had killed him? Why had the man in black killed Frank and not him? One of the cops seemed to be of the opinion that it had been a robbery gone wrong, but neither John nor Dell had bought that.

He thought of those eyes again, how they had looked at him with no trace of fear, no emotion. Chilling, to say the least.

And Lizzie – who was she? Was she behind it or was she dead now too? Where did Walter Hogan fit into this? What about Katie? Why were all these people dying? What the *hell* was going on?

He rubbed his hands over his head and opened his eyes. He noticed the shadow of an officer's feet outside the door and began to whistle softly. If there was one thing he had learned over the years about dealing with cops, it was not to let on that he was bothered. Once they saw you were, they just went on turning the screw.

It worked.

Half an hour later he was on the street with a flea in his ear and a headache.

He needed to find a hotel. He didn't really fancy traipsing back across town to the fleapit. He stopped a cab and told the driver to bring him to the nearest hotel. The cabbie looked him up and down, plainly unimpressed by what he was seeing. 'You sure, mate?'

'Yes.'

'There's one on Canary Wharf, that do ya?'

'Is it nice?'

'Very. Load of footballers and their missuses stay there.'

'Expensive then.'

'You'd better believe it.'

Fuck it. It was only one night. Sam Jones would be picking up the tab, and John felt he deserved it.

'Make it so, number one. Warp speed.'

The cabbie rolled his eyes and pulled away from the kerb.

John dialled Sarah's number. She answered on the second ring. 'QuicK Investigations.'

'It's me.'

'John! I've been trying to reach you. Didn't we talk about the phone thing?'

'I tried to call but there was no signal in the cop shop.'

He waited for her to be shocked and was disappointed when she wasn't. 'I heard.'

'From who?'

'Steve Magher called. He was worried. Are you all right?'

John felt as if he hadn't slept for days and his stomach felt as if his throat had gone on strike. 'I wouldn't say all right, but I'm still breathing.'

'What's happened?'

He explained exactly what had gone on, noticing that the cabbie had switched his radio right down and was listening intently. Well, why the hell wouldn't he be interested? John thought. I'm a walking soap opera.

'Okay,' Sarah said when he'd finished talking, 'some of this is starting to make sense.'

'Is it?'

'I went to see Walter Hogan's sister today and she was telling me all about her brother and his *good friend* Elizabeth Sheldon.'

John sat forward, his tiredness forgotten for a moment. 'Did you say Elizabeth?'

'Yes.'

'Frank mentioned someone called Lizzie. It could be the same woman.'

'Has to be. She was in Greystones in 1980 with some foreign guy. Yvonne Hogan wasn't sure but she thought they might have been boyfriend and girlfriend and, get this, they were driving a sporty car.'

'She remember the foreign guy's name?'

'Nico.'

'The Greek.'

'When you get to the hotel, text me its fax number and I'll send the photo from here. You can see it for yourself.'

'Great, thanks.' Suddenly John wanted nothing more than to be sitting at his desk across from her. He knew from her voice that she was on the hunt. She probably had her hair tied back, a pen over her ear, her brow knitted in concentration. He imagined her tapping her finger as she read.

God, he missed her.

'Did Yvonne Hogan remember what type of car Nico drove?'

'An Alpine.'

'Renault – and pretty nippy,' John replied. 'Not exactly common in Ireland back then.'

'So, what have this Elizabeth Sheldon and Walter Hogan got to do with each other?'

'Yvonne says she was a student doctor, same as her brother.'

'Check the college he attended, see if you can find her.'

'Yes, thank you, John. I *had* thought of that. And I will, first thing in the morning.'

John grinned. 'You think we have them, don't you?'

'We may be getting close. Her, him, the car. That's a lot of coincidences.'

'I thought you didn't believe in coincidences.'

'I don't. But someone had to have helped to get Katie out of the country, and someone created false documentation for those kids. I want to see if this Elizabeth might have been involved in the charity thing Walter was involved with, some group called the Cradle Foundation.'

'Never heard of them.'

'They've disbanded now, but I've traced two of the founders. One is a solicitor, Simon Phelps. He works for the Liffey Project, a charity for the homeless. Of course, the main office is closed now so I'll have to wait until morning to talk to him.'

'It's late, Sarah. Why don't you head home? You must be exhausted too.'

'I'm fine.'

'Who's looking after your mum?'

'She's with Helen. I'm going to stay here a while and see if I can't find some trace of Elizabeth Sheldon or even Walter Hogan. Then I'm thinking of heading to Wicklow to show Bernie Lynch the photo of the car, see if she can get her dad to look at it for me. It could be them, John. I think one or more of the people in that photo had something to do with Katie's kidnapping.'

'Okay, look, I'm going to talk to Drake again, and I'm going to try to raise this guy D'Angelo, see why he was asking questions about Katie. I gotta go now – the cab's pulling in. I'll give you a shout when I check in.'

When she spoke again, her voice was soft. 'Are you sure you're okay, John? It must have been such a shock for you seeing him die like that.'

'It was.'

'Stay safe.'

'I will.'

'Promise?'

'Scout's honour.'

He hung up and began to dig in his pocket for his wallet to pay the cabbie.

'That's some life you got going there, mate,' the cabbie said, eyeing him in the rear-view mirror. 'What do you do for an encore?'

'Naked tap dancing.'

John handed over ten pounds, asked for a receipt and clambered out before he had to answer any more questions. He looked at the liveried doorman, then up at the tasteful sign over the canopy. The Four Seasons Hotel looked inviting, and when the doorman didn't so much as curl a lip at John's – frankly – disgraceful attire, he knew it was going to be the best money Sam Jones had ever spent.

* * *

Forty-five minutes later, he was sitting on his bed, wrapped in the softest bathrobe he had ever worn, eating a club sandwich and staring at the photo Sarah had sent. It wasn't the greatest quality, but it gave him a clear view of Elizabeth Sheldon and Nico. It was hard to say for certain that the man in the photo was the Greek: he wasn't obese, and neither was his throat cut.

John opened his notebook and added their names, looked at the growing list and tried to make sense of what he had learned.

Katie Jones had been kidnapped by the Greek, according to this woman, Lizzie. But if Sarah was right, Lizzie had either been with the Greek or had known all about the kidnapping from the outset. She had procured more than one child and for a hell of a lot of money. There was still Katie's brother, who was in jail. He had to have come from somewhere, and the child of Frank's friend, Milo.

Then there was Harry D'Angelo. Who was he and why was he asking questions? What had driven Katie to Walter Hogan's home? What had made her kill him?

John knew he was close to figuring it out. He could feel it.

He had to find Lizzie and confirm that she was the woman in the photo.

He licked mustard off his fingers and picked up the phone by his bed. He dialled Harry D'Angelo's number. It went to an answering machine, but when John tried to leave a message, an automated voice told him it was full. Clearly, Harry hadn't been picking up his messages of late.

John hung up and stared at his notes again.

Backtrack.

He slid off the bed and padded across the carpet for his mobile. He opened it and dialled Drake's number.

'Hello?'

Damn.

'Yolanda, it's John Quigley.'

'Who?'

John rolled his eyes. 'The detective. I'm looking for your brother.'

'He's not here.'

'Yeah, right.'

'He's not.'

'Will you tell him I called?'

'*Yeah, right.*'

'Look, Yolanda, clearly you're still pissed off about yesterday, but that's too bad. I need to speak to your brother right now. He could be in danger. So could you.'

'What are you talking about? What do you *mean* "in danger"?'

'Something's going on. Katie's adopted father is dead – he was killed earlier this evening, right in front of me. Murdered. I think it's possible whoever killed him might have tried to make contact with Katie and your brother, I don't know – Drake said something about people harassing him. I need to know who they were and a description.'

'He thinks everyone's harassing him. He always has done.'

'This time he may be right.'

Yolanda didn't say anything for a moment. Then she snorted.

'Yolanda, *please*. It could be important.'

'Come over. I'll be here.' She hung up.

'I'm on my way,' John said to the dial tone.

He dug out his one remaining clean T-shirt and, reluctantly, got back into his filthy jeans. He combed his hair with his hands, snatched up his jacket, left his room and made his way out grimly into the cold night.

39

Sarah opened Bernie's gate as a bitter wind blew across the garden, blowing sand into her face. She turned her back against it. She shivered and felt the panic inside her struggle to the surface.

Victor was out there somewhere. He had been following her, watching her movements. He could be watching her right now for all she knew – she certainly wouldn't put it past him. Well, this time, she wasn't going to sit trembling, waiting for the blow. Let him come for her, because he would, no matter what. And sure as shit she wasn't going to make it easy for him.

She turned and walked up the path, stepped into the porch and rang the doorbell, wincing at the explosion of barking in the small house.

The door opened and suddenly the Jack Russells were milling around her feet, sniffing and yapping. It always amazed her that a big dog like Sumo didn't faze her, but ankle-biters did.

'You made it in good time,' Bernie said. 'You must have flown down.'

'The new road's brilliant.'

'Even so,' Bernie winked, 'I hope you didn't get caught on any of them cameras.'

Sarah laughed. 'I doubt it. If I did, I'm probably a blur.'

'Well, come on in. I told Daddy you were on your way to see him. I have to say he's better in the mornings normally, but he's not too bad.'

'I understand. I really appreciate him seeing me.'

Bernie ushered her into the front room, where Bernie's father was sitting by the fire in a big wooden chair. He was a big man, or had been. Now, he was gaunt, his cheeks hollow, his body frail. His hair was freshly washed and looked like cotton wool. He wore blue-checked pyjamas and a navy dressing gown. His chin was covered with white stubble. But it was his eyes that drew Sarah's attention: they were almost as dark as her own and lit with keen intelligence.

'Hello Mr Kelly, I'm Sarah Kenny. How are you this evening?'

'Very good.' His voice was frail.

'Sit down in the other chair,' Bernie said. 'Miggs, get down off that.'

She lifted a large black and white cat out of the chair and set him among the dogs. He swished his tail in annoyance. 'Go on,' she said to Sarah, 'sit in there now by the fire. You must be perished.'

The old man turned his eyes to Sarah and whispered something as she warmed her hands over the fire. She couldn't make out what he was saying.

'Do you mind if I sit here?' she asked.

He shook his head, cleared his throat and tried again. 'Rough old night.'

This time she heard him perfectly. 'Yes, it is. A bit of a gale's blowing up.'

The old man nodded and stared into the fire.

'Can I get you anything? A cup of tea?' Bernie asked, hovering.

'I'd love one,' Sarah said.

'Right so.'

Bernie went out, the dogs and Miggs in her wake. Sarah heard her opening presses, then the rattle of cups and saucers. She reached into her pocket and removed the photo. She didn't know whether to give it to him or not. Maybe she should wait until Bernie came back. However, the old man reached across the space between them and took it gently from her.

He stared at it in silence for some time. His huge gnarled hands shook uncontrollably, and Sarah thought how frustrating it must be to have your body fail you.

'Bernie says you're asking about the girl.'

'That's right.'

'Is it really her in the hospital?'

'Yes. Do you remember her, Mr Kelly?'

'I remember her.' He spoke haltingly. His voice was weak, as though it was reluctant to leave his body and did so only under protest. 'She was blonde, only a little thing.'

'That's right. Her name was Katie.'

'She was ... crying.' He tapped the photo with his index finger. 'The little girl was crying. I told them that. She was crying and this one was angry.'

'The man?'

'He told her to shut up. Very harsh.' He sighed. 'I told the gardaí at the time, but they didn't listen to me. I think they'd made up their minds.'

'Do you remember the woman?'

He looked at the photo again. 'Yes. She looked right at me. She said, "They never want to go home, do they?"'

'You still remember exactly what she said?'

'I remember, all right. Sure, how could you forget?'

He looked into the flames and Sarah saw a haunted expression on his face. This man, this kind man, had probably questioned his action all his life.

'Here you go.' Bernie bustled back in with a tray, bearing three cups and a plate of Jaffa cakes. 'Daddy?' she said, concerned.

He waved a hand feebly.

Bernie looked at Sarah. 'Is it them?'

'I think so.'

'Daddy, are you all right?'

'I need to lie down for a bit.' The old man motioned for Sarah to take back the photo. 'Bernie—'

'All right, Daddy.' Bernie put the tray down and went to him. She wrapped her arms round his chest and lifted him out of the chair.

Sarah stood up. 'Can I—'

'No, it's fine. I have him.'

The old man looked at Sarah. 'Thank you,' he said softly.

Sarah wasn't sure why he was thanking her – she should have been thanking him.

Bernie helped him out of the sitting room, probably to a back bedroom. Sarah heard her voice rumble through the thick walls, kind and unhurried.

'I'm sorry, I didn't realise he was so ill,' Sarah said when Bernie returned. 'I shouldn't have upset him.'

'You didn't. My father's dying.'

Bernie said it so matter-of-factly that Sarah wasn't sure if she had heard her properly. 'He's …?'

'Dying. He has cancer of the bowel.' Bernie smiled sadly. 'And God knows where else at this stage.'

'Can nothing be done? An operation? Chemo?'

'No. We did talk about it, of course, but the specialist said it was very advanced and Daddy didn't want to put himself through all of that at his age.'

'I'm so very sorry.'

'Thank you. I asked him if he was upset about dying and he's not.' Bernie took a sip of her tea. 'He says he's lived his life to the full and it's time to go.'

'It must be hard.' Sarah couldn't believe how calm Bernie was, how understanding and accepting of her father's wishes.

Bernie noticed her discomfort. 'I'm glad you're here, though. I'm glad you were able to tell him he was right. That day has haunted him. He always said he should have gone after them, tried to stop them – something. He knew something wasn't right, knew it in his gut. If it had been the man on his own he would have challenged him, but the woman threw him.'

Sarah splayed her hands. 'It wasn't his fault.'

'I know that.'

'I would have done the same. Ever see a kid throwing a tantrum in the supermarket? They always sound like they're being half killed.'

Bernie nibbled the edge of a Jaffa cake. The dogs sat under her, patiently waiting for their cut. Bernie did not disappoint – she dropped a small piece into each mouth. 'So what now?' she asked. 'You have some idea who these people are?'

'Not yet, but we're closing in on them. My partner's in England right now. I think the man might be dead, but the woman could still be there.'

'What kind of woman would do such a thing? It's pure evil taking a child like that.' Bernie shuddered. 'Her poor parents. I'll never forget their cries that day and the young lad in hysterics. Never.'

Sarah finished her tea and stood up. 'I won't take up any more of your evening, Bernie – and I'd better get back anyway.'

'How's the girl doing?'

'Still in a coma.'

'Will she make it, do you think?'

'I honestly don't know.'

Bernie stood up and brushed some crumbs off her jumper. 'I'm glad we were able to help.'

'Thanks, and please tell your dad the same. He's a remarkable man.'

Sarah turned to go, but before she reached the door, she turned back.

'Did you forget something?'

'No. I just wanted to tell you ...'

'What?'

'That was the best cup of tea I've ever had.'

'It was only Barry's.'

'Still, it was lovely.'

'Must be the water.'

Sarah opened the door and stepped out. 'Goodnight.'

'Bye now.' Bernie called the dogs back in and closed the door, leaving Sarah to brace herself against the wind and her demons.

40

'Why should I believe you? This whole thing is ridiculous.' Yolanda paced the sticky kitchen floor, her arms wrapped tightly round her chest.

John was seated once again at the breakfast bar. He noticed broken glass under his stool and some in the groove behind the toaster. He wondered which sibling had flung the glass.

'Ridiculous?' John's temper rose. He had come across town and explained in graphic terms exactly what had happened to Frank Todd and the Greek. The last thing he'd expected was for Yolanda to disregard him so completely.

'What has any of this got to do with us? What have we got to do with the likes of them?'

'Ah,' John said. 'The *likes* of them.'

Yolanda's face tightened. 'I'm sorry she's hurt and I'm sorry her father's dead, but I don't want my family dragged into this mess.'

'Too bad. You're in it.'

Yolanda fixed him with a malevolent glare. 'You don't get it, do you? I'm trying to protect my brother. I don't want him involved with an East End hussy who has a gangster for a father.'

John lit a cigarette. 'Yolanda, don't talk about your future sister-in-law like that.'

'She is *not* my future sister-in-law.'

'Your brother seems to think she is. Where is he anyway?'

'Thanks to you, he's gone to Dublin.'

'*Alone*?'

'Yes.'

John was impressed. He wouldn't have thought Drake had it in him. He really was serious about Katie. 'I'm trying to understand your reluctance to talk to me, Yolanda. Drake told me about the man who tried to break in here.'

'So?'

'You don't think there's anything odd about that?'

'Apart from him kicking in the landing window?' Yolanda sneered.

'Yes, apart from that,' John snapped. 'When was this exactly?'

'I don't know *exactly*.'

'*Think*.'

'I can't!'

'Had Katie moved in?'

'Yes.'

'Long?'

'No, a few days, maybe, I don't know – maybe a week?'

'So, it's conceivable that whoever broke in might have been after her.'

'Or he could have been a burglar.'

John looked around him at the shabby room. 'You don't really believe that, do you?'

'It's possible.'

'It's possible you're spinning me a line here. I know you're hiding something.'

Suddenly, Yolanda slumped into Drake's chair and buried her face in her hands. 'Can't you leave me alone?'

'I'd love to. I'd love to forget this day ever happened. I'd love not to have watched a man die – I'd love that most of all. But I need to know what the man who tried to break in here looked like and when it happened.'

'Well, shouting isn't going to help!'

'No, what might—'

'Please, I can't help you.'

'Can't or won't?'

'Does it matter?'

John nodded and made a note. Katie's apartment had been trashed. She'd moved here and someone had tried to break in a few days after. Security had been stepped up at her work and she had stopped going to see her father. It wasn't rocket science to grasp that the girl had been terrified. Whoever was after Katie was prepared to get to her in any way they could. But why had she not moved back to Frank's if she'd felt she was in danger? He would have been in a better position to protect her. What had happened between them? Who *was* the man with the moustache and why had she been avoiding him?

John pinched the bridge of his nose. 'Does the name Henry D'Angelo mean anything to you?'

Yolanda shook her head, but her eyes were averted and she flushed. She'd heard the name before. 'I've never heard of him.'

'You sure, Yolanda?'

'Of course.'

''Cause it wouldn't be the first time you'd told me a porky.'

'I said I didn't know him.'

John sighed.

'All right, fuck it. I've tried and I'm getting nowhere. Maybe I'm out of my depth here.' He grabbed his jacket and put it on. 'I thought I could help you, but I can see now I'm wasting my time. I missed my flight to talk to you and your brother and for what? The bloody brush off.'

'I'm not—'

'Save it. I'll go to the police and give them his name, see if maybe they can find him.'

'Why would you do that?' Yolanda sat up straighter. 'Where did you hear that name anyway?'

'What's it to you?'

Yolanda swallowed. 'I ... '

John waited, but continued to zip up his jacket. 'See ya.'

'Wait – I might have heard the name before.'

'Yeah? Where?'

'He was like you.'

'Handsome?'

Yolanda couldn't have looked more disgusted if she'd tried. 'I mean he was a private detective.'

John sat down. He'd thought as much and now he had confirmation.

'Okay, and how do you know that?'

She hesitated, her kohl-rimmed eyes lowered. Finally she said, 'Because I hired him.'

'*You* hired Harry D'Angelo?' John gaped at her.

'Yes.'

'Why?'

'To investigate Katie.'

'Again, why?'

Yolanda drummed her fingers on her brother's easel. 'She was going to marry my brother, and I had to be sure she wasn't a gold digger.'

'A *gold digger*?' John gestured at the dilapidated room. 'What was she going to run off with? Your mouldy old furniture?'

'You don't understand. I only wanted to be sure. Drake's been made a fool of before.'

'He's old enough to take care of himself.'

'Oh, I wish that was true. He's too innocent for his own good. He couldn't see it. He thought she could walk on water, with her cutesy ways and stupid voice. My grandmother was just as bad, always going on about her as though she was Mother Teresa.'

John thought of the story Frank Todd had told him, about his little girl rescuing the magpie. He thought of how the ward sister had smiled at her name. Of Katie's chosen profession, of how she could see past Drake's idiosyncrasies to the man he truly was.

He stared at Yolanda's ugly jealous face. If Drake was an innocent, John Quigley was fast beginning to suspect he wasn't the only one.

He flung his notebook across the room. It landed with a plop on

247

the easel. Yolanda jumped and jerked her head in his direction. 'Address. And don't mess me about. I'm getting sick of second-guessing you.'

'I don't want Drake to know I hired that man.'

'Yolanda, I don't know what fucking can of worms you opened when you got him to dig around in Katie's past, but I'd be willing to bet Drake finding out is the very least of your worries. Now, write that address down and then get the hell out of here.'

'Out? What do you mean, out?'

'Out of here, just for a few days.'

'Why?'

'Because it'll be safer. You've got friends, right?'

She nodded, pale now, the anger and self-justification gone.

'Good. Stay with them.'

'What about Drake?'

'I'll make sure someone watches his back.' John pointed to the notebook. 'Get scribbling. And then get packing.'

41

'She did what?' Sarah said, pulling into the drive.

'She said she hired this guy D'Angelo to check into Katie's history.'

'When?'

'Three weeks ago.'

'You think that's the catalyst – the reason Katie came here?'

'I don't know, but the timing's pretty good. Frank Todd told me this guy was asking questions and took a swing at him. But Frank would have been jumpy from the word go. If D'Angelo approached the Greek or this Lizzie woman Frank dealt with, it means they got heads up and that might explain why all these people are suddenly winding up dead and why Katie moved in with Drake.'

'But Katie shot Hogan.'

'Who says? Nobody saw her pull the trigger, did they?'

Sarah thought about it.

Before she could speak, John went on. 'I think Hogan and Katie being shot is very convenient for someone. I think someone's tidying up loose ends.'

'The taxi dropped her at Hogan's. She had gunshot residue on her hands, John.'

'She also had a hell of a bump to her head and the taxi driver didn't see her shoot herself.'

'You think someone shot her, then used her hand to shoot the doctor?'

'It's possible, isn't it?'

'Anything's possible.' Sarah pulled up, took the tyre iron from behind the driver's seat, got out and locked the car.

'Look, Drake's on his way to Dublin now. He'll probably land at eight so he'll get to the hospital around nine. Sarah, I have to tell you, he's a little weird.'

'So you mentioned.'

'He could also be in danger. Actually, if Frank told Lizzie that Katie's still alive, so could she.'

'You think whoever killed Frank will try to kill Katie?'

'I don't know, but you should watch out for her and Drake.'

Sarah made her way slowly up to the door, her ears cocked. A cat ran across the lawn to her left and jumped the wall. 'Jesus.'

'What?'

'Nothing.'

'Why did you say "Jesus" like that? And why are you whispering?'

Sarah's heart pounded in her chest. 'What are you going to do?'

'I'm planning to visit to the office and home of Harry D'Angelo. I need to find out who he spoke to and what he said.'

Sarah let herself in at the front door and waited in the shadows, her eyes scanning the darkened hall. Nothing seemed out of place and the air did not feel disturbed.

'Sarah?'

'I'm here, just thinking.'

'How's Jackie?'

'I don't know. I haven't seen her since this morning. I went to Wicklow.'

'Did you see the old man?'

'Yep. He confirmed the couple in the photo with Hogan are definitely the people he saw that day at Brittas.'

'It was a long time ago. Is he sure?'

'No question.' She switched on the hall light and used the tyre iron to open the kitchen door.

'It has to be the woman Frank went to see earlier. He called her Lizzie. Damn it, I need an address.'

'There's no one at the college until the morning. You got the photo, didn't you?'

'Yes, but I wish I had a bloody address. Maybe D'Angelo has one for her.'

'Maybe.'

'Will you keep an eye out for Drake? And remember, he's a bit of an oddball.'

'He wouldn't be the only one,' Sarah said, hitting the lights and peeping round the door. 'Don't take any stupid risks and call me as soon as you've talked to D'Angelo.'

Sarah slipped her phone into her pocket, then tiptoed across the room and unlocked the back door.

Sumo bounded in, tongue lolling, tail waving.

'Hey there, big fella.' Sarah rubbed his head and lowered the tyre iron. Then she closed the back door and waited for Sumo to settle down before she guided him into the hall. She clung to his collar. 'Okay! Anyone here might as well know I've got a dog with me!' she called.

She went into the sitting room. Sumo's ears pricked.

Nothing.

She checked the rooms upstairs, then came downstairs and plonked herself on a chair at the kitchen table. 'Phew,' she said to Sumo. 'I know. You think I'm a loony,' she told him. 'In fact, you might even be right.'

The mobile rang, scaring her half to death. 'Hello?'

'Sarah, it's Sam Jones.'

'Sam.' In the background she could hear someone shouting.

'Do you know anything about a Drake Vaughn?' Sam said, raising his voice over the noise.

'Yes. I was just about to call you about him.'

'Who is he?'

'Your sister's fiancé.

'Are you sure?'

'Yes.'

'Hold the line.'

She heard a slight scuffle, an incredulous squawk, and then Sam was back on the line, breathless. 'Sarah, are you absolutely sure about this?' He sounded gob-smacked.

'I'm sure. John just called and said Drake was on his way. I didn't realise he'd get there so quickly. Can you put him on to me?'

'One moment.'

She waited. Finally an outraged Englishman shrieked, 'Yes?'

Sarah winced. 'Please don't shout. Are you Drake Vaughn?'

'I would surmise so,' he said at a slightly lower pitch.

'Drake, I want you to listen to me. I'm Sarah Kenny, John Quigley's partner.'

'The detective, yes, I know him.'

'Drake, what's going on there?'

'I came to see Katie and I was attacked!'

'Attacked?'

'Yes! Katie's in a coma. This is *very* upsetting.'

'I know, Drake. I want you to calm down a little. I'll make sure you get to see your fiancée. Okay?'

'That would be acceptable.' He lowered his voice. 'Can you tell this man to stop squeezing my arm?'

'Of course. Wait there, I'll be at the hospital in half an hour and I'll help sort the whole thing out, okay? But try to stay calm.'

'Calm, yes.'

'Now, let me talk to the man, please.'

Sam came back on the line. 'You're telling me this clown's engaged to my sister?'

'Sam, let go of him. Drake won't harm her, but John says he's a little … unstable. Manhandling him won't help.'

'He just barged into her room … I didn't know what the hell to think.'

'I understand.'

'He started babbling and crying and grabbing at Katie, and my mother got upset. He wouldn't leave so I called Security. Next thing I know, he's lost it!'

'He's an artist.'

'He's a freak!'

'Sam, I want you to calm down too.' Sarah stood up and reached for the car keys. 'I'm leaving now, and I'll be there in twenty minutes. Okay?'

'Right,' Sam said, sounding less okay by the second. 'Thirty minutes?'

'Yes.' Sarah hung up. This was the last thing she needed. She looked at Sumo. 'You're going to have to go out again. I'm sorry.'

He wagged his tail at her and she felt a huge pang of guilt.

'Maybe I won't put you outside. It's freezing. Anyway, what you need is food.' She opened the fridge and rummaged, found a gammon steak and held it aloft. 'Well? What about this?'

Sumo licked his chops.

Sarah flung it to him. It disappeared in two bites. 'I'll make it up to you tomorrow, we'll go for the longest walk ever, I promise.'

Sarah locked the back door and picked up the tyre iron, then headed out into the night.

42

John climbed out of the cab and closed the door. He stretched, then limped past a kebab shop and a launderette. He was back in Kilburn. He felt as if he'd been going in circles all day.

Harry D'Angelo's office was at the top of a grimy block of flats. The stairwell was dark, dank and reeked of urine. He climbed up to the first floor, turned the corner and walked straight into a gang of teenagers. They were playing some kind of dice game, a stereo blaring high-speed rap, and stopped when John approached, their eyes indifferent, aware and watchful at the same time. They couldn't have been more than fifteen, but John could sense their hostility.

They wore pristine runners, beanie caps, hoodies and massive gold chains. Two moved their hands to their waists.

'Evening, lads,' he said. 'Cold old night.'

The boys watched him hobble past. He heard one snicker and say something rude about his 'threads' and thought it best not to respond.

He climbed eight flights of stairs and finally reached 32A, a little out of breath, his injured leg burning. He knocked on Harry D'Angelo's door. There was no answer and no sign of movement behind the glass. What to do? Leave a note? His card?

He bent down and pushed opened the letterbox to leave his business card. But it wouldn't budge. The flap was jammed with post, some of it folded tight and wedged in.

John dropped the flap and stood up. He rested his forehead against the glass. Okay. D'Angelo had probably gone to ground, or he was on holiday, or his rich mother had passed away and he was now poodling around on a cruise, somewhere hot maybe, the Caribbean.

Except John didn't believe he was – call it a hunch, call it a guess, call it the faint trace of blood beneath his fingernails.

What now?

He could brave the dice game, head back to the hotel and spend an hour in the bath. Keep ringing the number he had.

Or he could take a look.

No contest.

He got out his wallet and used his tools to open the front door. He switched on the hall light, which illuminated the pile-up of post behind the door.

That was the first thing he noticed. The second was the smell, which hit him like a two-ton truck. John gagged and reeled outside. He pulled the door to and tried not to retch. He took a deep breath, pulled his scarf over his nose and let himself back into the hall.

Careful to take shallow breaths, he checked out the flat. It was small and neat, cheaply furnished but clean. The kitchen sink was empty, the table and worktops wiped clean. Through the breakfast hatch John could see the living room. D'Angelo obviously ran his business from his home. There was a cheap chipboard desk pushed up against the far wall and two filing cabinets beside it. Other than that, there was an easy chair and a television, not much by way of personal items, a couple of photos and a pink throw, which looked out of place with the wooden furniture. There was a fish tank between the kitchen and the living room, but the water was cloudy and John doubted anything was living there.

He moved on. The smell got stronger as he worked his way to the back of the flat. There were two more doors. He chose the one on the left.

The bedroom was empty, but there were clothes on a chair, a pair of brogues beneath it, and the bed was unmade. It looked as though the occupant had been disturbed while he was reading – a copy of the *Daily Mail* lay folded on the bed.

John checked the paper. It was dated 19 November. Two days before Katie had killed Hogan. He picked up the trousers from the chair and found a wallet in the back pocket. He eased it out and opened it. Inside the plastic flap, he found a copy of the card Frank had given him and a driving licence. He took it out and stared at the face of Harry D'Angelo, a grey-haired man with an open, cheery expression. He was fifty-eight and he had lived in Bristol when the licence had been issued.

John put it back in the wallet and looked through the rest: credit cards, money … nothing had been touched. There was a grainy photo of a boy in the last flap. John could see the resemblance immediately: he had to be D'Angelo's kid.

He wondered if the boy kept in contact with his father. Did he know that there was a bad smell in the man's home, that his mail hadn't been collected?

The stench was so strong now that John's eyes were watering. Despite the scarf, John could barely breathe. He made his way slowly to the last door, resigned to what he would find.

He opened it and pulled it wide with his foot. A cord dangled just inside the room. He pulled it.

D'Angelo was in the bath. His head was thrown back and tilted at an angle, facing the door. Maybe he had hoped someone would come to his aid. Flies were crawling all over him and his eye sockets were empty. His skin had swollen and split, and had now almost drained of fluid. The body was beginning to dry out.

The smell was unbearable, although John could see that putrefaction was almost complete. The stench of decay – sweet, cheesy, cloying – filled the air. There appeared to be mould on the fingers of the right hand, and John could see maggots moving freely across D'Angelo's chest, disappearing into a cavity only to reappear elsewhere. He took a step closer, holding his breath. Something glinted on the floor near the feet. He bent towards it and blanched when he recognised teeth.

Harry D'Angelo had not given up his information easily.

John Quigley did something he never did. 'May the Lord have mercy on your soul,' he said and blessed himself.

He turned off the light and shut the door. He made his way back to the living room and searched it, then the kitchen and, lastly, the bedroom. There was no mention anywhere of Katie, Yolanda, Drake or Frank. No mention of Elizabeth Sheldon either and no word on the Greek. And yet D'Angelo was dead. Whoever had killed him had killed him for a reason.

Something connected with Katie Jones.

John was sick of death, sick of floundering around in the dark and being one step behind. He needed to get the hell out of this flat, but he was missing something. He knew it.

He looked at D'Angelo's brogues. They were old, but well cared for, like the flat. John lifted the right one and tilted it. D'Angelo's watch and a set of keys slid down to the heel. He took out the keys – to the flat, his car – a Golf – and a Chubb and a smaller one, probably for a padlock.

John let himself out, slammed the door, yanked down his scarf and gulped at the cold night air, drawing it deep into his lungs. He leaned over the railings and tried not think of D'Angelo's final moments.

After a minute, when he had regained his composure, he ran down the stairs, hoping the teenagers were still there.

They were, but they didn't look any friendlier. John jumped the last three steps, making the one nearest to him flinch.

'Yo, what you fuckin' at?' The kid's hands were already moving for the knife in his waistband. He pulled it out and flicked it open. 'What you mad-doggin' us for?'

John held up his hands in front of his chest. 'Sorry if I scared you.'

The boy's jaw clenched. 'You didn't *scare* shit.'

'Well, sorry for busting up your game, then.'

The kid glared at him.

'Hey, do you know if this place has garages?'

Now all the boys were on their feet. They looked at him as if they were a pack of wolves circling a wounded deer.

'Who's asking?' a boy wearing a blue beanie barked. 'You're not from here.'

'Well, do you know or not?' John said impatiently.

The atmosphere cooled a degree. Then the nearest boy's nostrils flared. 'Man git the fuck out, you smell *evil*.'

Now the others caught it and backed away from John, pulling faces.

'Garage,' John said, taking a step closer.

The kid with the knife looked as if he might vomit. 'Whoa, back up. Some a them oldies got a place. It's under the first building – man, *back* the fuck up. You smell like shit.'

'Close enough. Cheers.' John saluted and hurried away. This time, he didn't notice how bad the stairwell smelled.

He found the Golf at the back of the lock-up garage. It was a boxy number from the early nineties. D'Angelo had kept it in mint condition – it had all its original features and showed very little wear and tear.

The file on Katie Jones was under the mat on the passenger side. D'Angelo had either been a casual sod, which John didn't buy, or he had expected trouble at the flat.

'Good man, Harry,' John said. He sat behind the steering wheel, lit a cigarette, flipped open the file and began to read.

43

When John called, Sarah was standing next to a wary Sam Jones, drinking watery coffee from a plastic cup.

'You at the hospital?'

'Yes, with our client.'

'Go somewhere.'

Sarah pressed the phone to her chest. 'Sam, will you excuse me?'

Sam drained his coffee and flung the cup into the bin. 'It's getting late and I need to get my mother home. She's exhausted – I can't believe she's offered to let *that man* stay at her house.'

Sarah had been listening to him say that for a good ten minutes and she was bored with it. She wanted to ask him why he didn't offer to put Drake up if he was that concerned about his mother's well-being.

'Later then.' Sam stalked away.

Sarah watched him go. As soon as he turned the corner she lifted the mobile. 'Jesus, you missed the fun. Drake got here earlier than expected and there was uproar. I managed to calm him down, but Sam is—'

'Sarah, listen to me. I've hardly any battery and you need to hear what I'm about to tell you. Harry D'Angelo has been dead for a few weeks, probably since mid-November. Now, I know I should call the police and wait for them, but if I do that they'll lock me up and throw away the key.'

259

'John, you can't be serious.'

'I'm here just two days and so far I've got two bodies to my tally. I doubt they'd be letting me out to roam the streets any time soon.'

'Stop shouting.'

'I'm not shouting!' John shouted.

Sarah heard him take a deep breath and knew he was fast approaching the end of his tether. 'John, listen to me. If you don't go to the police and they find out you were there, you could be charged with obstruction.'

'I have an address for Lizzie Sheldon.'

'You got it?'

'Old Harry was doing some sterling work. He had copies of Katie's supposed birth certificate and her supposed adoption papers. They look kosher to me too, notarised, and complete with a doctor's report. He had Hogan's address and phone number. And you were right, Sarah, there are notes on that charity, the Cradle Foundation. He was very thorough, he even has a note of Katie's blood type, although Christ knows where he got that.'

'Maybe Hogan gave it to him.'

Sarah heard him flicking papers. 'There are records here on vaccinations and adoptions, names … a lot of names. There's one here I recognise – Frank mentioned it. Milo, down here as Milo Hennessy.'

'Was he involved in an adoption?'

'I don't know, Frank wouldn't say, but I got the feeling this Milo, whoever he is, went the same route as Frank and his wife. I can tell you who signed off on all of the medical paperwork, though.'

'Let me guess. Good old Doc Hogan?'

'The very one, and you want to hear something even juicier?'

Sarah smiled at his tone. 'Sure.'

'I'm looking at a copy of a marriage certificate. Elizabeth Sheldon and Nico Kastrinakis.'

'Really?' Sarah thought of how even, in the photo, Hogan hadn't been able to keep his eyes off the woman. She wondered how he had felt about the marriage. 'Kids?'

'Doesn't say.'

'You need to get to the police with this. This is evidence.'

'I want to talk to Elizabeth Sheldon first.'

'John, stay away from her. Think about it! Hogan's dead, Frank's dead, the Greek's dead.'

'Sarah, she could be in danger.'

'She could *be* the danger.'

'We don't know that. Sarah, I'm tired, I'm sore and I smell like death. I'm coming home tomorrow, so before I leave, I want to talk to her, see if she denies it all. Then I'll hand this shit over to the cops. But I want to look her in the face and find out what she has to say.'

Sarah knew there was no talking to him when he got that stubborn tone. 'Okay – but for God's sake, be careful.'

'I—'

His phone went dead.

Sarah tried to call him back but it went straight to voicemail. His battery had died.

She hung up and slipped the phone into her pocket. It was almost ten o'clock and she was tired and hungry.

Sarah made her way back to Katie Jones's room, trying to process everything John had told her, a little worried that her hot-headed partner might be putting himself in the firing line, either with the police or with the Sheldon woman. She considered talking to Steve Magher, see what he thought, but at the end of the day, Steve was still a cop and had a duty to report what he knew if John was mixed up with anything criminal. It wouldn't be fair to involve him.

Rodney Mitchell might know what to do.

Sarah thought it over for two seconds and abandoned the idea. He was a good guy, but she didn't want to deal with him tonight – she hadn't the energy for the small talk he'd inflict on her.

She walked back into the room in time to see Charlotte Jones lean across her daughter to kiss her goodnight. She nodded to Drake. Sam wasn't there and Sarah sensed the ease that Drake and Charlotte found in each other's company. They both loved Katie.

Earlier, Charlotte had helped the nurses to change her daughter and give her a bed bath. She had gone out and bought fresh flowers, clean cotton pyjamas and a pale blue dressing gown for 'when she wakes up'. She hadn't any doubt that Katie would make it.

John was right, Sarah thought. She was a remarkable woman.

'Oh, Sarah, there you are,' Charlotte said when she straightened up. 'We're going to head off now.'

'Okay.' On Drake's lap, Sarah noticed an open sketch-pad. She craned her neck to look at what he had drawn. It was a charcoal sketch of Katie, but in it, her hair was intact, not partly shaved. She looked like a sleeping angel. 'Hey, you're *really* good.'

Drake smiled shyly. 'It's for her.' He nodded to Charlotte. 'She doesn't have any photos ... I would surmise.'

Charlotte beamed at him. 'I'm going to frame it when we get home.'

Sarah was touched for both of them. 'That's a really sweet gesture.'

Drake flushed crimson. 'No, no. It is what I do.'

'John told me you designed jewellery – I didn't realise you were such an artist.'

'Yes, I'd like to draw and paint full-time, but Yolanda—' He stopped and studied his hands.

'Your sister wants you to continue designing?'

'Yes ... we have an understanding.'

'I see,' Sarah said softly.

'Come on, Drake,' Charlotte said, gathering up her things. 'We'll go on home and I'll put you up in Sam's old room. Do you like pork chops? Mushy peas? Potatoes and gravy?'

Drake gaped at her as though she was offering the ambrosia of the gods. 'I *do*,' he said emphatically.

'You look like there's hardly a pick on you.'

He began to close his own folder when suddenly he said, 'Oh.'

'What is it?' Sarah asked.

'I had this for John. I was not sure if I should give it to him.'

'What is it?'

'A rendition.'

'A what?'

But Drake was flicking through his pad. He found the page he was after and ripped it out. 'Here.' He handed it to Sarah.

It was a sketch of a man's face. Even though Drake had drawn it, Sarah knew straight away she was looking at a killer.

Drake had captured the rage, the murderous intent in the eyes, so clearly and with such accuracy the paper almost felt hot to touch.

'Drake, who is this man?'

'He tried to break into the house a few weeks ago.'

'When?'

'I don't always follow dates very well.'

'Was Katie living with you at the time?'

'Yes.'

'Did you report it to the police?'

'Katie said not to.'

'Why?'

'I don't know, but she asked me not to, so I didn't.'

A few minutes later, she saw Drake and Charlotte off, then she hurried to her car, trying John's number as she went. She needed to get to a fax machine and send this picture to John. She went to the office.

44

Willie parked a long way down the street and climbed out. He checked his watch and rolled his shoulders. He need to be sure he could get in at the back of her house. He walked up the quiet street towards Sarah's house, went straight up to the front door and made a big production of ringing the bell. Sumo barked furiously and Willie smiled, relieved that one problem was already solved.

He glanced over his shoulder, reassured himself that no one was about, then ducked down and skirted along the hedge. He nipped into the side passage and peered at the door. It was old, half rotted. He could get through it in seconds.

He went back to the car. He got in on the driver's side and slammed the door.

'So, what's your interest in her?' a voice said behind him.

Wexford Street was quiet. Sarah parked the Manta on the footpath and climbed out.

She locked the car and stretched, feeling the tired muscles in her back complain. This day seemed to be never-ending.

She unlocked the street door and made her way up the stairs, past the pirate radio station where the nine-to-one DJ was busy playing club classics. She hurried past Rodney's door – there was a light on inside, which could mean either Rodney was working or that he was drinking, and she didn't want to find out which.

She hurried on to her landing.

The office door was ajar, the jamb splintered.

Sarah stopped. John had reinforced it in the weeks after she had been shot to protect them from retaliation from the York gang. It would have taken brute force to kick it off its hinges. She was unsure about what to do. What if whoever had entered was still there? There were no lights on and she could hear nothing, but that didn't mean anything. Vic could be inside, waiting.

But why leave the door open if he wanted to take her by surprise?

Sarah clenched her fists. She was angry now – angry that her door had been broken down, angry that she was rooted to the stairs with fear. She slipped her mobile from her pocket and dialled 999, but didn't press the button to connect the call. Slowly, she made her way to the door, wincing at every creak and groan the wood made under her weight. She reached it and eased it open, hit the light switch and gasped.

The place had been destroyed.

The computers were smashed to pieces. The walls had been sprayed with bright-pink paint and a chair had been thrown against one of the sash windows, shattering it. John's desk had been flipped over. Fortunately, the filing cabinets had been locked and, for some reason, had not been forced. Her own desk had been kicked apart, paint splattered across the carpet. Even the kettle had been crushed.

QuicK Investigations was in ruins.

Sarah tried to keep it together, but failed. She wailed. It was a sound not quite human, not quite her. An outpouring sound of outrage, grief and fury.

Something answered that wail – a muffled groan from behind John's desk.

Sarah started, then turned to run, but something made her stop. She held onto the door and listened, tears coursing down her face.

There it was again.

She edged her way into the room and inched over to the upturned desk. She peered over the top. An arm was sticking out from under it.

Then she saw skinny legs clad in grey, ginger hairs clearly visible on freckled skin.

'Oh my God, *Rodney!*'

Sarah ran round the desk and dropped to her knees. Rodney lay half under the desk on his back. His face was cut and bruised, his nose looked broken and his lips were split in three different places. He moaned again.

'Oh, Jesus! Oh, Rodney. Oh God, Rodney – don't move, you might be badly hurt. Hold on, okay?' She moved some debris off his chest and wiped the blood from his forehead. Rodney opened his eyes. They were glazed and unfocused.

'Sarah … he …'

'Don't talk, Rod. I'll get help. Hold on a second.'

She hit the button to connect the 999 call and asked for an ambulance. When she was sure they had the right address she hung up and turned back to Rodney. He was unconscious again. She checked his wrist for a pulse and found it. She sagged with relief.

'Rod, I'm going to try to get this desk off you. I'll lift it, and you're out cold, so hopefully, you won't feel a thing. Then the ambulance will be here, and we'll get you cleaned up. Soon you'll be good as new.'

She was babbling hysterically, but at least it stopped her screaming or crying or flinging herself out of the window.

She heaved up the desk and began to pull it away. It wasn't particularly heavy and she wondered why Rodney hadn't tried to push it off himself. Maybe he had a head injury or—

He screamed. The sound was so piercing that Sarah almost dropped the desk.

'All right, Rodney! All right. It's off now.' She eased it clear, heart hammering with fright. 'See?'

Then she saw his leg. 'Oh, Jesus.'

Rodney's shin was broken. A piece of bone protruded through a jagged tear in his trouser leg, which was saturated with blood.

She turned away and put a fist in her mouth. It was Vic's favourite move. He was trained in Muay Thai, and he liked to boast about how easy it was to smash a man's shin. To *incapacitate* him.

'Oh, Rodney.' She dropped to her knees beside him. His eyes were open, but he was sweating, his teeth clenched against the pain. 'They're coming. Just hold on, okay?'

Rodney reached across his chest with his right hand.

'What is it? Maybe you shouldn't try to move, Rod,' she said, choking back her sobs. 'What is it you need?'

His long, sensitive, blood-stained fingers reached into his pocket and he pulled out a folded sheet of paper. He pressed it into Sarah's chest.

Sarah took it, unfolded it and read it.

If you don't meet me at midnight what I did to him will be nothing to what I do to you and you family. Leave your phone on.
V

She folded the note and put it into her back pocket.

'Rodney, I'm so sorry.'

But Rodney wouldn't meet her eyes, and when she reached to wipe the tears off his face, he moved his head away.

'Rodney, listen to me. I'll get him. Don't mention this note to the gardaí, Rodney, okay? Please, Rodney, if you get the gardaí involved we're all in danger. I'll handle it.' Tears rolled down her face, 'Just say you disturbed a break-in, a robbery. I promise, Rod, I'll take care of it.'

Rodney closed his eyes. Sarah wasn't sure if he had passed out again or it he just couldn't bear the sight of her.

She stayed by his side, holding his hand and crying, until the ambulance arrived.

Then after he had been taken away and after she had fed the gardaí who had appeared on the scene some ridiculous tale about disgruntled clients, she dried her eyes and swore that they were the last she would shed that night.

She forgot to send Drake's sketch to John.

45

After the second cab refused to take him, John was forced to use D'Angelo's car to make his way back across town to the Four Seasons. He got lost eight times and by the time he had finally found the right area, Harry's pristine vehicle reeked and had run out of petrol. John had no option but to abandon it.

He climbed out and left the keys in the ignition, hoping this would deter would-be thieves from damaging it. He looked at it fondly and patted the roof. He was a sucker for older cars and even more of a sucker for older cars that had been lovingly maintained.

He walked the rest of the way to the hotel, ignoring curious looks from passers-by, and took the stairs to his room on the fourth floor. He let himself into his room and began to strip even before the door had closed. He was getting pretty sick of D'Angelo's smell and, even though they were his least destroyed jeans, John had to put them with the rest of his clothes into a plastic bag and seal it.

He hopped into the shower and scrubbed himself until his skin felt raw. Then he soaped up and did it again. He brushed his teeth in the shower too, trying not to think about what might have been airborne in D'Angelo's bathroom.

When he was as clean as he could be, he stepped out of the bathroom, took some painkillers and redressed his leg. He opened his sports bag and dug out his clothing from the previous day. His T-shirt was stained and the jeans were ripped, and stiff now that the blood from his leg had dried. John grimaced as he pulled them on.

When he was dressed, he rang Sarah's mobile from the hotel phone, but it was engaged. He called downstairs and checked to see if she had left any message for him. She hadn't. He made another call, anonymous this time, to tip off the police about Harry D'Angelo. He couldn't bear to think of him lying there any longer.

Satisfied, he read through Harry's file again.

Elizabeth Sheldon, Walter Hogan, the Greek. The three had been involved in Katie's abduction, of that he was certain. The trouble was he had no proof that Elizabeth Sheldon had had anything to do with the deaths of Hogan, Frank, the Greek and Harry D'Angelo. In fact, John thought, he wouldn't be too surprised if he arrived at Elizabeth Sheldon's door and discovered her lying dead in the hall. The way things were going, he half expected it.

But there was no way he could leave this file lying around. He added his own notes to it and decided to lodge it with the front desk. If anything happened to him, he wanted to be sure that Sarah had everything at her fingertips.

It took almost an hour by taxi to reach Richmond and the mildly suspicious driver looked positively ecstatic when John handed over the crumpled banknotes to pay him. As he waited patiently for his receipt, he wondered just how much like a tramp he looked. Certainly, the night-doorman at the Four Seasons had eyed him disbelievingly when he had hailed a cab. John had resisted telling him he should take a leaf out of his predecessor's book and work on his blind eye.

He climbed out of the cab and watched it drive off into the night. When the taillights faded, he turned to survey the house.

It was a big Georgian affair, set back a little from the road in a mature garden. Expensive, tasteful, the kind of house most people coveted but would never afford. There was a light on in an upstairs window. John stepped into the drive and a security light blinded him.

He blinked and waited for his eyes to recover, then made his way up the flight of stone steps to the front door.

He smoothed his hair back and rang the bell.

After a minute, a light came on in the hall. John heard the sound of a chain being disconnected, then a bolt being drawn back, and another. Finally, the door opened. A small woman dressed entirely in black peered out. 'Yes?'

'I'm sorry about the hour. I'm looking for a Mrs Elizabeth Sheldon.'

'Well, you've found her.'

John smiled. Of course, update the clothing and add ten pounds, and she could have stepped from the photo Sarah had sent. She was older, a bit blonder, but essentially the same.

She gazed up at him questioningly. Her mouth was small and firm, the skin round her sea-green eyes woven with wrinkles. The lashes were pale red. Her expression was wary and intelligent. 'And who might you be?'

'My name is John Quigley, I'm a private investigator.'

'Really?' She didn't seem perturbed by this.

'Would you mind if I came in?'

'If you tell me why first.'

'I'd like to talk to you about Katie Jones. You might know her as Katie Todd.'

'Todd? That's poor Frank's girl.' She ushered him inside and led him into a formal sitting room to the left of the hall. 'Have you found her?'

'Yes.' John sat on a hard chair by an empty birdcage.

'Oh, thank God! Frank will be so relieved, poor man.' She sat in a matching chair opposite him, so close their knees were almost touching. 'Frank's dead.' She gasped at him. 'He was killed earlier – stabbed.'

'I don't believe you.'

'I'm afraid it's true. I was with him when he died.' John glanced down at his hands. When he looked up, Elizabeth Sheldon was weeping.

John shuffled his feet uncomfortably. He wasn't sure what he had been expecting her to say, but it hadn't been this.

And he hated it when women cried. He put out his hand and patted her shoulder awkwardly.

'Poor Frank,' she said.

'Em … there now. I'm very sorry for your loss.'

'Did you know him?' She raised her head and sniffed. 'He was a fine man.'

'I didn't know him that well,' John said truthfully, 'we'd only just met.'

'Oh, my! What a shock it must have been. Please, tell me he didn't suffer.'

'It was very quick,' John said, thinking of Frank's blood-stained teeth. He cleared his throat. 'Were you and he close?'

'Yes – I mean he and Sadie – she was his wife – we've known each other for years. Sadie, she was like a sister to me.' She began to cry again.

John continued patting.

Presently she pulled herself together. 'Forgive me, it's such a dreadful shock.'

John cleared his throat and sat back on the chair. 'Look, Mrs Sheldon—'

'Please, call me Lizzie – everybody does. The only person who ever calls me Mrs Sheldon is the greengrocer.'

John smiled stiffly. 'I'm afraid I need to ask you a few difficult questions.'

She tilted her head to one side. 'Difficult? I don't know what you mean.'

'About Katie – about her adoption.'

'Her adoption?' He waited for any reaction, but she just sat there staring at him. If she was guilty of anything, she sure was a superb actress – unless, of course, he had everything wrong.

'Frank came to see you today, didn't he?' he asked.

'Frank?'

'Yes.'

She waited a beat too long and in that instant John saw through her. 'I haven't seen him in weeks.'

John sat back in the chair. 'Oh. Well then, I was misinformed.'

There was a longer silence this time as she inched forward on her seat. 'You were …' She smiled. 'Who told you he'd been here?'

'Doesn't matter. They were obviously mistaken.'

The smile stretched, the skin around her eyes crinkled a little, but the expression in them remained cold and analytical. 'And Katie, what did you want to ask about her adoption?'

'Well, it's the strangest thing, but I was talking to Frank about it, and he said that it wasn't exactly legit.'

'Not – I'm afraid I don't understand what you're saying,' she said.

'I'm saying Katie Todd wasn't legitimately adopted.'

She sat perfectly still now, her expression frozen, but John could practically feel the cogs whirling behind her eyes. He decided to give her something to chew over. He pulled his notebook from his inside pocket and flipped it open, as though the particulars of the case were unfamiliar to him.

'Her real name is Katie Jones, and she was abducted from a beach in Brittas Bay, Wicklow, twenty-six years ago.'

'*Really*!' Lizzie Sheldon's eyes widened. 'Well, I'm stunned, I can't – I don't believe it. Frank and Sadie would never have involved themselves in something illegal. There must be some mistake.'

'I don't think Frank and Sadie knew the child had been abducted.' John said, watching her watching him. 'They thought she had come from an unmarried mother.'

'Really?' she said again.

'Their son too.'

'Robbie?'

'Yes. He came from the same facilitator.'

She said nothing, but her hands betrayed her nerves as they played with the fabric of her skirt.

'Do you know a man by the name of Walter Hogan?'

'No.'

'You don't?'

'No.'

'But didn't you go to medical college with him?' John flipped through his pages, and pretended to read. There was nothing written there and he was chancing his arm, but she didn't know that.

'What was the name again?'

'Walter Hogan. He was a retired GP.'

She kept her eyes on John, steady, unflinching. Then she made another mistake.

'Oh, Walter! Why yes, I do remember him now ... gosh, but it was so long ago I'd forgotten all about him.'

John kept his face neutral. 'I'm afraid I have even more bad news for you, then. Walter is dead too.'

'Really?' she said again, but this time she didn't bother trying to inject any emotion into it. 'That's terrible, of course, but we hardly knew each other.'

'He was shot.'

'Oh.'

'By Katie Jones.'

'How terrible! But I don't really see that any of this has anything to do with me, Mr Quigley.'

'Call me John.'

'John.' She said his name as though she was sucking a lemon. 'I mean, obviously I'm devastated that Frank has been killed – but to be perfectly honest, he was a man who ... how shall I put it? He was inclined to skirt the law. He was a live-by-the-sword man, and it would appear that he also died that way.'

'It certainly seems that someone wanted him out of the picture,' John said evenly. 'The man who kidnapped Katie is dead too. His name was Nico Kastrinakis. Do you know him?'

'No, I don't.'

John took out a copy of the photo Sarah had sent him. He passed it to her. She took it, looked at it and laid it face down on her lap. When she lifted her head again, her eyes glittered.

'That's some patchy memory you have, considering you two were married once upon a time,' John said amicably. 'Anyway, Frank was killed in your husband's office—'

'Ex-husband.'

John tilted his head. 'Glad you remember him now. Anyway, Frank went there to find out where Katie and Robbie had come from. He might have been a man who skated, as you say, close to the edge, but I don't think he would have deprived another family of their child. In fact, he seemed pretty angry when he discovered he'd been duped.'

'Did he indeed?'

'At first I thought Frank's death might have been a case of bad timing, but then there's Harry D'Angelo to consider.'

'Who?'

John smiled. 'That won't wash, Mrs Sheldon. You know it and so do I. I'm pretty sure old Harry might have had a chat with you recently. Although not too recently, if his current look is anything to go by.'

'If I didn't know better, Mr Quigley, I'd almost have gained the impression that you think I'm involved in this somewhere.'

'Oh, I'm just speculating. There are a few things I'd like to chase up first before I start accusing anyone of anything. A charity called the Cradle Foundation, for one. I'd ask you if you'd heard of it, but your memory doesn't seem to be at its best this evening.'

Lizzie Sheldon seemed to weigh up the implication of what he was saying. She stared at him with naked loathing. 'John, it's been a trying day. I think I've had enough company for one evening.'

'Yeah, I'm pretty beat myself. Looking forward to going home tomorrow.'

She stood up. 'You never told me who you were working for.'

'Didn't I?' John stood up too. 'I'm working for Katie's real family. Her flesh-and-blood family.'

She frowned. 'But how did they get involved?'

'She sent them a locket she had been wearing the day she vanished.'

Lizzie Sheldon seemed about to spit. 'I see. So what you're saying is the Irish police are involved in this ... mess too.'

'Yep.'

'And you're probably going to give them everything you've learned over the last few days, including your *speculations*.'

'Well, like I said, I'm hired by the family, but I imagine they'll want the gardaí to know all the details, especially since the gardaí think Katie shot Hogan.'

'You don't?'

'I'm not too sure. Maybe she did – but from what I gather about the girl, she'd be the type to try to save him rather than shoot him.'

'I see. And do you—'

The door opened and a young man walked a few feet into the room. He was about twenty, slim and pale with a sprinkling of freckles over the bridge of his nose. His dark red hair was thick and glossy. He moved with the grace of a dancer.

'Ah, Mark,' Lizzie Sheldon said, smiling.

'Sorry to interrupt, Mother. I just wanted to know if the gate needed to be locked.'

He glanced at John but did not acknowledge him. His eyes were almost amber and John felt sick as he remembered where he had seen them before.

'Thank you, darling.'

Mark nodded curtly, spun on his heel and left the room, shutting the door behind him.

'Your son?' John asked.

'Yes.'

'He's a handsome lad. Striking eyes.'

'Mr Quigley, if you wouldn't mind, I'm very tired and this has been a long day.' She sat down and waved at the door. 'I don't want to hear any more about this hideous business. I just want to go to bed and sleep.'

John watched her. He had never in his life seen someone with such a range of acting skills. She looked now as though she might drop dead from exhaustion, but moments before she had bristled with nervous energy.

He took out a business card and left it on the table by her elbow. 'I'll be at the Four Seasons until tomorrow morning. If you suddenly feel the need to talk, that's where you'll find me.'

'Go, please.' She turned her head.

John nodded and strode across the room. He opened the door, stepped out and was in the process of closing it when he sensed rather than saw movement. He jerked his head just in time to avoid the stiletto blade in Mark Sheldon's left hand. It whistled past him, grazing his cheek, and embedded itself in the heavy wooden door.

Mark – teeth bared – tried to yank it free.

John punched him in the gut as hard as he could. Mark hissed and doubled forward but didn't fall. John hit him again, but it was like hitting concrete. Mark backhanded him across the face and John fell back from the door. Before he could register what had happened, Mark had side-kicked him in the chest and sent him crashing into the coat-stand on the other side of the hall.

Okay, so the kid could fight and he was in good shape, John thought, trying to untangle himself from the coats.

Mark advanced on him, dancing lightly on the balls of his feet. John put up his fists to protect his face, like they do in the movies, and Mark rabbit-punched him so hard in the kidneys that John dropped to one knee and thought he might puke.

This was not going the way it did in the movies.

As Mark swung a downward right, John tilted to one side and kicked the lad square in the kneecap as hard as he could. He felt it give and relished the shock and pain on Mark's face. Before the lad had a chance to recover, John scrambled to his feet and charged him. Mark landed hard, cracking his head on the black and white tiles. He was stunned, but still managed to bring up his hands and grip either side of John's mouth. He locked his arms and began to pull. The pain was so intense that John thought his lips might rip clean off his face. He did the only thing he could. He made as if to pull his head away from Mark's hands, and when the lad's grip lessened he planted a ferocious head-butt in the middle of his face.

Mark grunted. Seconds later, his head lolled to one side and his hands fell away.

John rolled off him and lay there gasping. 'Bet they don't teach that in fucking karate.'

He heard movement in the sitting room and watched the door open.

Lizzie Sheldon peered out and shrieked. She turned and, with both hands, tried to wrench the knife from the wood.

Suddenly, John found the reserve of strength he needed to get to his feet. He picked her up, shoved her back into the sitting room, slammed the door and turned the key on her screams. Then he grabbed a scarf and the belt of a raincoat from the coat-stand, rolled

Mark over and bound his hands behind his back, then tied his feet to them. With Lizzie Sheldon's fury ringing in his ears, he located a phone and made a call to the emergency services.

Really, he thought, lighting a cigarette and pressing a wad of tissue to the graze on the side of his face, by now, they must recognise my voice when I call them.

46

She was running. No, just walking fast, calling. She was searching for Ziggy. She knew where she was now. She was back at the flat – the same wallpaper, the same furniture, the same smell, the same fear.

She went from room to room, calling him. Where was he? He never hid from her. Normally, he rushed to greet her as soon as she got home, crying to be cuddled so he could rub his cheek against hers.

She checked under the bed and in the wardrobe, keeping her fear in check. 'Okay,' she muttered, 'he's probably asleep somewhere and hasn't heard me.'

She went into the kitchen and started opening and closing the presses. 'Ziggy!'

Maybe he'd got out. But they were five floors up – where was there to go?

She tore into the sitting room and dropped to her knees to look under the sofa. He had to be asleep. So why hadn't he woken? 'Ziggy? Ziggy! Where are you, baby?'

And where was Victor? He was always here when she got in. That was what frightened her most.

She walked round in a circle, her hands on the small of her back. Think, think.

She went back to her bedroom. Maybe he'd climbed into the laundry …

That was when she saw that the toilet lid was down. She stopped by the bathroom door. Victor never left a lid down. He hated it, said it made the toilet smell.

So why was it down today?

The answer hit her.

She walked slowly to the toilet, sat on the bath beside it and said a little prayer. 'Please God, don't let it be. Please.'

She took a deep breath and lifted the lid. 'Oh, Ziggy ...' She put her hands in and lifted out the sodden little cat. He was cold and lifeless, his eyes tight shut, his tiny teeth protruding under his lips.

She yanked a towel from the handrail and wrapped him in it. His neck rolled as she moved him. She felt the tiny bones. Broken.

For some reason, that helped. At least it had been quick. The thought of him struggling for hours in the water would have been too much to bear. She ran her finger over his head, smoothing his stripy fur, tears sliding down her cheek.

'I'm sorry, Ziggy,' she whispered as she held him close to her.

'I told you not to be late back.'

She turned her head. Victor was watching her from the door. She hadn't heard him come in. 'Why do you make me do this?' He stepped into the bathroom, reaching for her. 'Why do you make me hurt you?'

Sarah watched the lights from the cars on the street cross her mother's living-room ceiling. She sat up, shivering with cold. Sumo whined from the floor under her. She stretched, switched on a lamp and glanced at the brass carriage clock on the mantelpiece.

It was twenty past eleven. She had forty minutes to make her peace with the world.

She picked up her phone and tried John's number again, but it went straight to voicemail. She rang the Four Seasons and asked to be put through to his room, then waited, listening to the phone ring endlessly. In her mind's eye, she could see John, grinning his boyish grin, his eyes full of mischief.

She hung up. She hoped he was okay wherever he was and whatever he was doing.

Her mobile rang as she was putting it on the table.

'Hello?'

'Did you get my message?'

It was Victor.

'You bastard! You didn't need to do that to Rodney. He's harmless.'

'He came barging in like a lunatic. Should have kept his nose out of my business, shouldn't he?'

'You broke his leg.'

'He's lucky it wasn't his neck. How do you do it, Sarah? How do you get the fucking saps to roll over for you? You giving him the old five-finger shuffle? You should have seen him, all puffed up. Fuckin' joke, I—'

'What do you want?'

'Didn't you read my note? I want to talk to you.'

'So come here, then. You know where I am.'

He laughed. 'Oh, yeah. You must think I'm a mug. I ain't callin' in for a cuppa, no way – fuck knows what you've rigged. Nah, you're going to come and see me. I'll make it easy for you, sweetheart.'

Sarah waited.

'Know that wooden bridge thing down the road from your house?'

'You know I do.'

'Come down there. Sit in the men's shelter. Make sure you're alone and don't try any funny stuff. You do and I'm gone. Next time I'll carve the fucking note into your sister's back.'

'I'll be there.'

'One hour. And don't be late.'

'Victor—'

'Bring that dog and I'll kill it. Understand?'

'Yes.'

'I just want to talk to you and clear a few things up. Maybe catch up on old times.'

Sarah closed her phone. She thought of Jackie and Rodney, of what Victor could do to Helen or her mother if she disobeyed him. She had to go.

What choice did she have? If she called the gardaí, what could they do? Nothing. It wasn't against the law to be in a beach shelter and it would be her word against his that he had been threatening her.

Why had he picked that spot?

If he had been watching her, he probably knew she often walked out to the point there and, chances were, he probably knew one of her ankles was weak. Maybe he'd make it look like she'd slipped on the rocks. Stupid gimp slips, bangs head and drowns. Yep, nice and neat.

Victor was nothing if not thorough.

So this was it. He was planning to kill her. Was she was going to walk straight into his murderous arms?

She got up and walked into the kitchen, Sumo trailing behind her. She looked around her homey room. She could leave a note, saying that if anything happened to her, he was to blame.

She took a notebook and pen from a drawer and sat at the table. 'Dear Mum,' she began, but she couldn't write another word.

It would be of no solace to her family to know that she had walked into a trap to protect them. Maybe it would be better if they thought she'd slipped.

She put down the pen, closed her eyes and rested her face on her arms.

'Lord, give me the strength I need,' she whispered.

The wind was piercing and the wooden slats of the bridge were greasy from the earlier rain. Thick clouds moved across the moon, threatening another downpour. As she walked across the narrow link to Dollymount Strand, Sarah inhaled the rich sea air. The tide was in and she could hear water slapping at the support posts beneath her. The sounds of the city fell away.

She passed a man in a yellow windbreaker walking his spaniel towards the main road. He nodded to her as they passed. 'Rough old night,' he said.

'It's not too bad,' Sarah smiled. 'Least it's dry.'

She wondered why she no longer felt afraid. Perhaps this was how soldiers felt before they went into battle. When there was no hope of a good outcome, calm descended. Maybe it would hold, maybe not, but whatever happened, she had decided, she would no longer allow Victor any power over her life.

She walked on. There were no cars and no other walkers, and by the time she reached the first shelter, she was resigned to what was about to happen.

She walked on towards the men's shelters. The wind here whipped the sea spray across her, threatening to blow her clean off the walkway.

She stepped inside and sat on the concrete bench. The water was halfway up the steps and the squalls threatened to bring it right over the rocks.

Sarah shivered as she gazed over the bay towards the flashing beacons of the Poolbeg electricity towers. It was too dark to make out their barbershop red and white, but something about their shape comforted her. They looked so solid, immovable. A friend had once said they looked like sentinels.

She slid her hands into her coat pockets and sat back. She remembered hot summer afternoons on this beach, she and Jackie searching the rocks for crabs and little fish. Once they had found a small shark washed up. They had had to fight off the seagulls to get a good look at it. She visualised it now, dead or dying, caught in a rock pool by the outgoing tide. It had been no longer than her arm, and silver, with rows of tiny teeth: a perfect miniature of the one in *Jaws* that had terrified her. She and Jackie had wanted to catch it and take it home, but Helen had stopped them and when Sarah had gone to check on it later that afternoon, the gulls had torn it to pieces.

The predator had become the prey.

'You want to hear something funny? I could smell you before I saw you,' a voice said to her left.

She turned her head. Victor stood outside the shelter smoking a cigarette. He seemed impervious to the wind and cold.

'Chanel, ain't it?'

'Yes.'

'I always liked that on you.'

Sarah stared at him in the moonlight. He had changed. He was older, heavier, but just as handsome and just as dangerous. He turned his head to blow smoke and she saw that one of his eyes was white. 'What happened to your eye?'

'Little welcoming present from when I went inside.'

'Oh.'

'I don't mind it. I'm told it adds real character to my face.'

'What do you want, Victor?'

'You mind if I sit down?'

'Suit yourself.' Sarah edged further along the bench and deeper into the shadows. Victor sat down on the edge. 'That's better, more civilised. We can be civilised, can't we?'

'Can we?'

'Sure.' He looked at her in the half-light. 'You're back working with your old boyfriend, then.'

Sarah didn't reply. It wasn't a question. He just wanted her to know he knew everything about her. Classic Vic.

'Nice little set-up you have, by the way. I bet he was glad to have you back in his arms.'

'I'm not in his arms.'

'Wonder how he'd feel about you if I paid him a visit.'

'He doesn't have anything to do with this. I work with him, that's all.'

'You tell him about me?'

'What do you think?'

'I think you like fucking with people.' He took another drag at his cigarette, then pitched it into the water.

Sarah heard it hiss in the darkness. She swallowed. To be so close to him again made her feel almost as though she had entered the twilight zone. Him, her, the sea, the rising wind. It was almost beyond creepy. 'What do you want, Vic?'

'I've had three years to think about why, you know, and I still can't figure it out. I gave you everything. I gave you a roof over your head, a life, money—'

'Vic—'

'No.' He held up his hand, palm flat. 'Let me talk, I've waited this long. Least you can do is hear me out. I think I was more than a man.

I had bitches throwing themselves at me daily, but I didn't cheat, I had offers – oh, you better believe I had offers – but I said no. I tried, I really did.'

'You beat me up.'

He looked at her, hurt. 'I thought I explained that. I was only trying to make you see—'

'You gave me black eyes, a broken rib. I lost two teeth and I've got a scar on my arm longer than my index finger.'

'You blaming me for that?'

'You did it.'

'You made me! You pushed me, all the way.'

'Why did you run Jackie off the road?'

He snorted. 'Answer me this first. Why did you set me up?'

Sarah sighed and looked out over the choppy waves. She should have known better than to expect an answer from him. 'It doesn't matter now.'

'Oh, it matters all right. I want to know.'

'There's nothing to tell.'

'You didn't do it alone.'

'Who says?'

'I know you.' Vic turned to her. 'You might have been the one to plant the drugs on me, but I want to know who helped you and what the fuck made you do such a stupid thing to *me*?'

Sarah heard it then, the outrage, the underlying fury. And his voice had held the note that usually preceded violence. So much for being civilised, she thought.

'You killed Ziggy,' she said.

Victor stared at her. 'What?'

'You killed Ziggy,' she repeated.

'Who the fuck's Ziggy?'

Sarah glanced at him. 'He wasn't that important to you, except as a tool to make my life a misery.'

'The fucking cat?'

'Yes.'

He stared at her for a long moment. At first she thought he was going to explode, but then he laughed.

Sarah watched his face, remembering every line, nook and cranny, how he would smile as he 'explained' to her that he was not hitting her to hurt her, oh no, he was hitting her because she 'made' him do it. His laugh was like fingernails on a blackboard.

'A fucking cat! You got me locked up in jail – lost me my flat, my business, my *eye* – for a cat?'

'Yes,' she said simply.

It was true.

When she had fished Ziggy's tiny body from the toilet, something had shifted inside Sarah Kenny. She could cope with Victor's bullying, his demands for complete obedience. She must have known somewhere within her the type of man he was. But for him to have wrung the life from something so loving, so defenceless as Ziggy ... It was as if she had opened her eyes for the first time. She finally understood that she had allowed herself to become attached to a man with no moral centre, who did not feel, who only wanted to control. She knew then that she had to get away from him. She had known even as the blows rained on her that she would take him down.

And now he was back, like a cockroach after an explosion.

'I don't believe it,' he said.

'I don't care if you do or not,' Sarah said.

'Who helped you?'

'Nobody.'

'Don't give me that. I fucking know that fat knob Sid had something to do—'

'He didn't.'

'You tell me or else.'

'Nobody helped me.'

'You're going to tell me who helped you.'

'Nobody helped me.'

The blow knocked her off the seat onto the filthy concrete. For a second, she blacked out. When she came to, her ears felt red hot, and he was hauling her up by the front of her coat. She tried to get her feet underneath her, but they refused to obey even the simplest command.

Too late, she thought, *you've left it too late*.

He lifted her up and flung her onto the seat. She hit the back wall, which knocked the wind out of her. As she struggled for breath, Vic loomed over her. 'You banged me up, girlie. Did you think I'd let you walk away? I want you to know I'm going to make you suffer, but first you're going to tell me who helped you. I know you didn't get your hands on that quantity of drugs by yourself and I know you hadn't the fucking gumption to set it up alone, so I'm asking you again, who helped you?'

'No one helped me,' Sarah gasped.

He hissed air through his bottom teeth. 'You think this is a game?'

'No, Vic, but you have to understand that—'

He pulled her up and slapped her across the face with the back of his right hand. Sarah's head flew back at the force of the blow. She tasted blood and felt it trickle down the back of her throat from her nose. Her eyes watered and, for a split second, with the light behind him, Vic glowed red.

'Who set it up?'

'Nobody helped—'

He hit her again, even harder. Sarah's head rang.

'I'm asking you nicely, *who helped you?*'

'No one.'

Vic had grabbed her left hand and was doubling it back on itself. Her wrist was about to snap. Sarah opened her mouth to scream.

'Don't scream – if you do, I'll break it.' His voice was soft, almost cajoling. 'I don't *want* to hurt you, Sarah. You understand that, right? I just need to know who my enemies are. Come on, darlin', you know I don't want to do this. You're making me hurt you and I don't want to.'

'Please, Vic.' She was crying now, her tears mixing with the snot and blood on her face. 'Please ...'

He smiled and Sarah knew he thought he had her. 'Just tell me what I want to know, okay? We can settle this. I don't want to hurt you, Sarah.'

He twisted her arm closer to his. The pain was unbearable. Every tendon and ligament threatened to snap.

'Okay, okay.'

Vic lessened the grip on her wrist. Sarah sobbed uncontrollably.

'See, darlin'? It don't have to be this way.' His voice was still low but filled with malice. He tapped her cheek with his knuckles, not hard this time. 'You always make me hurt you. Now, why is that?'

Sarah opened her eyes. 'Please, I need to sit down. I think I'm going to be sick.'

'Who helped you?' He shifted his weight and yanked her backwards, towards the seat. As he did so, Sarah swung her right arm in an arc.

'You're going to give me a name, Sarah.'

She had a free swing, and, unfettered, she buried her mother's good carving knife as deep as she could in the side of Victor's exposed neck and twisted it.

His breath hitched. He made a funny gurgling sound. He pitched onto his knees, falling half into the shelter. Sarah landed heavily on her back as he released her arm. She lay there for a second, stunned, unable to do anything but watch as Victor tried to grasp the handle of the kitchen knife that now stuck out from his neck at a ninety degree angle.

'Sarrgghh.'

His fingers slipped on the handle – it was slick with his blood and he couldn't get a purchase on it. He reached for her and she tried to scrabble backwards with her heels. He caught her shin and she kicked out at him, catching his jaw and forcing his head back. He grunted as blood poured from his neck, and she knew she had severed an artery. He tried to get to his feet and slipped. He rolled onto his back, bringing his hands up to his throat, tearing at his clothing and skin.

Sarah scooted closer to the step and tried to get to her feet. She heard a strange rattle behind her, then silence.

She looked at Victor. He was still. She waited a full minute before she moved towards him. She checked his pulse. Nothing. She looked down at his face. His eyes were open and he seemed to be looking directly at her.

She took a deep breath, grabbed the handle of the knife with both hands and yanked it as hard as she could out of his neck. She wiped the blade on his coat and threw it up onto the shelter seat.

She searched him, removing his watch, his wallet and his money. She found a set of keys with a plastic tag saying they belonged to a guest house on Dorset Street. She pocketed them too.

Finally, satisfied that he had no more identification on him, she rolled him onto the steps and towards the water, using the slimy, seaweed-covered concrete to slide him to the water's edge. She slipped twice and by the time she had got him to the water's edge, her strength had all but gone, her ankle was on fire and she barely had the energy to hold up her head.

With one last, desperate shove, she launched Vic into the black water. He bobbed there for a second, his face obscenely pale against the inky blackness.

'Just go, will you?' Sarah whispered, gripping the metal handrail.

Then the current caught him and he slipped below the surface.

Gone.

She remained where she was, crouched in the blackness, for some time, but eventually the cold forced her to move.

She used sea water to wash the blood off her face, choking at the taste. She did the best she could, rinsing her hands and sleeves, then kicked water up onto the concrete, but in the dark she couldn't tell shadow from blood and eventually she had to leave and hope that the tide would deal with it.

She picked up the knife and made her way wearily back across the bridge and onto the main road. She hurried along, keeping her head down and staying close to the walls and houses.

But that night, some guardian angel was watching out for Sarah Kenny and she made it back to her house without meeting another soul. As she closed the gate and staggered up the path, the rain began to fall heavily.

Sarah raised her face to the sky. She let the water wash over her bruised skin and her dark heart, cleaning away the stain of Victor. 'Thank you,' she said to the heavens.

* * *

Sarah went inside and walked to the back of the house without switching on a single light. Sumo rushed to greet her, but she did not stop. She walked upstairs and into the bathroom and vomited into the toilet, spewing sea water and bile until her throat hurt.

Finally, she grabbed a roll of tissue, blew her nose and flushed the toilet. After a few minutes she felt strong enough to stand up.

She switched on the light over the mirror and groaned. Her face was a mess. Her nose was swollen and crusted with blood. Her eyes were beginning to swell and she was bruised and torn where he had struck her.

She ran a hand towel under the cold tap and tried to clean away the blood with one hand while she searched the cabinet for pain-killers with the other. Then she went downstairs and filled the towel with ice cubes.

John would be back tomorrow. How would she explain her injuries?

Back upstairs, she swallowed two paracetamol tablets, holding the towel to the bridge of her nose, she went to her room and lowered herself gingerly onto the bed. Sumo followed her and lay down on the rug. She put out her hand to him and he licked it.

She tried not to think of what she had done. She tried not to think of the heat from Victor's blood, the sound he had made as he died. She closed her eyes and tried to steady her breathing.

She had killed him.

Stop.

She could go to jail for this.

It was self-defence.

She had brought the knife with her.

For protection.

She had pushed his body out to sea, concealing evidence.

Stop thinking about it.

She had killed.

It's not the first time.

Sarah began to cry.

47

Helen drove quickly, blasting the horn at hesitant drivers and lane jumpers. It was barely eight-thirty and already the traffic was snarled and crawling. 'Come on. *Move.*'

Her fury increased as a bus pulled out three cars ahead. She glanced at her watch again. She was tired and irritable. She hadn't slept well. Her mother, disturbed by her new surroundings, had woken her twice and, eventually, she had locked Deirdre's door.

She had called Sarah's mobile first thing that morning. Her sister hadn't answered. By the time Belinda had arrived, she was angry and a little worried. She was on her way to her mother's house now to have it out with Sarah once and for all.

If she ever got there.

She rested the heel of her hand on the horn again.

By the time she swung into her mother's drive and pulled up behind John Quigley's beaten-up old hulk of a car, her temper was at an all-time high. She climbed out, slammed the car door and marched up to the front of the house. She tried to let herself in with her key, but the door was on the chain.

She rang the bell.

An explosion of barking came from within and she rang again, leaving her thumb on the bell for almost ten seconds. After a minute, she thought she saw a figure move through the heavy bubble glass.

'Sarah! It's Helen! I know you're there! Open this door. I want to talk to you.'

'Helen, can you come back later?'

'*Come back*? No, I can't!' Helen rapped on the pane angrily. 'Open the door *now*.'

Finally, she heard the chain slide free. 'What the hell are you up to? Why didn't you answer your phone? Sarah, Mum's been up and down all night and I'm in no mood for games. I – Jesus Christ!' Helen stepped into the hall. 'What happened to you?'

Sarah's eyes were swollen. The skin across her nose was split and she had bruises to the left side of her face. Helen stepped to her and raised her hand.

'Don't.' Sarah turned away and padded towards the kitchen.

Helen followed. 'What the hell happened?'

'I was jumped.'

'Jumped?'

'Mugged.'

'Mugged?'

'Are you going to repeat everything I say?' Sarah filled the kettle and switched it on.

She ached all over. She feared that her nose was broken and one of her back teeth felt loose. She had taken some of her mother's sleeping tablets and slept fitfully, with Sumo sprawled across her bed. Now, in the cold light of day, she felt sick at the memory of what she had done.

The last thing she wanted – or needed – was a confrontation with Helen.

'Sarah, what the hell is going on?'

'I told you, I was mugged.'

'Did you go to the police?'

'No.'

'*Why the hell not?*'

'Don't shout.'

Helen put down her handbag and ran a hand through her hair. 'I don't know what I'm going to do with you, I really don't.'

Sarah took two mugs down and spooned coffee into them. 'Who says you have to do anything? I'm not a project, Helen. I don't need you to fix me.'

'Sarah, I'm worried about you. You – you live this crazy life – the risks, the danger. You can't keep doing this to yourself. You can't keep doing this to *us* – to your family.'

Sarah got the milk out of the fridge. Her hand shook and, try as she might, she couldn't stop it. The pain in her head was getting worse, too.

Concentrate on the coffee.

'Where did it happen?'

'What?'

'Where were you mugged?'

'Down the road, near the promenade.'

'When?'

'Last night. Look, Helen – what are you doing?'

Helen was taking her mobile out of her bag. 'I'm doing what you should have done. I'm calling the gardaí.'

'No, Helen!'

Helen paused. 'What?'

'I told you, I don't want them involved.'

'Sarah, what's going on?'

'Nothing, I just – I just—'

But before she could think of a good enough reason not to call the gardaí, her own body came up with one. She fainted.

48

John hurried out of Arrivals and glanced around frantically.

'John, over here!'

He turned and spotted Helen bundled up in a cashmere coat by the railings. She raised her hand. She didn't look happy to see him. He made his way toward her. 'Thanks for coming.'

'She insisted.'

'How is she?'

'Still pretty out of it. She's got a broken nose and possibly concussion.'

John was stricken. 'Have they identified the guy who attacked her?'

Helen shook her head. 'She says she doesn't remember what he looked like, and anyway, it was dark.'

'Dark?'

'She's lying – I know she is. She mentioned something to the gardaí about a pub. Nesbitts, I think.'

'Jesus fucking Christ!' John flung his bag over his shoulder and walked with Helen out of the electric doors towards the car park. 'I *told* her, I god-damned *told* her not to go near that place!'

Helen glanced at him with barely concealed loathing. 'Well, she did go near it and here we are again, with my sister in a hospital.'

'Stop talking like I don't care about her, Helen.'

'Oh, you care now, do you?'

John skidded to a halt. He had been in the police station giving a statement until twenty past three that morning and when he'd finally got back to the hotel, he had passed out on the bed with his clothes on. Helen's call to let him know that Sarah was in hospital and that she would pick him up from the airport had done nothing to calm his nerves. He was dirty, unshaven and as close to breaking point as he liked to get.

He flung his bag onto the ground with such force that Helen jumped.

'Enough!' He raised his finger until it was inches from her face. 'You don't like me, you're never going to like me, and you know what? That's fine. I don't give a shit what you think, but understand this. Your sister means more to me than you will ever know.'

'Right, and we both know that means so much.'

John clenched his jaw but held his tongue. Helen was Sarah's sister. She had every right to be angry and frightened. 'I don't want to fight with you, Helen.'

Helen squared her shoulders and began to walk again. John picked up his bag and fell into step beside her.

'Who is Willie Staunton?' Helen eventually asked.

'He's the man who probably sold Katie Jones the gun she was carrying. Sarah wanted to check him out and I told her not to.'

'Sarah is tenacious.'

'Stubborn, you mean.'

'I'm afraid there's more bad news,' Helen told him.

'What?'

'Your office has been trashed.'

'Fuck the office,' John said. 'That shit can be replaced.'

Helen nodded. 'Do you want me to drive you home first, or—'

'No,' John said. 'Take me to her.'

* * *

The ward sister was delighted to see Helen. 'Oh, good, there you are. She won't listen to reason – she's trying to discharge herself. '

Helen frowned. 'Last time I saw her she was almost comatose.'

'She's very distressed. I was about to call you.' The nurse cast a mildly curious glance at John, then turned back to Helen. 'Come with me, please. Maybe you can talk some sense into her.'

Helen and John hurried after her down a corridor. Sarah was sitting sideways on a trolley, unhooking herself from an IV drip. Or trying to – both of her hands were bandaged.

'Sarah,' John said.

She looked up and his face tightened. Her face was black and blue, her eyes cloudy and swollen. She gazed at him through her hair, as though she had no idea who he was.

He reached her and lifted her chin with his hand. 'Oh, Jesus, your face.'

She frowned. 'John?'

'She's on very strong painkillers,' the nurse said, and added to Helen, 'I don't know how she's still upright. She really shouldn't be going anywhere.'

'It's all right, I'm here now,' John said softly. 'It's all right.'

'Take me home, John, please … please.'

She slid off the trolley and folded into John's arms. She pressed her face into his chest and wept as if she was a child, with no embarrassment, as though she would never stop.

John was appalled. He wrapped his arms round her and held her tightly. 'It's okay, Sarah, I'm here. I'll take care of you. Don't cry now, come on, sweetie, don't cry, I'm here.'

Helen stared at the side of John's face. At that moment, she saw something in him that up till then she hadn't thought him capable of. It was pure love.

She turned to the nurse. 'Perhaps you could get me her discharge sheet. My husband's a surgeon, we will take good care of her.'

'Well…' the nurse said, clearly unhappy.

Helen took her wrist squeezed it.

'Come with me, then,' the nurse said.

Helen followed her to the nurses' station. She glanced back once. They hadn't moved and Sarah was still weeping.

* * *

John kicked his feet up onto his desk, shook out the newspaper and groaned. 'They never get the fucking name right, do they? It's QuicK! Capital Q and capital K.'

Sarah glanced at him. 'I can't believe they're still going on about it.'

'Slow news week.'

'Still, I wish they'd stop.'

'Are you nuts? It's great publicity.'

'Mm.'

'Well, come on,' John said. 'It's a big story. Think about it. How many adoptions was that Lizzie Sheldon behind?'

'Twenty-five that they know of,' Sarah replied. She was tired of this conversation. She seemed to have had it nearly every day for two weeks – first the gardaí, then two English detectives, Sam's family, the press and her own family. It was exhausting. She wanted to put the case behind her and move on.

'Right. It's going to take months to track everyone down and even longer to get to the bottom of it all. That solicitor, the one who founded the Cradle Foundation.'

'Simon Phelps.'

'He's skipped out of the country, got everyone hot on his tail.'

'They'll find him. He can't hide for ever.'

'It's a can of worms. And to think if Yolanda Vaughn hadn't been such a filthy snob, none of this would have been uncovered.' John snorted. 'Just goes to show.'

'What?' Sarah said wearily.

'That you can't get away with something for ever. Eventually it'll come back to bite you in the arse. It's the circle of life.'

Sarah felt sick. 'How so?'

'Well, if Yolanda hadn't hired Harry D'Angelo to go digging about in Katie's past, Katie wouldn't have heard of Hogan. If Hogan hadn't learned he was dying, he wouldn't have been so keen to talk to Katie and she wouldn't have come to Ireland. If she hadn't come to Ireland, Lizzie Sheldon might not have sent her bastard son to take out Hogan and Katie and she would have carried on selling babies to sterile rich folk and Katie would never have found her real family. See?' John smiled. 'You want to hear something else interesting?'

'Do I?'

'Britney Spears has shaved all her hair off.'

'That's nice.'

Sarah tried to smile, but she couldn't. Her head hurt and her teeth hurt. She turned back to her new computer. If John was right, when was her circle going to be complete? When did she get to pay for what she had done? In the two weeks since that fateful night, she had scanned the papers every day for news that Victor's body had washed ashore, but there had been nothing.

She wondered how long the sea would keep him.

Although the swelling to her face was going down, she was a mess. She couldn't sleep or eat and she had lost almost ten pounds. Everyone was worried about her. She knew it, she understood it, but it infuriated her.

Willie Staunton – whose body had been discovered in his burned-out silver Toyota at the back of a bakery on the same day that Sarah had collapsed – complicated matters further.

The cops knew Sarah had been to Nesbitts investigating him, and were initially sceptical that Willie had not been the cause of her injuries. But Sarah had persisted in telling them she had not met Willie Staunton, and when Jimmy Dunne had been located, the little shyster had settled some scores. Once he had an assurance of immunity, Jimmy squealed with gusto about how Willie had been dealing guns and how he had scarred Jimmy for life. After that, the cops had considered widening their list of suspects, and anyway, there was no evidence to tie Sarah to his death.

John glanced over at her. 'I got a call from Sam this morning.'

'Oh?'

'He wants to know if we'd like to come to his mother's home for a bite to eat on Friday.'

'I don't think so.'

'Might do you good to get out for a few hours. Drake's crazy about you. Mind you, Drake's crazy full stop.'

'I don't feel much like socialising at the moment.'

'Suit yourself.' John was clearly pretending he didn't care. 'Hey, look at this! Do you know why penguins' feet don't freeze?'

'No.'

'Then let me enlighten you.'

He waffled on, attempting to make Sarah smile, trying to breach whatever void had opened between them. He couldn't understand what had changed and he desperately wanted things to go back to the way they had been before he had gone to England.

When he had taken her home from the hospital, she had asked him to bring her to her own apartment. Despite Helen's misgivings, he had done as she'd asked and stayed with her the whole night, watching over her as she slept, gently smoothing her hair when she whimpered in her sleep. But the next morning, pale and stiff, Sarah had thanked him for staying and shown him the door.

He knew straight away that she had closed off from him again and, no matter what he said, she hadn't wavered. She wanted him gone.

Bewildered, he had driven to Sarah's mother's home to collect his car and his dog.

But John was no fool. He had gone to see Rodney and after questioning him about the man who had attacked him and trashed the office, he had figured out that Rodney was hiding something too. When John told him that Sarah sent her regards, something in Rodney's expression had spoken volumes. 'Did she now?'

'Everything all right, big man?'

'Fine,' Rodney said.

And, like Sarah, he had refused to be drawn on the subject.

But despite the weirdness, not everything had turned out badly.

Drake had been practically adopted by Charlotte Jones and when Katie showed signs that she was responding to his presence, Charlotte's adoration of the skinny, jerky artist had doubled. Sam still regarded him with deep suspicion, but when Katie opened her eyes three days after Drake's arrival, he was prepared to accept that maybe, just maybe, Drake wasn't the loon he'd thought him. Certainly, he had been much impressed by the man's absolute devotion to his sister.

Katie Jones had told an incredulous Detective McBride the truth about that day at Walter Hogan's house. As John had suspected, she had not shot the doctor. Rather, she had been ambushed the moment she had set foot in the house by Mark Sheldon, who had been lying in wait for her for almost forty-eight hours, with the good doctor held hostage. Mark had hit Katie, shot Hogan, using her hand, then shot her, making it look as though she had turned the gun on herself. But he had botched it and had no option but to flee when the taxi driver had started banging on the door.

Katie had told the gardaí all about Harry D'Angelo, how he had approached her about her adoption and told her it was false. He had given her Hogan's name and, after she had contacted him, Hogan had asked her to come and see him. She had demanded her real mother's name and he had given it to her. But she had also known that someone was after her – her apartment had been broken into and her paperwork stolen, but no money or jewellery. She had known then that she was in danger and had moved into Drake's house for protection. It was only after someone tried to break in there that she had decided to go to Ireland and find out who she was and where she had come from.

She was not to know that Harry D'Angelo had also contacted Lizzie Sheldon, thereby tipping her off that her lucrative empire was under threat. Katie couldn't have known that such a heartless, ruthless woman as Lizzie Sheldon existed.

Initially, Mark Sheldon would admit to nothing, just as his mother claimed innocence, although she could not produce any plausible reason for the presence of the two sleeping babies found at her home. She claimed she was minding them for someone, describing her actions as charitable and altruistic. The police eventually located the babies' real mothers, but they wouldn't talk either. When questioned about her involvement in Katie Jones's abduction, Lizzie had wept bitterly, claiming Nico Kastrinakis had abducted her and that she had known nothing about it. Yes, she said, she had been with him that day, but she had been terrified of Nico and hadn't questioned him when he warned her to stay out of his business. She claimed that she'd fled from him the next day and had lived in guilt ever since.

So convincing was her act, and so outraged was her expensive lawyer, that the case might have been stymied then and there if not for the quick thinking of Ahmed Kahn, a forensic specialist with the Metropolitan Police. He had tested blood from the scene of Mark Sheldon's fight with John against DNA belonging to Lizzie Sheldon. As Ahmed suspected, it turned out that Mark and Lizzie Sheldon were not related by blood.

When the stunned boy learned this, he talked, and talked, and talked. And oh, what a story he wove.

Elizabeth Sheldon was placed under arrest, charged with murder, theft, kidnapping, forgery, GBH, trafficking and conspiracy to commit fraud.

Katie had wept bitterly over Frank's death, but Charlotte had held her close and soothed her, speaking softly as only a mother can. It was not a perfect start to her new life, Charlotte had told her, but then, what had perfection ever done for anyone?

This led Drake to surmise that Charlotte was really very smart indeed.

Sarah felt John's eyes on her but she didn't look up. She knew he was confused and hurt and it broke her heart to see the pain she was causing him. But she couldn't risk letting him in, allowing him to become close to her. She was a mess.

She had become everything she hated most in a person – a fraud and a liar. And her lies had hurt everyone around her. Jackie, Rodney – even stupid Jimmy Dunne had paid for her blunders. She couldn't risk letting John love her. She wouldn't risk loving him.

Not with her secrets. Not knowing what she knew. What was the point?

Sarah Kenny kept her eyes down. She knew if she lifted them, she would tell John Quigley everything she had done and then he, too, would share the burden.

And she wouldn't do that to him. Not now – not ever, if she could help it.

49

Evan Williams raced across the dunes of Colwyn Bay, trying to control the huge kite. It was a dragonfly, made from the lightest plastic and oiled paper. He had been given it for his birthday and he took every opportunity to fly it.

The wind off the Irish Sea was strong and as the kite dipped and swirled, he was almost being lifted off his feet.

'Dad! Dad! Did you see that?' he yelled over his shoulder.

'Hold on tight, Evan! Don't let go,' his father hollered back, tugging at Bonnie, the West Highland terrier's lead. 'Come on, lass, you can't have a drop left at this stage, can you?' he said to the little dog.

But Bonnie wouldn't be rushed and by the time she had finished, Evan was out of view, although his father could still hear his excited laughter.

Cyan Williams wasn't concerned. Colwyn was quiet at this time of year, free of the weirdos and transients that littered so many beautiful Welsh beaches during the summer months. 'Come on, Bonnie.' He crested the nearest dune and was surprised to see the kite lying forgotten in the sand.

Evan was further ahead, staring intently at a load of old drift-wood on the shoreline.

'Evan? What you got there?'

Evan didn't turn round and Cyan knew from the boy's posture that he was keenly interested in something.

He picked Bonnie up and carried her over to the surf. 'Evan, why didn't you answer—'

And then he saw what had transfixed his son.

Lying among the kelp and the pieces of driftwood was a man's bloated, half-eaten body.

'Jesus!' Cyan said. He grabbed his son and yanked him away. 'Come on, son, we've got to get back to the car.'

Evan's face was as white as a sheet. 'Daddy, w-where are his eyes?'

'Come on, son. Let's go.'

'But Daddy—'

'Grab your kite, there's a good lad.'

Evan did as he was told and Cyan hurried him along the sand and back to the car.

Overhead, a gull shrieked and wheeled away on an updraught.

Cyan shivered. The warmth and laughter had gone out of the day.

Victor had that effect on people.

Acknowledgements

My deepest thanks to my agent, Faith O'Grady of the Lisa Richards Agency, my excellent editor, Ciara Considine for always knowing when to nip and when to tuck, and to Hazel Orme, my new copy-editor. (Normally I don't like change, but I am so impressed with Hazel's work I can only hope she runs her remarkable fine-tooth comb through any future books I produce. Tana French, my previous copy-editor, came over to the dark side and published her first novel this year, *In the Woods* – go buy it). And to the terrific team at Hodder Headline Ireland, what can I say except thank you?

My gratitude also to Bill Wallsgrove for all his patient help when I pestered him about London, a hearty wave to Tom too, for no reason other than that he is adorable. Thanks as usual to Bryan for his tireless cheer and ability to think on his feet when asked any question, no matter how ridiculous it might seem.

My deepest love to Anna 'Lady of the Manor' Kenny for being as fabulous as ever. We'll be rocking the patio soon, I'll bring rum.

Antonia, for being the best lunch date a gal could ever have. Sarah and Tara, mwoah mwoah, and a quick 'eek' to Sarah, who will be getting married to the lovely Daragh this year. Chris, double mwoah for you and a heartfelt congratulations. I must mention a special thank you to Teresa from Elite International Detective Agency for answering all my queries and being good enough to invite me to ask more should I need to.

To Terry, Tim and the family, my continued love and

appreciation. May we barbecue and drink beer 'til our hearts' content.

To Jordan, an unabashed kiss and a hug – every year I watch you grow into a kind and intelligent woman and my heart wobbles with pride.

My husband Andrew, reader, editor, confidant and coffee maker, all my love, as always, and forever.

There are loads of others I would like to mention (hi Muriel!), but I can't go waffling on forever and a day (well, I could, even if it meant thanking the wood pigeons for keeping me amused on the days when I'm gazing out the windows not working when I should be). But I would like to take this opportunity to thank all my readers – without you I'm just a voice in the wind. I want you to know I enjoy all the emails you send and it delights me to hear from you. Thank you for all your continued support and I hope you enjoy *Missing Presumed Dead* as much as I enjoyed writing it.

Take care,
Arlene Hunt
April 2007